THE DANGEROUS MARQUIS

For long moments Huxford stood gazing down at her. He wanted to tell her she was beginning to haunt him. That his desire for her was making sleep impossible. He wanted to tell her of his decision that she must be avoided.

When he spoke at last, his voice was hard. "What can a girl like you know about a man's feelings, Miss Taylor? Can she know that merely seeing her, so unbelievably beautiful, can make him want her so badly he will go to unbelievable lengths just to touch her? And can she understand this might lead him into forming an unwelcome alliance, thereby compromising his ideals of what, or who, is right for him?"

Audrey gasped. Huxford was saying, in effect, that he wanted her but was unwilling to offer marriage. It was an insult calculated to stagger the mind. But then, she thought, she'd asked for it.

The Dangerous Marquis

BARBARA REEVES

AVON BOOKS ◆ NEW YORK

THE DANGEROUS MARQUIS is an original publication of Avon Books. This work has never before appeared in book form. This work is a novel. Any similarity to actual persons or events is purely coincidental.

AVON BOOKS
A division of
The Hearst Corporation
1350 Avenue of the Americas
New York, New York 10019

Copyright © 1994 by Barbara Reeves Kolaski
Published by arrangement with the author
Library of Congress Catalog Card Number: 94-94080
ISBN: 0-380-77672-3

First Avon Books Printing: September 1994

AVON TRADEMARK REG. U.S. PAT. OFF. AND IN OTHER COUNTRIES, MARCA REGISTRADA, HECHO EN U.S.A.

Printed in the U.S.A.

RA 10 9 8 7 6 5 4 3 2 1

1

London—1813

No matter what time Gideon St. Aubin, Marquis of Huxford, arrived home the night before, he rode in the park at dawn and ate his breakfast at eight.

Few persons in the ton would have dared disturb the marquis so early. His ward, the Honorable Sir Paden Offutt, lately down from Oxford, did not hesitate.

Arriving in Brook Street shortly after the hour, Sir Paden was thankful finally to find the marquis home. "It's about time, Twickem," the young man told the butler.

Twickem murmured something soothing and escorted Mr. Offutt upstairs, bowed him into Huxford's dining parlor, and with a fine distinction, omitted to announce him.

Huxford's expression held none of its usual hauteur as he watched Paden Offutt saunter into his breakfast room. Instead, he allowed his harsh features to relax into something close to a smile and resumed buttering his roll.

"Hallo, halfling," he called, gesturing toward the sideboard. "Hungry?"

Paden, forced to rise at dawn for this interview with his trustee, swallowed convulsively. The sight of kippers, scrambled eggs, and sauteed mushrooms made him grimace. "What I don't understand, Hux, and never will, is how the devil you manage to eat all that at the break of day." He shuddered.

Huxford grinned, his lean cheeks creasing. "What brings you to Brook Street, Paden? And so early? I confess I'm surprised to see you out of bed at this time of day."

"Couldn't be helped, Gideon. Wanted to see if you was home." This brought to mind his grievance of the past week. He gave his friend a black look.

"Blast it all, Huxford!" he exclaimed. "This is the fourth morning I've been here! Yes, and I'll tell you something else! You're a damned hard man to find if a fellow needs a conflab! I'd swear you'd disappeared from the face of the planet! Couldn't find you anywhere!"

Paden pulled off his hat, a wonderful article boasting parti-colored bands and two green partridge feathers. He tossed it at one of the side chairs. It missed and fell to the floor.

Still thinking of all the trouble he'd been put to, Paden continued in an aggravated tone. "I can't imagine where you've been, old man. No, and I ain't meaning to ask," he added hurriedly, "because I won't risk another set down like last time!"

When his friend merely crooked an amused eyebrow in his direction and resumed eating, Paden hitched his chair close and lowered his voice. "Thing is, Gideon, I had me a notion and wanted to ask what you thought of it."

Gideon St. Aubin choked. Mr. Offutt looked alarmed, jumped to his feet and thumped his friend on the back. "Here," he cried and handed the marquis his wine glass. "Drink this!"

Gideon swallowed and composed his face. "You . . . you say you had a notion. You mean you've had an *idea,* Paden?" he asked in a carefully controlled voice.

Paden nodded. "Yes. And it was this: Got to thinking it might not be a bad thing if I bought myself a pair of colors and went into the army. Thought I might try and take Victor's place, you know?" Paden's voice shook slightly on his late brother's name and he fastened his eyes on the Marquis of Huxford, waiting hopefully for the verdict.

Gideon St. Aubin drew in a long breath. Rosedale, the country home of the Offutts, was situated just through the home wood from Baddingly Castle, Huxford's seat in Sussex. From his infancy Paden had trotted after Gideon and Victor, joining their games and depending on them to tell him what to do. Since Victor was killed two years ago in the first siege of Badajoz, Paden had relied on him alone.

Gideon took another bite of his breakfast and chewed it slowly. "Have you mentioned this to Lady Offutt?" he asked at last.

Paden blanched. "M'mother? I should think not! Well, you know what she is, Gideon. Besides, you might say no and then where would I be? Nothing said, no one the wiser."

"Very prudent."

"Well, should I do it? Shall I join up?"

The marquis shook his head. "Better not."

Paden blinked. "No?" he asked. Although he had turned twenty-one, Paden sometimes seemed younger. He waited while Gideon, his senior by ten years, pulled the jam pot closer. Presently, his patience had its reward.

"You're the only surviving Offutt, don't you see?" came Huxford's gentle reminder.

Paden absently retrieved his hat from the floor and chewed the brim awhile. "That never occurred to me," he admitted.

"No, I thought it couldn't have," murmured his friend politely.

Paden sighed. He'd been indulging himself in a reverie these past few days. It was the least important aspect of the whole affair, of course, but he did think he might look rather nice in regimentals. He sighed again and cast the alluring image aside.

"Have you seen the American?" he asked eventually.

"No." Gideon smiled. "Who is he?"

"Isn't a he," Paden said, tossing his hat at a tall silver epergne on a stand in the corner. "It's a Miss Audrey Soames-Taylor and she's been in England two weeks. She has taken London by storm. Can't think why you ain't bumped into her somewhere. Oh, I forgot! You've been away, haven't you?"

"Visiting London, is she?" the marquis asked.

"Yes. Lady Marpleby—well, you know her, Gideon— she's your own godmother. Lady Marpleby is her aunt. Girl's here for the season."

"I think . . . yes! I remember hearing of her now," Gideon mused. "No doubt she's husband-hunting from America. That's a long way to come for one, don't you think?"

"Miss Taylor says she ain't here for a husband. You'd like her, Gideon. Speaks out when she has something to say, don't rattle on for no reason. And she knows horses. Anyway, she says her coming was a whim of her papa's before he died. He was Lady Marpleby's brother, you know. The one who settled in the colonies. Only, whatever you do, don't say *colonies* to Miss Taylor. Puts her in a regular blaze! She says her country is independent; that's why the Americans are fighting this war. Is that right, Hux? And she says their president had mush on his brain when he passed this trade embargo of theirs. Says it wiped out her papa's business, and a lot of others' besides."

Paden shook his head. "I didn't understand what the girl was trying to tell me. But you would, Hux. You always know about political things, the ins and outs of 'em, and so I told her, 'Talk to m'friend St. Aubin. He knows all that stuff; he'll know what to advise you.' "

"And what," the marquis inquired with a lift of his brow, "was Miss Taylor's reply to that?"

Paden squinted, trying to remember. "She said she wasn't looking for advice, precisely. Said there was nothing to be done at any rate."

Thumping his fist on his knee, Paden nodded. It was coming back to him now. "And I said for her not to trouble her pretty little head about it. Said when you got back from wherever you'd loped off to, you'd fix everything up right and tight."

The Marquis of Huxford, trying to reconcile his expression with Paden's conviction that he could alter the trade policies of the American government, asked, "And Miss Taylor—was she relieved?"

Paden pursed his lips. "I think so, for she turned the subject and I assumed she didn't care to discuss politics any longer. But she ain't husband-hunting. Says she don't want a husband. Wouldn't expect anyone to offer for her anyway. Says her fortune went down the drain with her papa's ships. She plans to enjoy her season and sail back to Boston when the war is over."

"Is she pretty?"

"Lord, yes! Speaking eyes. Chestnut hair. That filly of mine I had from Smedley last year has the same glint in her coat. Beautiful color. You know the one."

"None better." Gideon felt uneasy. If some woman—especially a dashing young beauty—reminded Paden of a horse, chances were he was fairly smitten. And if she had no money, she wouldn't do. As Paden's trustee until he was twenty-five, he was determined that the boy marry well. Paden was quite wealthy, but a man's title and estate were earmarked for his eldest son. A rich wife could provide his other children, especially his daughters, with respectable portions.

Like as not the American girl was no threat, the marquis thought. All things considered, it could be worse. There was excellent blood on the Soames side of her family. They'd been landed gentry in Kent for countless generations. As for the Taylors, Gideon recalled that they were connections of the Soames family several generations back.

"Visiting Tatt's today?" Paden asked suddenly, the subject of horses having brought it to mind.

"No time," Gideon told him. "There are people I must see; I have appointments all day."

"Will you go to Lady Marpleby's ball Friday? You realize it's Miss Taylor's formal come out?"

"No, I didn't. Haven't had time to check my mail. However, it's likely I'll drop by sometime during the evening."

He would make a point of it. Standing in Victor's stead as Paden's mentor, he was determined to see for himself this paragon who was casting out lures to his young friend.

Later that day, Huxford arrived at the foreign office, where he'd been summoned by the third secretary, Lord Brumley.

Brumley shook his hand. "Splendid job you've done these past few weeks, St. Aubin."

He glanced up at the marquis with the peculiar sidelong

glint he had. He's gone to school with this cub's father, Hugo. Stood up with Hugo when he married the boy's mother in Hanover Square. Sad business that, Hugo and Madelaine, dying within a week of each other. Some sort of epidemic. Scarlet fever, that was it. Only four years ago—seemed forever. The boy sold out his commission, of course. Couldn't have him fighting in the Peninsula after he'd succeeded to his father's honors.

"Sit down, m'boy." Lord Brumley gestured toward the chair beside his desk. "Have a new proposition for you," he said casually.

Gideon grinned. At least two of Brumley's *propositions* had very nearly gotten him killed.

Lord Brumley's hairless pate glistened as he bent to rummage in a desk drawer. Coming up with a small red book, he studied it closely. "Did you ever come across a Frenchman named Arnaud de Vinnay? Must have! I see him at every rout, ball, or what have you m'wife drags me to these days."

"I've seen him once or twice, sir, but I don't go into society much," the marquis murmured.

"Going to have to! Mix and mingle; stir about. Set up flirts and all that."

"Why?" Gideon asked baldly.

"Scheme of mine. Thing is, we have someone passing off information from one of the government offices. You and de Vinnay are going to catch him for us." His lordship screwed his face into the grimace that signaled his amusement. "Except this time," he said with a snort of laughter, "the Frenchies will be receiving only the information we want them to have. Because we're setting up a little game of counterespionage." Brumley's eyes gleamed merrily and he ejaculated, "Eh? Eh?" several times, raising his brows at the marquis.

Gideon smiled at his chief, then finally asked, "You're sure of de Vinnay, sir?"

His lordship sobered. "Oh, yes! Yes, he's a Royalist, you see. The last of a famous French family. Hates the name of Napoleon. He's done a number of things for us—he and Hunt Wymon. Yes, and Egan Spencer, too. De

Vinnay was in on the Scruffield affair. You were in Spain at the time. Yes, carrying despatches for Lord Wellington at Ciudad Rodrigo. That's where you got that wound in your leg, wasn't it?"

"Oh, that was nothing, sir," Gideon protested. "The bullet went clean through." After a slight fever he'd been able to get in some hunting on the Spanish border with one of his friends, Brigade-Major Harry Smith of the 95th Rifles. Pushing Smith from his mind, the marquis asked, "How will I be working with de Vinnay?"

"Ah!" Brumley exclaimed. "You'll be his standby, the liaison between him and me. Won't do for him to appear to be in *my* pocket or to come near this office."

Gideon nodded his understanding. "What shall I do first, sir?"

"Nothing much. Let it be known Arnaud de Vinnay is an acquaintance of yours. Be seen with him. Then we shall see where it all leads us."

The Marquis of Huxford meant to pay his godmother, Lady Marpleby, a morning call that week but, with one thing and another, he found himself unable to do so. Thus it was several days before he met the American girl.

Lady Marpleby's ball was exactly the sort of thing he tried to avoid. No one was more surprised than she to see the marquis amble into her foyer. And just as she was about to disband the receiving line, too. Gideon St. Aubin visited her privately—he was her godson, after all. She never failed to send cards of invitation round to his Brook Street address. But it had been years since any of the fashionable hostesses had been able to rely on his presence. Lady Marpleby, never one to deny her own worth in polite society, was certain his appearance tonight was owed to her friendship with his dear departed mama. None of these reflections was allowed to show on her dish-faced countenance, however. She extended her gloved hands and smiled.

"Gideon, my dear boy! You can't know the joy it gives me to welcome you." She gazed dotingly at her tall godson, her cheek raised for a kiss.

The marquis smiled, which had the astonishing effect of unfreezing his face, so that Audrey Soames-Taylor, standing a few feet away, had a first glimpse of him rarely afforded others.

Audrey was aware that people in the ton claimed Gideon St. Aubin was a hard man to know. She'd been warned that he was arrogant and insufferably proud. Unimpressed with Englishmen, ready to believe the worst of a breed she held in disdain, she felt that such charges must hold at least a modicum of truth. Apparently the marquis spent all his time in the idle pursuit of pleasure. This did not surprise Audrey. He was a member of the Corinthian set, a nonpareil sportsman. He could afford to waste his time, for his fortune—so her Aunt Letty informed her—was one of the largest in England. Audrey could well understand why the marquis was considered the greatest catch of the 1813 London Season.

She watched St. Aubin as he took her aunt's hands and bent to kiss her.

"How could I stay away?" he murmured.

Her ladyship gave a gurgling cry of protest. "Oh, easily, I'm sure! Your sweet mama always claimed you'd do anything to avoid being bored."

The expression on Huxford's face softened still further. "She spoiled me dreadfully, didn't she, ma'am?"

"No," Lady Marpleby asserted. "You and your sister were the dearest treasures of her life."

Godmother and godson looked at one another for a long moment in shared sympathy, his lordship's jaw clenched.

Brought to herself, Lady M turned to the young lady beside her. "Gideon, allow me to present my niece from America. This is Miss Audrey Soames-Taylor from Boston. Audrey, the Marquis of Huxford and Baddingly, Gideon St. Aubin, my godchild."

As the marquis turned to greet her, Audrey received a remnant of the smile he had given her aunt. Clearly not for her, it faded and was immediately replaced by his usual stiff mask.

Audrey had been informed that Gideon St. Aubin was

attractive. This was a fine example of English understatement, she thought.

Huxford's classically shaped features produced a stark masculine beauty. He was dressed in the most impeccable evening attire, obviously made to fit his excellent figure perfectly by that haut men's designer, Weston. His gleaming white shirtfront was slightly ruffled, allowing a mere glimpse of a magnificent diamond stickpin—his only jewelry—and his shirt points were sufficiently high to proclaim the marquis conversant with the best in current fashion. As for his cravat, it was the best example of the exquisite—and very difficult—Oriental that Audrey had ever seen. He had long military sideburns and wore his dark hair in a style that suggested the Brutus. But it was his pale eyes, winter-gray and set well apart, that dominated his face. They were hooded and cynical, their flinty gaze shielding his thoughts, shutting out the world and revealing nothing of himself. Audrey was at once fascinated and repelled.

"Miss Soames-Taylor," he murmured, as Lady Marpleby finished her introduction.

Audrey struggled to return some innocuous reply but found she had an insane urge to say something that would bring back his smile.

Absurd, she chided herself. What a ridiculous notion! Her sense of humor rescued her as it had countless times in the past. Audrey laughed ruefully as she turned from Huxford to greet the next person in her aunt's receiving line.

2

The marquis frowned as he made his way to the card room. The girl had been amused—he hadn't missed the twinkle in her violet eyes—and he was unaccustomed to affecting marriageable young women that way.

Paden Offutt spied him, came across the room and cried, "Here, Gideon. I say! What has you looking so black? Oh! Met the American, have you? Didn't I tell you she wasn't in the common style? Well, what do you make of her?"

Gideon's face relaxed and he surveyed his protégé benignly. "You can't be drunk already, Paden. Only just met the girl. How can I know her after a simple how'ja do?"

Mr. Offutt, struck by this clever line of reasoning, nodded and watched as Huxford removed a silver snuffbox from his pocket. The marquis held it a moment before snapping it open. Taking a pinch, he looked about him.

Only someone well acquainted with Gideon St. Aubin would have detected the slight alteration in his manner as his attention fell on a man bending over one of the card tables, speaking to those seated there.

Following his friend's gaze, Paden grunted. "What? The Frenchman? Nothing amiss there. Arnaud de Vinnay appears everywhere in society. Entry in all the high places, you know. Hostesses dote on him. Has all the *on dits* at the tip of his tongue. Good man to know. He helped Reggie Selkirk redecorate Beakum House after the dowager baroness popped off. Selkirk refused to let her touch it before, you know," Paden confided.

The marquis elevated his eyeglass and surveyed his companion for a full half minute before he finally spoke.

"Now, Paden. Surely you can't think I'd have the slightest interest in the trifles and furbelows in the Baroness Rayne's drawing room?"

Mr. Offutt flushed. "Can't have been thinking, Hux. Tell you what you will like to hear. Bought m'self a pair of sweet goers at Tatt's yesterday."

"Not those bays of Motley's? Had to sell, did he? I was looking at them the day I left town. How much?"

"Four hundred guineas. Not dagger cheap, but I didn't want to haggle." Paden knew he was a good judge of horseflesh, yet his habit of relying on Gideon's counsel surfaced and he couldn't help feeling a trifle anxious.

"It's what I should have offered," Gideon said carelessly.

Paden breathed a sigh of relief when he discovered that Huxford admired the bays. Persons in the ton—both men and women—were known for the cattle they kept. To be driving a pair that excited the admiration and envy of friends, to ride a fine barb along Rotten Row each day, these were essentials necessary to members of the beau monde. Duels had been fought over a remark disparaging one's mount. Paden's father had been known for his bloodstock. His mother was one of the finest horsewomen in England. He stuck his hands in his pockets and assumed an air of nonchalance. "Glad you like the bays," he said, as they made their way to the card tables.

Two hours into the ball, Lady Marpleby watched Huxford approach the gathering around Audrey. Her niece was resting on a couch and laughing at something one of her admirers—Captain Ware—had said.

Paden sat by Audrey's side and plied her fan to cool her. Kit Hartwell, Lord Chartley, stood to one side, leaning negligently against the wall—his favorite pose. Kit was Gideon's best friend. Hanging across the back of the sofa, Lord Sir Giles Fawlkes concentrated his myopic gaze on Audrey's profile.

As the marquis drew near, a young man carrying a glass of lemonade advanced on the group. After maneuvering his way gingerly through the crowd, he handed the refreshment to the American, much as an offering to a goddess.

Audrey smiled. "Thank you, Mr. Eddington." She drank it half down. "I needed that," she assured him.

Her benefactor colored, stepped back, and collided with the Marquis of Huxford. "Sorry, m'Lord," Mr. Eddington began to apologize.

A shake of Huxford's head dismissed offense. "No harm done, Eddington," he drawled. He raised his eyepiece and aimed it at Audrey. "Doing the pretty to Miss Soames-Taylor, I see."

Audrey turned to confront the marquis. She'd been stared at often enough since she'd arrived in England. She thought it very rude in people. But no one had the audacity to raise his glass and subject her to an actual inspection! She felt her face grow hot.

His lordship dropped the offending glass but continued his examination. Turning his head to one side, he asked himself just what it was that made the girl so beautiful. Her eyes? They weren't overly large, but they held a violet brilliance he could recall seeing nowhere else. And they were beneath a brow of perfect symmetry. Shadowed temples and high cheekbones. A determined little chin. That chin, he noticed, seemed to be thrust in his direction at the moment. He folded his arms and continued his perusal. As Paden had mentioned, her hair was unique, a glorious shade of reddish-gold, uncut and exactly the color of ripe chestnuts. The girl was no slave to fashion. No short curls for her! Her locks were banded and braided to form a high crown. As regal as it was charming, Huxford thought. Like most men, he preferred long hair. He could imagine what Audrey Soames-Taylor would look like with it down. A single diamond star, fixed to the front and center of her heavy braids, created the effect of a diadem.

Huxford raised his eyeglasses again for a closer inspection. He dropped it when his gaze encountered Miss Soames-Taylor's. To his surprise, he perceived an angry glow. However, she placed her hand in his when he reached for it.

Lifting her fingers to his lips, he said, "Make you my compliments, ma'am. The reports were true."

Audrey's spine grew rigid. "Reports, my lord?"

"Tales of your beauty flying around me this past week."

Her eyes held a challenging glint. "Your lordship can't think I take credit for something bestowed on me by nature! Compliments are unnecessary."

Audrey was appalled as the words slipped past her teeth. She elevated her chin still further.

Her court fell abruptly silent. Miss Taylor, as she preferred to be called, had graciously received congratulations on her looks these past weeks, however little value she seemed to place on them. They turned as one to see the effect of her words on Huxford.

His mask cracked and a smile tugged at the corners of his mouth. He chuckled. His eyes lit. He threw back his head and laughed aloud. Tightening his hand on her fingers, he drew Audrey to her feet.

"Who," Huxford demanded, "has the next dance on your card?"

Audrey, so angry she was trembling, collected her wits enough to say, "My card is blank, my lord. The next dance is a waltz and I haven't been to Almack's yet."

Her Aunt Marpleby had been most adamant on this point. "No one, my dear, dances the waltz without having first been presented by one of the hostesses at Almack's as a desirable partner."

The first strains of the music were sweeping the ballroom. "But Miss Soames-Taylor! I cannot think *you* would care for that!" His tone was satirical.

"Certainly not! It's Aunt Letty. She wishes me to conform to the mores of London society, however I may view them."

The marquis took her lemonade, handed it to Mr. Offutt, and said, "Paden, would you hold this? Miss Soames-Taylor and I shall promenade."

They proceeded to do so, strolling along the edges of the crowded room. Huxford tucked one of her hands in the crook of his elbow and Audrey could only conclude he meant for them to be considered a couple. They stopped often as he spoke to those he wished to recognize, introducing her as his partner for the set.

Their progression around the long salon brought them at last to Lady Marpleby, who appeared fidgety and extremely uneasy.

"Huxford!" she cried. "Here you are with Audrey! I see you didn't care to waltz. But then ... that is to say ... what a very novel idea, I'm sure! Merely to walk about while others are dancing, thereby setting a new fashion! How ... but perhaps another time!"

Ignoring his godmama's disjointed attempts at conversation, the marquis thanked Audrey and reached for her card. He located Paden's name engaged for a quadrille after supper, scratched through it, and wrote in his own. With proper compliments all round, he took himself off to the card rooms once more.

It was almost twelve when the marquis and his party arose from the card table in the blue salon.

Stretching as he stood, Arnaud de Vinnay politely stifled a yawn. "My game was out tonight," he remarked to Kit Hartwell. "As was yours, my friend."

The viscount shrugged; Kit cared little for games of chance. "I've been distracted all evening. But Motley's luck was in. More so than usual, I believe."

This individual bowed and scooped in his winnings. Sir Malcolm Motley's smile was thin as he said, "You must avail yourselves of the opportunity to recoup your losses as early as may be, gentlemen."

Sir Malcolm knew himself for a gamester of the worst sort. Long ago he had realized his whole existence focused on the wager, the prospect of proving himself invincible in the face of unbeatable odds. Now, after a long dry spell, his luck had turned—capriciously as it did once in a while—so everything he touched, every card he turned and every bet he made, was his.

Except in retrospect, Sir Malcolm was never able to enjoy such a run. He knew he must spend every possible moment in play. So long as Fortune smiled, he must win enough to see him through those arid days, inevitable as the sun, when nothing he did was right.

Motley was especially pleased to take St. Aubin's money. The marquis had a disagreeable way of seeming to know how desperate he was to win. The nonchalance Sir Malcolm affected had the dismal habit of abandoning him, almost on cue, whenever Huxford was present. And there were other factors that made his lordship less than easy to love. This hatred for Huxford had long fueled Motley's one-sided enmity. It was an enmity he cherished and lovingly sustained. Huxford's titles and honors, coupled with the fortune he'd inherited, brought home exactly what Sir Malcolm was: the third son of a country squire, forever on the scramble for funds enough to subsist on the fringes of society.

Motley went down to supper. He must eat enough to sustain him through tomorrow; he had no intention of squandering money on food. He was lost in his favorite fantasy. It was this: He and Gideon St. Aubin were engaged in cards, alone and with no distractions, when one of Motley's golden runs was on. A wave of something almost sensual crept over him. Motley paused, clutching the stair rail, the imaginary scene vivid in his mind.

As hand after hand fell to himself, the marquis at last admitted he was done up. In the hard dawn St. Aubin's face was haggard. He stammered that he needed time to make good his IOU's while Motley graciously insisted he take all the time necessary.

Sir Malcolm drew a deep breath. It wasn't impossible. It could happen. It *could!* In a cloud of euphoria, he ascended the stairs and hurried to the supper room.

Satisfied that Paden had secured Miss Soames-Taylor's company at supper, Huxford made his way toward them. They were at a table occupied by Lady Marpleby and her ancient cicisbeo, Lord Egbertt Higglesby. His lordship was about seventy, a tall, heavy man, still powerful, and with a large leonine head of curly white hair. He was jovial, laughed readily, and was quite good-looking. He was habitually absent-minded, somewhat deaf, and completely devoted to "his Letty."

Lord Egbertt, discovering the marquis looming at his elbow, gave a grunt and boomed, "Gideon, m'boy! Haven't seen you in an age. Must have been two—no!—three weeks. Well, it was! In White's the night Chartley bet Salford he could stare longer without blinking his eyes. Laid a pony on himself, as I recall. Won it, too! Probably been practicing all day, you know. *Would* that thing need practice? Maybe not. Might very well be something you were born with. Where were you?" he asked *volte-face*, directing a keen gaze at the marquis from under bushy white brows.

Audrey, whose acquaintance with Lord Egbertt had gone forth alarmingly well these past few days, suddenly coughed into her napkin to hide her smile.

Paden, however, was betrayed into outright laughter. "Never ask Huxford where he disappears to, sir, unless you want to be raked over the coals," Paden advised.

Sir Egbertt stabbed the air with a blunt forefinger. "Ha! He'll never use me as he does you, m'boy! I've known Gideon St. Aubin all his life. Dandled him on my knees when he was an infant. Was in love with his grandmother once for three whole weeks. Calf love, m'dear," he informed Lady Marpleby. "She was older than me," he explained. "That was years before I laid eyes on you, m'love!"

Still pursuing the mystery of Gideon's disappearance, his lordship returned his attention to the marquis. "I know: secret business—Brumley and the foreign office, eh?" He winked one rheumy eye. "Say no more, m'boy," he begged Gideon, who had not uttered a word. "Spy stuff," he announced at top register. "Sh! Don't worry. Mum's the word, what?"

"Just so, sir," Huxford said, his sleepy gaze assessing the laughter in Audrey Taylor's eyes.

He laid his hand on Lady Marpleby's shoulder. "May I join you, ma'am?"

Paden Offutt, taking Lady M's welcome for granted, leaped up and began rearranging chairs, nabbing one from the adjoining table. "Here, Hux!" he cried. "Sit between Lady Marpleby and Miss Taylor."

The marquis agreed and excused himself to fill his plate at the buffet. It was some time before he returned. The others, except for Lord Higglesby, were starting to eat.

His lordship, finishing a lengthy speech with Sir Cosmo Orphington, turned after telling Sir Cosmo in no uncertain terms there was no room at the table. Egbertt smiled complacently at Lady M. "Told the damned fellow he wasn't wanted, m'dear."

Eyes sparkling, Lady Marpleby begged him to eat.

As Egbertt reached for his fork, he recoiled. "Here, I say!" He stared suspiciously at his plate, loaded with lobster patties, pearled onions, filet of sole, and green peas.

"What is it, my dear?" Lady Marpleby asked.

"Peas!" exclaimed Egbertt.

Her ladyship was bewildered. "What?" she asked.

"Peas!" Egbertt reiterated. He threw his napkin on the table and complained in exasperation, "I'll tell you what it is, Letty. It's that damned cook of mine. I'm going to have to get rid of him!"

Sadly shaking his head, his lordship proceeded to apologize to the Marquis of Huxford. "Beg pardon, I'm sure. If I've told the fellow once it's a hundred times! 'Don't put chunks of red stuff in the peas,' I said. Who wants to be put off his food having to dodge a bunch of red spots in his peas, now I ask you?"

Lady M was tugging at Egbertt's sleeve and he turned. "Letty, didn't you have a cook who made peas like this?"

It registered that her ladyship was trying to communicate something. Egbertt leaned closer and patted her hand. "What is it, m'love?"

"It's my cook, Egbertt."

"Eh?"

"We're at Marpleby House and it's my cook who made these peas."

Higglesby glanced vaguely about. "By Jove, so it is! Forgot where I was, m'dear." He patted Letty's hand again. "I remember now: your niece. It's a ball in her honor. And there she is," he said, beaming across the table at Audrey. Suddenly he leaned back in his chair. "Gad, what a relief!"

"Relief, Egbertt?" Lady M asked faintly.

His lordship spoke around a large bite of lobster. "Won't have to hire m'self a new cook," he mumbled in simple satisfaction.

3

Toward the end of their meal, Lady Marpleby turned to her godson. "Gideon, when is Victoria coming to London?"

"I'm going into Sussex in a few days; she's returning with me then."

"Wonderful!" trilled Lady M. "I'm looking forward to so many exciting events this season! Audrey, you remember my telling you about Gideon's sister and how she stays with me whenever she's in town. Well! Gideon's is a bachelor household and what would Victoria do there? Anyway, it's going to be such fun, having you girls with me!"

The ball lasted until two o'clock. Lady Marpleby had enjoyed herself immensely, but she was so worried and exhausted by the time everyone left, she couldn't sleep.

The moment she closed her eyes, Letty's brain persisted in casting images. All of them were of Audrey and Huxford. His dark head bent to catch what she was saying. The girl's eyes laughing at some outrageous utterance of his at the dinner table. The way he looked at her when she turned to speak to someone else. And worst of all, the very attractive picture they made when he handed her through the quadrille.

Lady M was sure that more eyes than her own had noted the grace with which they performed the figures of the dance. And then, having done away with Audrey's unfortunate partner, Huxford had thoughtlessly executed another of those promenades around the hall.

It was, her ladyship recalled, a country dance, for she had been forced to endure an endless interval of straining to catch a glimpse of them through the pattern of dancers. Gideon might just as well have danced with the girl again! No, not that precisely, but the intimate way he kept his hand on the small of Audrey's back as they stood talking to Lord Palmerston was . . . Words failed Lady M; she could have screamed. And to compound matters, what had poor Egbertt done except raise his glass and proclaim at the top of his lungs that the handsomest couple at the ball was Miss Soames-Taylor and the Marquis of Huxford? Lady M moaned. Couple, indeed! Calling attention to them that way! But what did it matter? Most of her guests had already discovered the interesting spectacle of her niece and the marquis as they made that second fatal progression around the room!

Lady M fell asleep at last, but rest eluded her. Morning found her cross and more worried than ever, still preoccupied with the problem of her niece and Gideon St. Aubin.

Audrey mustn't be allowed to develop a tendresse for Gideon. It simply would *not* do! And so Lady Marpleby meant to tell Audrey the moment she returned from her morning ride with Paden Offutt.

This, however, Lady Marpleby was unable to do, for who must enter her sitting room with her niece and Paden except Huxford himself, followed by her own dear Lord Egbertt Higglesby? Lady M's tête-à-tête must be postponed.

She watched Gideon laughing at something Audrey had said. Lady M felt her pulse leap in her throat. The girl must not be allowed to fall in love with him! If she did, her heart would surely be broken.

Marpleby House had another caller that morning, and never had Lady M had a less welcome guest. Mr. Archibald Emmerhite was as much of a gossip as old Creevey, she thought. One thing she had to admit: he was a stickler for the prevailing niceties. Thirty minutes was the proper lapse of time for paying a morning call, and Mr. Emmerhite seemed to pride himself on being precise to a hair. He always arose on the stroke of the half hour.

Lady Marpleby knew that Archibald Emmerhite had a mission in life. He had once informed her he intended to go down in history as one of the great diarists of his period. An assiduous man, Mr. Emmerhite assured her, couldn't waste time in rewrites. Therefore, he was forever double checking his data. Such was his apparent determination on the morning following Lady Marpleby's ball.

Audrey looked away from the quizzical glance Huxford had just given her to see Mr. Emmerhite crossing the yellow salon where she, her aunt, and their callers were seated.

Aunt Letty had brought Mr. Emmerhite to Audrey's attention within days of her arrival, so she had been acquainted with him for several weeks. Audrey almost expected Mr. Emmerhite to rustle when he walked; he was a thin man and dry looking. "Be careful how you use Emmerhite," her aunt had warned. "He is amiable, friendly, and credulous to a degree you can't imagine. He believes whatever he first hears and his coin in one house is what he gleans in another. I have found it profitable, over the years, when I had news I wished placed, simply to whisper it in Archibald Emmerhite's ear. It will be all over town within hours."

Mr. Emmerhite crossed the yellow salon. After proper salutations, Mr. Emmerhite adjured everyone to ignore him and continue their visiting. "I'll just sit beside Miss Soames-Taylor," he said, "and check a few details I jotted down last week." And so saying, he took his familiar notebook from his pocket and beamed at Lady Marpleby's company.

But Lord Higglesby heaved himself from his chair. "No, no, Emmerhite. You go ahead. Carry on your interview with Miss Taylor. As for me, I can't *jauk* about here all day, y'know. Only came by for a moment."

Egbertt and Lady M passed out of the room, leaving Paden and the marquis to audit the catechism Audrey was forced to endure.

Mr. Offutt moved his chair closer to help Mr. Emmerhite with his facts. "Yes," he said. "I think I might start my own diary in a year or so. Be a good thing; I can include a lot of stuff about my stud. Useful information, that. Interesting, too." He smiled.

Audrey tried to ignore the satirical look on the marquis's face as she was forced to dredge up dates and information Mr. Emmerhite felt necessary for his account of their meeting.

". . . Boston," she was telling him. "Yes, a town house there and a plantation about twelve miles out. It's a horse farm, a country estate. Papa was famous for his stud, you know. We raise a breed of thoroughbreds Papa developed from an Arabian strain—the Byerly Turk line, crossed with descendants of the intrepid Bulle Rock. The Rock was the first thoroughbred imported from England to America, in about 1730, I believe Papa said. You remember, Mr. Offutt. I was telling you about it."

Audrey saw that Paden was showing unmistakable signs of a desire to launch into a long discussion of judicious crossbreeding. Luckily Huxford came forward just at that moment.

"Sorry to interrupt," he apologized as he took her hand. Audrey had heard of warm tingles, but this was the first time she had experienced them.

"Have you engaged yourself to drive in the park today?" Huxford asked.

Paden broke in before she could answer. "You'll like that, Miss Taylor! Those grays of Gideon's are famous! It will be the grays, won't it, Hux?"

"Yes." The marquis's eyes were grave. "It will certainly be the grays if Miss Taylor grants me the pleasure of her company."

"Oh, she will!" cried Paden. "Well! What I mean is, who wouldn't? Team like that?"

"Still," his lordship said, "I should like to hear it from her own lips." He surprised Audrey by breaking into a grin that lightened his expression and warmed her like the sun.

Audrey was unable to withhold an answering smile. "As Mr. Offutt says, my lord, anyone would be desirous of being taken up after your grays. I shall be delighted."

Huxford laughed and grasped her hand more tightly before releasing it.

* * *

At five Audrey was dressed in a close gown of loden green with a matching bonnet. She carried a small muff and wore kid gloves and dark half boots. She was about to be driven in the parade the beau monde engaged in each afternoon, meeting in the park to ride, walk and gossip, to see old friends and meet new.

They arrived in the park, and Huxford drove them around the track. Lord Petersham was there and hailed them, waving one of his famous canes.

Audrey had heard his lordship never left home until late afternoon. He was a great womanizer, Aunt Letty said, with a penchant for actresses, an out-and-outer. Now he seemed to be eyeing her with the warmest approbation.

"Have Huxford bring you around to my house, my dear. I shall concoct you a jar of snuff of your own special sort."

Audrey, who would as likely be caught killing rats as sniffing snuff, knew when a signal honor was bestowed on her. She smiled as prettily as she could and thanked Petersham.

Lord Petersham dragged his gaze from her and ran his eyes caressingly over Huxford's team of grays. "They're beautiful," he lisped, "but wouldn't do for me, you know. I never drive anything except browns."

As they drove away, the marquis explained. "It's true, you know. Petersham dresses in brown, his cattle are brown, and so are his harnesses and leather riggings. Brown as his snuff. A small affection. They've even coined a new color: It's called Petersham brown."

A faint shadow of the distaste Audrey felt must have crossed her features. This caught Huxford's attention. "Can you not approve, Miss Taylor? One must have something to fill one's time. Petersham's little preoccupations—his snuff, his canes, his tea—are his hobbies, you see. A man could have worse."

"As you say, my lord," Audrey replied carefully. She was determined not to rise to the marquis's bait. As a visitor to England, she mustn't reveal what she thought of a man who had nothing better to do with his life.

Something—his own peculiar demon, Audrey thought—

prompted the marquis to dig a little deeper. "Do no Americans collect canes or mix snuff?" he asked.

"They may very well do so, my lord," Audrey answered repressively.

They drove past a matron with two bracket-faced daughters. The marquis ignored the lady's attempts to hail him, lifted his hat, and drove blithely on. He glanced down at the figure beside him. "They may very well do so . . ." he repeated. "But what, Miss Taylor? Your answer was incomplete." His tone was lightly mocking, as if he were idly amusing himself by ragging her.

Audrey's tenuous grip on her temper snapped. "American men may very well do so, my lord, but *only* in spare moments to relax from their *work!* Their business, if you will, is to make a living to support themselves and their families and to build estates to succor them in their old age!"

Her face felt flushed when she finished and her breathing was clearly audible. Audrey clenched her fists and ground her teeth as the marquis unhurriedly pulled his team to a halt. Placidly, he eyed her countenance.

Audrey hadn't the faintest idea how she must look.

"What fuss, Miss Taylor! What passion! I take it that you are infected with this work ethic your countrymen are so justly famous for." There was a faintly perceptible smile on the marquis's lips and one of his eyebrows quirked upward. And something, she didn't know what, made Audrey suspect he was containing his laughter.

She went from pink to white. Never in her life had she felt so murderous! Gideon St. Aubin was the rudest, positively the vilest man she'd ever had the displeasure of meeting. He was precisely the sort of Englishman she despised—proud, superior, and superficial!

Audrey closed her eyes and took control of her emotions. When she opened them, she set her wide-eyed gaze on his and said in mock concern, "Your poor cattle, Huxford! Should they be left standing in this wind?"

At dusk, Audrey was dressing for dinner when Lady Marpleby entered her room.

Gazing with pleasure at her niece in chartreuse gauze, Lady M sighed. The dress, daringly bereft of lace, was shirred and layered in panels of white. "No one, my love, could carry that gown off half so well as you."

Audrey smiled her thanks and held up a diamond drop, suspended from a long chain. She motioned for her dresser to fasten it at the nape of her neck. Then she stepped back to inspect herself. She nodded in an offhand way to Matlock, the sturdy woman who waited for her verdict.

"Yes. Thank you, Matty, that's fine." Turning to her aunt, Audrey asked if she were ready to go down.

"No," her ladyship said. She took Audrey's hand. "My dear," she began hesitantly, "I don't quite know how to say this, but I fear that I should warn you."

At Audrey's raised brows, Lady M rushed on. "A young woman in the beau monde, especially if she's as beautiful as you are, is often subjected to the most concerted rush. I . . . I have no doubt you'll know how to keep the gentlemen in line. You are quite level-headed, I'm thankful to say. But the gossips will have a field day, and possibly do irreparable damage, if they think you might be encouraging Huxford. His reputation is such . . . he is thought to be very . . . fast, my love. He could ruin you, if the mood struck him. I don't know what he might not do, if he took it in his head to . . ." Lady M faltered before her niece's glittering eyes.

"Is this really necessary, Aunt?" Audrey asked sharply.

"Yes. I understand your reluctance to hear it, but I'd never forgive myself if I didn't give you fair warning. You mustn't allow your head to be turned, even the slightest, by Gideon's attentions. You're not used to the ways of London society, and perhaps . . . Audrey, my godson has been on the town for years. No one who knows Gideon expects him to marry before he must, except for family reasons, such as securing an heir to the St. Aubin name.

"He doesn't carry on light, harmless flirtations like most men in society. In fact, he isn't in the beau monde much. No, he confines himself to the world of the demireps. I don't think I've seen Gideon at Almack's half a dozen times these past ten years, and then it was to escort his mother or sister Victoria. Nor is he likely to appear at balls, or rout parties or—oh, never at musicales! He comes here, of course, but that's because I'm his godmother. He shuns the polite world, and—truth to tell—most of the society mamas have grown wary of him. Besides, he's sporting mad, you see, and belongs to all the clubs and important hunts. He even boxes, they say. Although why anyone should climb into a ring of ropes and try to stand there and get hit is beyond me, and so I've told him. Audrey, please don't fall in love with him! I couldn't bear to see your heart broken!"

Lady Marpleby's face suddenly crumpled and she was in the midst of one of her damp spells again. Audrey had learned she cried as easily as a child.

Audrey embraced her aunt in an effort to soothe her, but when she replied, her voice was not at all comforting.

Lady Marpleby jerked the handkerchief from her eyes when she heard her niece's brittle laugh. There was a militant expression in Audrey's features, and it was plain to see she was laboring under a fit of agitation.

"Fall in love with Gideon St. Aubin?" she cried. "Why, ma'am, I'd as soon fall in love with a fence post. Sooner! The marquis has about as much compassion and is proud and arrogant besides!"

Audrey bit her lip, seeing her aunt's eyes go round. "I'm sorry if such plain speaking hurts your feelings, Aunt Letty. I know you care for Huxford for his mother's sake. But you may rest easy. If ever I develop a tender emotion for a man, I can promise he won't be an Englishman. As for the marquis, I wouldn't have him if he were the last man in the world!"

By the time Audrey reached the end of this impassioned speech, her voice had risen. She was breathing rapidly. She pressed both hands to her cheeks in an effort to cool them. After a moment she hugged Lady Marpleby again. "So do come along, Aunt Letty," she said more calmly. "And don't worry. I shan't lose my heart to the Marquis of Huxford!"

But as Lady M accompanied her niece down the stairs, she felt no particular ease. She found herself wishing her godson was away on a foreign mission or visiting in the country. Anywhere, in fact, except London.

4

Almack's Assembly Rooms were all Audrey expected them to be. Her vouchers had arrived from Lady Emily Cowper. A small note accompanied the tickets. In it, Lady Emily mentioned that her brother Melbourne had solicited them for Miss Soames-Taylor at the behest of the Marquis of Huxford. She looked forward, her ladyship wrote, to seeing Lady Marpleby and her niece at the next subscription ball.

The assembly rooms were quite crowded when Lady Marpleby's party arrived. Most of Audrey's particular friends were on hand.

Paden Offutt busied himself with getting Audrey's dance card filled. Mr. Eddington, Lord Fawlkes, and several others seemed anxious to dance with her. He signed them all up and included two special friends he had dragged along for the occasion. He introduced them as Ambrose "Pinky" Tadburn and Farquar Fulverton.

"Went to school with me, don't you know?" Paden told Audrey. "Found 'em at Tatt's today laying down a couple of bets and made 'em promise to come." Then he exclaimed, "Ho, ho! Almost forgot!" He proceeded to sign Audrey's card again, writing in Huxford's name for a quadrille and the first waltz. "Orders," he added cryptically.

"But the marquis is nowhere in sight," Audrey protested.

"Will be. Said to expect him. Said to sign his name twice. A country dance and the first waltz. There—I've done it."

Paden waved Audrey's dance card in front of her nose and excused himself. "Must go now. See a fellow across the room. Here, talk to Tadburn and Fulverton about horses. Had to promise you would or they wouldn't come."

Audrey found herself staring at the two young men standing before her.

Mr. Tadburn bowed. "Paden said you might know, Miss. Soames-Taylor."

"Yes?" Audrey smiled encouragingly. "Know what, Mr. Tadburn? And please call me Miss Taylor."

Pinky coughed and nodded. "Should tell you. I'm a member of the Auld Masters Coaching and Harness Society," he began by way of explanation. "Paden's a member, too. Fulverton here ain't. He can't drive."

Lord Fulverton blinked once and bowed.

"Cow handed," Pinky added.

Lord Fulverton bowed again and blinked twice.

Mr. Tadburn plunged on. "Thing is, Miss Taylor, I've got this leader with a bad place on his shoulder. Can't get him cured up. Even Fulverton can't cure him. Anybody cure a horse of anything, Fulverton can. Only he can't cure my Tony horse. Can't harness poor old Tony with a bad shoulder, now I ask you. So what's to do, Miss Taylor?"

Audrey had begun to be amused as she listened to the conversation, but the plight of poor Tony soon took hold of her imagination. Before she knew it she was deep into horse doctoring. She asked for a description of the injury that afflicted Tony, its size, exact location, and duration.

"I expect your groom used a collar that was too short," she murmured. Then she inquired about Tony's size and age.

Tony was found to be six years old, stand sixteen-and-a-half-hands high, and weigh one hundred and ten stone.

Audrey did some rapid mental calculations. *Fourteen pounds to the stone.* "Fifteen hundred and fifty pounds!" she exclaimed. "My, he sounds like a fine animal!" She fell silent and stood gazing off into a corner of the ballroom, trying to think what could be done for the carriage horse.

Pinky and Lord Fulverton were respectfully attentive until she finished her cogitations.

Finally Audrey roused herself and said, "Well, I once saw my father cure a drayman's draft animal of a shoulder rub that wouldn't heal. Here's what he did. He took some arsenic . . ."

Both young men drew in their breaths.

"Yes, arsenic!" Audrey continued. "And he separated the hairs right at the tip of old Jack's tail and made a tiny slit. Each week, on the same weekday mind you, he repeated the operation, increasing the dosage a little each time. That was to accustom Jack's system to the effects of the poison, you see."

Mr. Offutt had returned and was listening. He, along with Tadburn and Fulverton, nodded, spellbound.

"By the end of the fourth week, Jack's shoulder had begun to heal. In three month's time it was well. But!—and now, gentlemen, this is *most* important—each week thereafter, my father had his groom continue the operation. Only this time he worked in the reverse, don't you see? So as to detoxify Jack's body. That was seven years ago and I saw Jack pulling his beer wagon not two months before I left Boston!"

They stared at her in the liveliest astonishment. Mr. Tadburn reached for her hand and shook it heartily. "Thank you, Miss Taylor," he said fervently. "I'm going to m'stables right this moment and start Tony on that stuff!"

"Here!" Paden interrupted. "You can't go now; the dance is starting. You'll leave four blanks on Miss Taylor's card!"

"Oh," Audrey waved this objection aside. "Never mind that. We can all dance another time!"

"Yes, by Jove!" Pinky cried. "Anyone ever tell you you're a capital girl, Miss Taylor?" He became aware that Lord Fulverton was plucking at his sleeve. "Don't do that, Farq," Pinky admonished, shoving his friend's hand away. "Ruin the set of m'coat!"

Lord Fulverton blinked. He leaned over and whispered in Pinky's ear.

"What?" Pinky exclaimed. "You're sure?"

More whispers from Fulverton, whereupon Pinky turned to the bemused girl. "Miss Taylor," he intoned, "Lord Farquar Fulverton asks me to say he wishes to meet with you and your aunt tomorrow to offer you a marriage in form."

Audrey felt her mouth drop open, and Paden cried, "No! Now, see here! Miss Taylor ain't in the marriage mart. Besides, she don't have a portion. Her papa got rolled up in trade or some such. There isn't a thing in the kick."

Lord Fulverton whispered earnestly in his friend's ear.

Pinky turned to Mr. Offutt. "Fulverton tells me that makes no difference. Says he's got enough juice for the both of them. Says he's always wanted a wife who understands horses. Well! If I didn't need to marry money, I'd offer for the girl m'self!"

At that very moment, Huxford arrived to take Audrey away for the quadrille.

Quite forgetting their former constraint, she vowed she was never so glad to see anyone in her life. "For you must know, Huxford, that I found myself utterly speechless!"

The marquis threw back his head and guffawed when she explained what had happened. "Fulverton proposed because you told Tadburn how to cure his horse?" He grinned.

"Yes! And you may laugh, but I can't think what I'm to say tomorrow when that pair descends upon Aunt Letty and me!"

"Do you want to marry him?" Huxford wasn't laughing anymore; there was a peculiar set to his mouth.

"Absolutely not! Nor anyone else in England, my lord."

"Then say only that you are honored but regretfully decline."

"That's all?" she asked, turning her face up to his.

"Certainly." His eyelids half hid his hard gaze as he stared at her for a long moment. "No explanation is necessary."

As Audrey looked up at him questioningly, he put his hand on the small of her back. "Come," he said. "They're beginning our set."

After their dance Huxford disappeared into the card rooms.

The next time Audrey saw him he was talking to Viscount Chartley. She felt the weight of their gaze. Surely they weren't discussing her, Audrey thought. But when she looked again, they were still watching her. When Lord Chartley came to claim her for a country set, Huxford never took his eyes off them.

Chartley escorted Audrey to her chair, and she took her seat beside Melbourne's sister, Lady Emily Lamb Cowper.

Lady Emily's husband, Lord Cowper of Althrops, was absent from the scene, but her ladyship wasn't unescorted. Hanging over her chair, laughing infectiously, stood Henry Temple, 3rd Viscount Palmerston, England's young secretary of war. Palmerston greeted Miss Taylor and shook Huxford's hand when he came to join the group. Cocking his brow at the marquis, Palmerston invited him to sit by Emily Cowper.

"Take Lady Marpleby's chair," his lordship said. "She's gone off for some punch." Palmerston winked at Huxford and glanced meaningfully at Audrey.

The marquis nodded, took Lady M's vacated chair, and leaned forward to say something in Emily Cowper's ear, murmuring so that only she and Palmerston could hear.

On the opposite side, Audrey couldn't imagine what he'd said. But she thought it must have been quite *broad*, for suddenly her ladyship shrieked and laughed.

"Stop that, Huxford! You're a bad, naughty man! Henry! Make him stop." She stuck the marquis lightly with her fan. He grinned and whispered to her again.

She glanced sideways at Audrey. "But this is her first visit to Almack's! Surely Miss Soames-Taylor should wait until next time to dance the waltz!"

At Gideon's level gaze, and urged by Lord Palmerston, her ladyship capitulated. "Oh, very well." Smiling, she stood and pulled Audrey to stand with her. Huxford stood also.

"My dear marquis," Lady Emily said. "May I present Miss Soames-Taylor as a most charming partner for the waltz?" She placed Audrey's hand in Gideon's as the first lilting strains of the season's most fashionable waltz—"Ah du lieber Augustine"—wafted through the room.

Audrey decided that Huxford's arms were quite different from those of the short little dancing master Aunt Letty hired two mornings a week. Monsieur Furet was plump and perspired heavily; his gloves were always damp.

Huxford's hands, bare of gloves, were lean and strong. Audrey felt her fingers warmed by his grip. His arm, clasped about her waist, pulled her close. Whenever she glanced up, his eyes searched her face.

Averting her gaze, Audrey found herself lost in a dream. Her world telescoped as she and Huxford whirled round and round to the music. They made a lightning reversal and turned with the music. The prescribe twelve-inch separation vanished as she was drawn against him. Audrey would have fallen then had he not steadied her.

When the violins finally died, they were left breathless, eyes locked. Releasing her, Huxford stepped back, his face assuming its enigmatic expression.

Audrey found that he had steered her back to her aunt.

Thanking Audrey absently, the marquis bade her goodnight. He left without speaking to anyone.

The night was dark and threatening rain. Huxford ambled along Picadilly, then traversed Berkeley Square and walked along Davies until he reached Brook Street. In his study, he tossed aside his evening jacket and loosened his cravat. This game he'd been playing with Audrey Taylor had suddenly gotten out of hand. He'd known how much he wanted her physically. Simply thinking of her—even casually—could bring him to a state of instant arousal.

And tonight, when she'd said that Fulverton wanted to marry her, he felt as if some force had hit him in the middle. He'd laughed, but until Audrey assured him that she didn't want to marry Fulverton, something had squeezed his heart. That was when he realized he was in danger of falling in love with the girl. That would never do. He didn't want to get married, and Audrey wasn't someone he could take and forget. If he capitulated and asked her to marry him, and if she agreed, she'd never be happy living in England. Frustrated, he climbed the stairs to bed. He would draw back from the friendship that had been developing between them, giving her a chilling set down or two, and therefore, a reason to dislike him. Then he'd make himself scarce. It was all he could think to do.

Two mornings later, astride his black stallion Erasmus, Huxford met Audrey, surrounded by her escorts. He reined in and watched the girl approach with Paden Offutt, Viscount Chartley, and Captain Ware. Paden had the right of it, the marquis thought. Audrey Taylor looked a vision on a horse. She was dressed in a blue habit that turned her complexion to peach. Her eyes under the small, curly-brimmed hat were deep violet, almost plum colored.

Audrey greeted him but seemed more interested in his mount, Erasmus. It was common courtesy for one rider to admire another's mount, but Huxford could not doubt the girl's sincerity, for her eyes lit with pleasure and she cried, "Beautiful! And up to your weight, my lord. Most horses large enough to carry you would appear ungainly. But not this fellow!"

The marquis saw that she was actually cooing at this barb, and Erasmus, fool animal, looked straight at his admirer, tossed his head, and snorted in a companionable way.

Laughter erupted from Miss Taylor's cavalry, as Paden had so aptly described it.

"Here, Hux," Mr. Offutt called. "This is the mare I found at Tatt's for Miss Taylor. Ain't she a pretty thing?"

With a swift side-glance at the girl, the marquis commenced inspecting the new mount. The seconds lengthened while he silently noted the thinly arched neck, the small beautiful head, smooth rump, and dainty fetlocks.

Glancing once again at Audrey, Huxford drawled, "I never especially liked bays."

He saw her visibly flinch. After one startled look that pierced Huxford's flinty gaze, she dropped her lashes.

Audrey's escort seemed astounded. Paden stuttered in astonished accents, "But Gideon, that can't be true! Only last month you said . . ."

Feigning a convenient deafness, the marquis raised his hat and rode away, down Rotten Row. It took every bit of his determination not to look back. He admitted he was in full retreat, realizing that it might already be too late. He was perilously near to falling in love with the girl. All the arguments he'd given himself last night still held: he and Audrey Taylor weren't right for each other. She must never know how he felt about her, never suspect that she—of all the women he'd ever met—could affect him the way she did.

Left behind in the park, Audrey stared at Huxford's retreating back. She was puzzled . . . and . . . yes, hurt. She lifted her chin and smiled brilliantly through threatening tears. Keep smiling, she told herself, as she led the way down the bridle path.

Lord Chartley was silent amidst reassurances from Captain Ware, Paden, and Mr. Eddington, all of whom set themselves to make Miss Taylor feel better.

The viscount frowned and narrowed his eyes as he watched his friend Huxford disappear. He turned to look at the American. She was forcing a smile that didn't quite reach those remarkable eyes. Kit pursed his lips and whistled softly.

When she arrived back at Marpleby House, all Audrey could think about was gaining her room. She'd never been so thoroughly snubbed in her life!

But her aunt was entertaining morning callers. Mr. Emmerhite and the Baroness Whitehead and her daughter were ensconced in the blue drawing room.

Audrey was forced to subdue her desire for solitude. Never had morning callers dawdled so, staying until Audrey was quite out of patience. Old Emmerhite was bad enough, but the baroness was a nasty tabby who never failed to remark that she couldn't imagine why American men had let Audrey get to the advanced age of twenty-three without snapping her up in matrimony. This was a theme Lady Whitehead expanded upon each time she found herself in company with Audrey. The woman seemed to have no other topic of conversation.

The Whiteheads left at last, accompanied by Mr. Emmerhite.

During lunch, each time Audrey thought of Huxford's provocative—one might almost say *mocking*—statement about her mare, she had difficulty swallowing. His words were deliberate, a carefully veiled insult; there was no denying that. But what was his motivation? Not that it mattered, but only two nights past he had seemed to like her very well.

She spent an interminable afternoon trailing through the Pantheon Bazaar, shopping with her aunt. When they arrived home Lady M commented on all their purchases and debated at length the advisability of returning two ells of puce satin trim.

At long last, Audrey escaped to her room. Lying across her bed, ignoring her headache, she spent an hour wrestling with her anger. Who did Huxford think he was? If anything could confirm her convictions about Englishmen, this last was it. Resolutely deciding the marquis was a boor, Audrey firmly put him out of her head.

But to keep him out required such effort that she fell asleep and had to be awakened to dress for dinner.

In her aunt's carriage that night, rumbling over the cobblestones toward Lady Lancaster's ball, Audrey's brain felt sore from the strain of exorcising Gideon St. Aubin. If only he would remain there, she would gladly have consigned the man to the nether regions. He had a way of appearing in her mind's eye that was most disconcerting. If only he would always frown and look black, Audrey thought, she could have borne it. But he persisted in laughing—really, he had the most attractive laugh—with a gleam in his eye she found almost impossible to resist.

Audrey leaned her head against the seat of the carriage. It was a relief not to talk; the din of the wheels precluded speech even from Lord Egbertt.

It wasn't until the horses were stopped that his lordship roused himself to ask where they were.

"Lancaster House," Lady Marpleby told him. "It's the ball for their second daughter. Her come out. I told you, Egbertt."

Egbertt gazed down at her ladyship. "Did you, m'love? Forgot. That's a devilish pretty dress you have on, Letty. You'll put all the young girls to the blush. Have the gallants falling all over themselves to dance with you."

Lady M shushed her cavalier, but once inside, they found themselves in a clutch of Letty's elderly admirers and his lordship's prediction came true. Audrey sat beside Lord Egbertt for the better part of an hour watching her aunt dance first with one and then another.

In the fond belief that he was speaking intimately with Audrey, Egbertt lowered his voice to a mellow roar. This was still several decibels above the general buzz of conversation and clearly audible to those who cared to listen.

With his quizzing glass raised to his eye, his lordship advised Audrey that his Letty was looking as neat as ninepence. "She's still beautiful," he said. "Older, of course, but there you have it! All of us are. Oh, not you, my dear, but me and Letty and our crowd: Osgood Felcher and Cosmo Orphington. Yes, and Ophelia Redfern, though she dyes her hair red and crimps it. But Letty is as well looking as ever. Better, if I do say so m'self. Does me proud, Letty does. Did Marpleby proud. A credit to the both of us." Lord H vented a long sigh. "Yes, he was the lucky one. He got to marry her!"

Audrey looked at him with curiosity and Egbertt proceeded to enlighten her. "Well," he recited, "there we were, both in love with Letty. A Miss Soames-Taylor she was in those days. Like you, m'dear. But you know that! She was your own father's sister. Older sister," he amended. "The old baron—your grandfather, you see—he threw Letty onto the Marriage Mart, London season of . . ." Lord Higglesby squinted. "I have it! Year of 1773! So there we were, both of us, Jasper Marpleby and me, in love with your aunt.

"I said, 'What's to do?' And Jasper answered, 'We'll have to flip for her.' So we did. Used my lucky gold piece.

Only it brought me no luck that day. Lost me Letty, it did.
I threw the damned thing in the Thames after that. Said I
wouldn't carry a coin about that lost me Letty."

His lordship shook his head, then brightened. "But she
made a beautiful bride. I was best man, you know," he told
Audrey. "Ah, here comes Letty now, looking every bit as
lovely as she did forty years ago when Jasper and I stood
up with her."

Even to Audrey's partial eye, and allowing that she was
very fond of her aunt, no vestige of beauty remained in
poor Lady Marpleby's raddled countenance, which, as her
ladyship came rapidly toward them, showed every sign of
exasperation.

"Audrey!" she cried. "I just felt a flounce rip; we must
pin it up. You will excuse us, Egbertt?"

Without waiting for his answer, Letty turned to her late
partner. "Lord Cromyn, I'm sorry to interrupt our dance. It
can't be helped. Another time. Come, Audrey!"

In a retiring room, Lady M sank onto a tiny sofa and
stretched a trembling hand to her niece. "Audrey! I've
been so remiss! It's quite my own fault. Oh, I could just
scream. I should have warned you!" She pressed her
brow with a lacy handkerchief and plied her fan rapidly.

Completely at a loss, Audrey frowned. "But what has
you in a taking, Aunt Letty? What's the matter?"

"It's Egbertt! Never let him engage you in a coze whilst
in company, love. Might as well hire a town crier. Even
Emmerhite's broadsides are slower than Egbertt's. He, at
least, knows he's spreading gossip. Poor Egbertt does it
unconsciously. Simply opens his mouth and everyone from
here to Dover may be privy to his conversation!"

Lady Marpleby closed her eyes and shuddered. "And
I've no doubt that next he would have been telling you
and the whole world about my marriage to Marpleby, details I'd rather keep secret."

"Is it true?" Audrey couldn't help asking. "Did my uncle and Lord Higglesby flip a coin for you?"

"Oh, yes." Lady M waved a small hand. "It's common
knowledge. Well, that's neither here nor there. I couldn't
choose because between them there was no appreciable

difference. Both were presentable, although to my mind
Egbertt was more handsome than my husband. They came
from good families; each possessed a fortune. I had to
marry money. For three generations the Soames men had
wasted their substance. My own father was a gamester of
the worst sort. Your father, my dear brother Ronald, was
different. He wanted to go to America. But he could never
have gone without my marriage settlements, you see. So I
needed to marry and I was well pleased that two such el-
igible and unexceptional young men offered for me. And
within weeks of the opening of the season, too!"

Lady M smiled. "But try as I would, I couldn't
choose. They were best friends, you know. I told them to
settle it. After that," she reminisced, "they had no reason
to be jealous of each other and we could all three still be
friends."

"And you felt no partiality?" Audrey asked.

"No. None."

"Yet your marriage was happy, I understand."

"I was satisfied," Letty said slowly. "Actually it was
rather like having two husbands, for what must poor
Egbertt do but swear never to marry! He hasn't looked at
another woman from that day to this, insofar as I know."
The smile on her face was half proud, half wistful.

Audrey took her aunt's hand. "He acts as if he has been
your husband all these years," she commented gently.

"I suppose he feels he was in a way," Lady M said.
"Yes, and that's another thing, Audrey. Egbertt keeps saying how well I look, and good God! I never *was* beautiful.
I wasn't even pretty! The best that could be said of me
was that I had pretty hair and a good complexion. And a
neat figure. I was very slender and my posture was perfect. My grandmother saw to that. How I hated that board
she had me strapped into each morning! But now Egbertt
must always be saying how beautiful I am, and it makes
him look foolish beyond permission!" she finished crossly.

Audrey remained silent for a moment. "Why don't you
marry him, Aunt Letty?"

Lady Marpleby dabbed at her tears. "Oh, Audrey," she
sighed. "I asked Egbertt to marry me when Jasper had

been dead a year and a half." She sniffed and gave a watery laugh. "Do you know what he said?"

Audrey shook her head and Lady M lowered her voice in an uncanny imitation of Lord Egbertt. "No, m'love. Can't do that. Mustn't take unfair advantage. Man's dead, y'know!"

5

When Audrey and her aunt returned to the Lancaster ballroom, they found the Marquis of Huxford sitting with Higglesby.

"Here they come now," Lord Egbertt was heard to remark clearly. "Was telling St. Aubin about your torn flounce, m'love. He came to dance with Miss Soames-Taylor," he finished, gazing waggishly from one of the young people to the other. A light dawned. "Letty!" Egbertt cried. "Do you think these two ... eh?" he interrupted himself as Lady M laid a finger across his lips.

"Egbertt," her ladyship uttered breathlessly, "could you take me to a retiring room? I need a glass of ratafia. And I want ... I need to tell you something!"

"By Jove, m'girl!" his lordship beamed. "That's a splendid scheme. Get away from this crowd. Have a glass of wine and a coze. Just the two of us."

They left Audrey alone with the marquis. She didn't know where to look.

"Shall we sit?" Huxford asked abruptly. He'd tried to stay away, but his desire to see Audrey had driven him to don formal dress and drive to Lancaster House, simply to be with her, to touch her hand, to gaze—just once more—into her violet eyes. He couldn't forget how those eyes had looked when he acted so churlishly in the park. The shock and pain she couldn't hide had goaded him cruelly, keeping him from sleep, inspiring a rash desire to go to her, to hold her, to say he hadn't meant a word, that he wouldn't hurt her for the world. This scheme of his to repudiate Audrey was proving more difficult than he'd thought.

41

Since his attitude seemed so uncivil, Audrey wondered why he'd come. Before she thought, she asked him just that.

"Oh, to see you, Miss Taylor." His laugh was harsh, his irony unmistakable. "We rub along so well I found myself unable to stay away."

At Huxford's violent tone, her eyes fastened on his.

Her distress must have been obvious, for he said roughly, "Pay no attention to my starts. I'm known far and wide for my unruly tongue."

"You . . . you don't like me, do you, my lord?" There was the tiniest tremor at the corner of her mouth.

His cold eyes assessed her for a long moment. "No. I don't believe I do." His expression was obscure.

The music started and the marquis rose to his feet. Audrey saw that he was holding out his hand for her. "I came to waltz with you," he said.

That night, long after she was clutching her pillow, Audrey stared into the darkness. Over and over she reviled herself for giving him her hand with such bovine docility. Huxford had swept her around the ballroom, whirling her in circles until she was dizzy. He didn't speak again, but his eyes never left her face. He held her in such an iron-like grip that Audrey thought she must surely break. Hours later, she still could feel his touch.

She was so heavy eyed at the breakfast table next morning that Lady Marpleby accused her of sickening for something. "Perhaps you're over tired, my dear. We've been spinning about town like a pair of tops."

Audrey sighed. "I believe I am a little tired, Aunt Letty." Her gaze drifted outside the morning room window. She couldn't face the prospect of meeting Huxford in the park. She couldn't bear another of his set downs. "I think I shan't ride today. I'll attend to some letter writing instead."

"I'm sure it's just as well that you rest, my love," Lady M said, as she accepted a small envelope handed her on a silver tray. The letter was accompanied by a single, long-stemmed yellow rose.

Audrey watched as her aunt lifted the rose to inhale its fragrance and began to read her note from Lord Higglesby. Every morning such a billet was delivered to Marpleby House and with it, some small gift or a flower.

Audrey looked out at the sunshine again, but what she was seeing was the image of Huxford's face. Not the hard chill face he presented to the world. Swimming before Audrey's eyes was his smiling face, the one he had shown her only a few precious times, his eyes alight with laughter.

Audrey emerged from her chamber that evening dressed in white crepe *peau d'ange* banded in silver. A sleeveless overdress floated in transparent folds about her slender form. Her only adornment was a long strand of seed pearls braided into her hair. Her coiffure, swept up and back from her face in smooth layers, was heavily bound with pearled braids. This effect lent a serenity to her features she couldn't feel.

Determined to enjoy herself this night, Audrey responded to Sir Paden Offutt's greeting with a smile.

"I say!" he cried. "That's a dashed clever thing you've done to your hair."

"Thank you," Audrey said. "And look at you! What a wonderful coat."

"Well, yes." Paden cast a contented glance at himself in the mirror over the inlaid mahogany console. "But only think! It's Holland House we're visiting tonight. Ain't ever been invited to a sit-down dinner there, you know. Had to do m'self proud."

Lady Marpleby came in on the tail of this ingenuous speech and was struck silent at the sight of her niece.

"Audrey!" she managed at last. "You are so . . . you look so . . ."

"Like a devilish snow maiden!" boomed Lord Higglesby as he entered the library. He raised his glass to inspect Audrey more closely. "Beautiful girl, your niece," he remarked and swung about to face Lady Marpleby. His love, in navy with jet beading, fairly snatched his breath.

"Letty," Egbertt demanded. "Where did you say you

were going? Ought not to let you out of my sight looking like that! Good God, the Soames-Taylors certainly knew how to breed up their women for beauty!"

Very correctly ignoring this last piece of gallantry, her ladyship said, "Holland House, Egbertt. We're going to have dinner with the Holland's."

"Oh, yes! And where am I going, my love?" Higglesby genially inquired.

"Cosmo Orphington has invited you, Osgood Felcher, and Lord Cromyn for dinner and some whist."

Egbertt threw up his head. "That's right! I remember now. You're to take me there and pick me up on your way home."

Lord H turned to Audrey. "Holland House is down past Kensington," he kindly informed her. "Used to spend the night there. Cold! Damn me if it ain't the coldest house you ever saw. Might meet anyone there. Fox ... well, Holland is Charles Fox's nephew, don't you see? *Was*. Fox died in ... What year did Fox cock up his toes, Letty?"

"In 1806, my dear."

"That long ago! Must be six or seven years. This is 1813, isn't it, Letty?"

"Yes, it is." Her ladyship nodded.

"Thought I had the right of it. Imagine that! Fox dead seven years! Doesn't seem possible. You sure Huxford wants your niece at Holland House?" Egbertt asked in one of his startling reversals.

Her ladyship, noting the sudden flags in Audrey's cheeks, intervened before her niece could say something unbecoming. "I haven't asked him, my lord. Why should I?"

"Yes, but you said ..." sputtered Egbertt.

"That's neither here nor there, Egbertt," Lady M said severely. "Do let us be going."

As they got their wraps, Audrey asked Paden a hurried question. "What's this about Holland House?"

"Old stuff," Padden replied in an undertone. "Lady Holland is divorced. Years ago she ran off from her first husband to elope with Lord Holland. Ain't received by some of the society dragons. Come to think of it, ain't received by any of 'em. Well! I once heard her complain that nobody but men ever come to Holland House. And all the great ones *do* go there, y'know: Palmerston, Melbourne, Earl Grey. And that's to name only a few. It's the stronghold of the Foxite Whigs, you see. Huxford dines there almost every week. Might see him there tonight."

An hour later, Lady Marpleby's carriage swept up the long drive of an expansive park. Audrey could see Holland House, set well back from the road. It was a Jacobean mansion of red brick, a house she'd heard of all her life.

Shortly afterward Lady Marpleby's party passed through its doors into one of the carved and painted rooms. As they approached the receiving line, they could hear their hostess complaining in her husband's ear.

Lord Holland was short and stout, exactly as her father had described him to Audrey. "Holland is a great man, but in a white waist coat, he looks exactly like a fat penguin," he had said fondly.

Looking at Lord Holland, Audrey saw that her father was right. His lordship's pleasant countenance, punctuated by bushy black brows, beamed as he welcomed his guests. His manners were exquisite.

He greeted them cordially when it came their turn, kissing Lady M's hand and saying something kind to Mr. Offutt. He asked after Lord Higglesby and then turned to Audrey.

"And here is the little American girl," he remarked. He presented her to Lady Holland, reminding his wife that they had known Audrey's father.

Her ladyship sent a page running for someone and Huxford appeared.

Audrey thought Lady Holland seemed well content with her handiwork. She was obviously delighted when the confrontation threw her guests into conscious looks. Huxford assumed a glacial aspect and Audrey felt herself go pale.

Glancing slyly from one to the other, her ladyship said to Gideon, "You must escort Miss Soames-Taylor this eve-

ning. Mr. Offutt shall squire your godmama." Then Lady
Holland grandly waved them toward one of the crowded
salons and seemed to forget them.

Audrey saw at once that Huxford was in a rage over
something. He installed her and Lady M on a sofa in an
out-of-the-way spot, excused himself, and took Paden to
another room.

Audrey breathed slowly and forced herself to look about
her. They were in a beautifully painted chamber with some
of the carving the house was famous for.

When Lady Marpleby paid no attention to Audrey's
comments on the beauty of the compartment, she saw that
her aunt was highly agitated.

Patting her bosom, her ladyship seemed almost overcome. "Oh, dear. Oh, dear!" she was heard to murmur.

"What's wrong, Aunt Letty?" Audrey asked.

"It's Huxford!" Lady M cried in failing accents. "He is
angry because I brought you here."

"But why, Aunt?"

"Oh Audrey!" Lady M exclaimed in a hushed voice.
"How could I have forgotten that Holland House is so-
cially taboo? Lady Holland is beyond the pale, especially
where young ladies are concern. It is never considered
proper to bring them here."

"Because she is divorced?" inquired Audrey with a
frown. "I can't think *that* would corrupt me in one short
visit."

"No, of course it wouldn't. However, it's not only that,
my dear. The woman is coarse. I come here occasionally
with Higglesby, you see. I'm used to her. But Gideon's reaction to your presence has brought me to my senses."

"Well ... still ..." Audrey began.

"You don't understand," Lady M cried. "The woman is
vulgar." She glanced about, dropped her voice to a whisper, and said, "Once, when Ophelia Redfern and I were
ushered into Lady Holland's private sitting room, we
found her with her page. The young servant was kneeling
on his knees, massaging her ladyship's legs with his hands
thrust under her skirts. And hardly had Ophelia and I gotten ourselves settled—trying desperately to ignore the

performance—than the butler brought in calling cards. Upon Lady Holland's request, two gentlemen were shown into the chamber!"

Lady Marpleby pressed her fingers to her mouth and uttered a low moan. "No wonder Gideon is on his high ropes," she said. "What possessed me to bring you here, Audrey, I'll never know. Although to be sure, my dear, you did express a desire to see the famous house your father always visited when he returned to England. Oh! If only I'd thought a little before we came. Gideon was right, as usual!"

Eyes sparkling, Audrey muttered defiantly, "It's none of Huxford's business that I am here."

Lady Marpleby opened her mouth to reply. Fortunately an interruption occurred at this point. A large, handsome man approached and took Lady M's hand.

"Lady Marpleby." He smiled. "And don't tell me! Huxford's pretty American!"

Audrey, hearing herself described in this manner, suppressed a very natural flash of anger. She watched as William Lamb, 2nd Viscount Melbourne, pulled up a chair and acknowledged her aunt's introduction. He plopped himself down, plainly ready to indulge them in a cozy chat.

Like all the Lambs, Melbourne was tall, good looking, vital, and loud. Audrey knew his wife, Caroline, was creating a scandal with George Gordon, Lord Byron, but she couldn't see any signs that his lordship minded. Here was what Audrey deplored in these sophisticated English marriages. A man's wife made a great parade of her love affair, and it seemed he didn't care in the least.

At dinner, Audrey found herself halfway down the table, with her aunt on her left and Mr. Emmerhite on her right. So many guests were crowded about Lady Holland's table that they were forced to squeeze uncomfortably close together. Audrey understood that this was normal for Holland House.

Lady Holland, holding court, blandly ignored the rules that decreed that guests should never talk across the table. She practiced an embattled style of conversation, challeng-

ing anything her guests might say as freely as she expected
to be challenged in return. She could be skeptical, stimu-
lating, and abrasive, all in one sentence.

It was during a discussion of the American War that her
ladyship's glance fell on Audrey.

"Here's an American among us," she pointed out. "Who
shall win the war, Miss Soames-Taylor?"

As Audrey collected herself to form an answer, Lady Holland interrupted. "Emmerhite, get up. Huxford, you take his
place. Told you to escort Miss Soames-Taylor tonight; you
should eat with her. You'll like that! Emmerhite, take
Huxford's seat by Melbourne. Get something for that diary
of yours. Ask him his views on marriage." Her smile was
malicious.

There was nothing to be done except that the marquis
and Mr. Emmerhite must exchange seats. Lady Holland
calmly watched until this operation was complete.

With her chair pushed against Huxford's, Audrey cast
him a look of dismay. His expression was stern. She stared
at her plate and prayed her ladyship's attention might be
diverted.

Prayer denied, her hostess demanded to be told exactly
what the Americans were about, starting this war. Audrey
realized everyone was looking at her. Beside her, Huxford
had stiffened alarmingly. Could he possibly be angry on
her behalf? Audrey laid her hand on his sleeve.

"That is exactly what was discussed all over New England, my lady," she replied easily. "My father decried the
war as an expansionist scheme brewed by the southern and
western sections of the country. Who shall win? The general consensus amongst my father's friends is that no one
can. The Americans have no money and no navy. And the
main thrust of England is necessarily here in Europe
against France."

"Yes, yes!" said Lady Holland impatiently. "But you,
Miss Soames-Taylor. Where do your personal loyalties
lie?"

Audrey heard the marquis draw a sharp breath. It was
an unscrupulous question. She touched his arm again. Her
manner was still calm, her voice steady, but there was a

glint of anger in her eyes as she answered. "Now, there you have a curious thing, your ladyship. I seem to be neither fish nor fowl, for I've come to believe that in America I feel British and in England I am made to feel an American."

Audrey rushed on before her courage could fail her. "However that may be, I must thank you for inviting me to your home. You must be aware that my father held this house in fond regard. With your permission, I should like to propose a toast on his behalf."

Audrey lifted her wine glass. "To England, the home of my father's heart, and to the memory of his great and good friend, Charles James Fox." She raised her glass and drank, not at all surprised when the company stood and joined in her toast.

With a slight smile, Lady Holland nodded at Audrey, who found herself shaking badly. She knocked her wine stem over when she attempted to place it on the table.

Gideon righted it, his glance keen. "Steady, now." His whisper was for Audrey alone. "Good girl! That was excellent." Leaning closer, he added, "Dinner will be over soon and I'll take you home."

6

Only when the ladies left the gentlemen to their cigars and brandy was Audrey able to speculate on what the marquis had said to her. She couldn't imagine how he would contrive to leave with them, nor did she pretend to understand why he should want to.

When Huxford and the others rejoined the ladies in the salon, he came directly to Lady Marpleby. A glance at his face told Audrey he had regained his detachment. Was he regretting his partisanship?

Apparently he wasn't, for he said abruptly, "Godmama, I came with Melbourne. He has decided to spend the night. Could I snag a ride in your carriage? And isn't it time we made our departure?"

Appealed to in this way, Lady Marpleby could only agree and set in train the marquis's plan.

In a very short time, a bewildered Paden Offutt found himself in her ladyship's carriage, with Huxford beside him.

"But Lady M," Paden complained, "it's not yet twelve o'clock. Why are we leaving so soon?"

"We must gather up Higglesby, my dear," Lady Marpleby told him.

Audrey saw Paden open his mouth and then close it. In the light of a flambeau, he had sustained a look from Gideon St. Aubin that would have singed a goat. Involuntarily, she smiled.

Paden wasn't alone in his bafflement. Lord Higglesby, routed from his whist, protested loudly. Handed into the carriage, he sat heavily beside Paden.

"Letty," he demanded, "why have you come before my game was over?"

"I wanted to see you that much sooner, my dear lord," Lady M cooed.

"Oh!" Egbertt returned blankly. Then he smiled and proceeded to entertain them with details of his evening.

In a seat just wide enough for two, Audrey sat wedged between her aunt and the Marquis of Huxford. His lordship had climbed in beside her when they picked up Lord Higglesby and had one arm thrown along the back of the squabs. She was pressed to his side, in the close half-circle of his embrace.

She'd never been so near a strong and vital man before. Audrey could feel the length of the marquis's body along her own, his hard thigh crushing hers. Whenever Huxford leaned around her to address Lady M, or forward to hear what Lord Higglesby had to say, his breath stirred her hair, gusting against its curling tendrils. When he laughed, she could feel it. And at one time during that ride home, the marquis touched her arm and pointed out his window at a great lighted mansion on Kensington Road.

Leaning to look past him, Audrey became aware that he was watching her face, which was no more than an inch below his own in the dark carriage.

A tide of warmth swept her; she was resuming her position when the wheels struck an object in the road and she lurched even closer to him. Her face was pressed against his neck and she was secured by his arms, which closed strongly about her.

Huxford released her almost instantly. Then he shifted slightly away, and Audrey wondered if it had really happened.

At Marpleby House, she and Huxford were left in the library while Lady M, Paden, and Lord Higglesby searched in the small parlor for Egbertt's snuffbox.

The marquis stood distant and impassive, gloves in one hand and hat in the other. He seemed impatient to be gone.

Audrey straightened, hugging her white satin evening cloak more closely about her. "Tell me, my lord," she said, looking directly at him. "Something has been puzzling me all evening. You were angry when we came to Holland House. Why was that?"

Huxford came to her, standing so close she had to throw her head back to look at him.

For long moments he stood gazing down at her, his mouth a grim line in his harsh, lean face. He wanted to tell her she was beginning to haunt him. That his desire for her was making sleep impossible. He wanted to tell her of his decision that she must be avoided. And he wanted to explain his feelings when he had walked in and found her in Lady Holland's foyer. It was a place Audrey never should have been, but there she was, wearing this damned white gown, with her hair begging to be taken down so a man could run his hands through it. When Lady Holland had sent for him—Huxford was aware how avidly her ladyship had watched their reactions—Audrey had raised her chin and looked at him with wide violet eyes.

Now those violet eyes were dark with shadows, and the corners of her lips trembled so that Huxford found himself wanting to kiss away her hurt and inflict a sweeter pain that would leave her breathless and clinging.

When he spoke at last, Huxford's voice was hard. "What can a girl like you know about a man's feelings, Miss Taylor? Can she know that merely seeing her, so unbelievably beautiful, can make him want her so badly he will go to unbelievable lengths simply to touch her? And can she understand this might lead him into forming an unwelcome alliance, thereby compromising his ideals of what, or who, is right for him?"

Audrey gasped and turned pale. It was an insult calculated to stagger the mind. Huxford was saying, in effect, that he wanted her but was unwilling to offer marriage. She was stunned. But then, she thought, she'd asked for it.

Afterward, she could never remember bidding him goodnight. Perhaps she didn't. Nor could she recall climbing the stairs to her bed.

It was two days before she discovered the marquis had left town. "And without a word to anyone," Paden told her. "Probably gone on a spying mission, y'know, so we'll stand mum on *that!*" he warned.

Once again Audrey put Gideon St. Aubin out of her mind and made an effort to gather up the pieces of her existence.

Kit Hartwell, Lord Chartley, was twenty-seven years old and probably the most beautiful young man Audrey had ever seen. His face was dark and thin and his blue eyes so lucent they appeared light-giving. Black hair, cut in the cherubim, curled carelessly round his head. Flashing white teeth and a well-defined mouth made him so attractive that she found it almost painful to look at him.

Naturally he didn't have the magnetism of the Marquis of Huxford. Few men would fare well in comparison with Huxford. When the marquis entered a room, all eyes swung in his direction. There was an aura, a force, about him that drew attention. His size also eclipsed Kit Hartwell's. The marquis, so tall and broad shouldered, seemed massive beside the more slightly built viscount. Chartley, though tall, was loose limbed. And his lanky form was graceful wherever he draped it, for he had the peculiar habit of crossing his arms over his chest and leaning against walls, mantels, door facings, or whatever was handy.

Why Kit should attach himself so particularly to her, Audrey had no idea. His attentions were casual and completely unloverlike. At first, the only thing she knew about him was that he was a particular friend of Gideon St. Aubin's. He and the Marquis of Huxford were neighbors in the country.

It wasn't long before she realized that everyone liked Kit Hartwell. He was brilliant, with an ironical wit and a vital energy. In spite of his starts of savage recklessness, he was welcomed by whatever company he chose to honor with his presence.

It bothered Audrey that Chartley was so often drunk. And she wondered about his marriage. His wife stayed in the country and was never mentioned.

An air of indefinable sorrow hung over Kit, of tragedy

so close he must be constantly battling to push it behind him. More than once Audrey caught a look of pain in his eyes, fleeting and evanescent. It was readily apparent that Kit had friends who cared deeply for him, and there seemed to be a conspiracy amongst them to protect and lavish attention upon him.

Women, Audrey had noticed, found Viscount Chartley irresistible. The barely leashed violence, the laughing mockery he offered when they would have clung—these made him highly attractive. Of course the older ladies adored him. They weren't threatened, she thought, by his overt sexuality as were the younger ones. The unmarried ones were never easy under his careless scrutiny. Audrey felt sure that was why they fell into nervous giggles whenever he happened to address them or asked them to dance.

How, Audrey asked herself, could she find Kit so charming when the life he led, so nearly profligate, was all she'd been taught to despise? Gaming hells and low dens, she learned, were his habitual hangouts, and Kit didn't deny it.

He would disappear, returning in a day or two pale and haggard and with so desolate an expression that instead of shunning him as she'd intended, Audrey found herself searching for something to excite his caustic wit and to lighten his look of wasted suffering.

For reasons she couldn't discover, Kit seemed drawn to her and whatever crowd she was part of, watching her and those around her with a closeness Audrey found unnerving. And when Gideon St. Aubin had been one of the company, the viscount's interest had been even more evident.

The Marquis of Huxford seemed to have vanished the week after the Holland House fiasco. Audrey spent Sunday morning in church, and later, she rested. She couldn't be sorry that Lady Marpleby reserved that day for staying home, neither inviting nor receiving visitors. Audrey needed a period of quiet reflection.

When lunch was over, she left Lady M and Lord Higglesby napping in the small parlor, her aunt on the sofa and Lord H in his overstuffed chair with a handkerchief thrown over his face. Audrey knew they would awaken later and spend the hours until dinner playing at piquet. This was a longstanding habit with them, a custom cherished by both.

"For you must know, my love," Lady M had confided, "Egbertt and I could never keep to the pace if we didn't have our Sundays."

In her bedchamber, Audrey tried to read, found she couldn't concentrate, and tossed her book aside. She had just decided on some letter writing when the footman came with the message that Kit Hartwell was downstairs.

Her first inclination was to refuse herself. But curiosity overcame her and she went down to find the viscount dressed in his driving coat, slapping his hat against his leg. Chartley straightened from his negligent pose leaning against the library door frame and watched her descend the stairs.

"You really are a pretty thing, aren't you?" he remarked, but in such an impersonal tone that Audrey couldn't restrain her laughter.

Kit grinned, and she asked, "Did you come, my lord, simply to reassure yourself on that point?"

He was pallid, but entirely sober for once. "No, I didn't. That was merely a by-the-way. I knew Huxford was out of town, Offutt too, and came to rescue you. Do you want to drive out?"

An eager smile betrayed Audrey before she frowned. "I'm afraid . . ."

"No need to be." Kit grinned. "I won't bite you. Would if you were mine, but you ain't!"

"Chartley," she cried, laughing. "That's outrageous!"

"Yes. Pretend I never said it." He laughed again, then drew himself up and assumed a mock formal manner. "Viscount Chartley desires the honor of driving out with Miss Audrey Soames-Taylor this fine Sunday afternoon. Propriety is observed, for the aforementioned viscount's tiger, name of Samuel, shall sit behind to satisfy convention."

Audrey hesitated. She really wanted to go. "Chartley, are you sure?"

He raised his brows. "Certainly am! Gideon would call me out if I led you into anything the society dragons could look at sideways."

Audrey's eyes snapped. "Why do you keep dragging Gideon St. Aubin's name into this?" she asked with some asperity. "That's twice and I do not see—"

"I also mentioned Paden Offutt," came Kit's immediate riposte.

"Oh!" Audrey almost stamped her foot.

His smile was wide and winning. "Do you want to go?"

"Yes!"

"Good. Grab your bonnet and tell your aunt and we'll be off. Can't keep my team waiting, you know."

His rig was a racing curricle, hitched to the finest pair of chestnuts Audrey had ever seen. "My God, Chartley. They are something special!" she breathed reverently.

Kit watched her evaluate the points of his cattle with a glint of appreciation. He liked the girl better each time he saw her. Gideon was luckier than he knew, and he was glad for him.

Later, when Chartley brought her home, Audrey thanked him sincerely. She held out her slim hand, saying boyishly, "They're sweet goers, all right! I don't know why you invited me, but I'm glad you did. I know you don't ask many, so must count myself lucky. No, don't get down. I'm capable of seeing myself to the door. Thank you again. This is the best Sunday I've had in London." She waved and went up the steps of Lady Marpleby's mansion.

Audrey rode into Hyde Park the next morning trailed by her groom. Kit encountered her near the gate.

He noticed that she was dressed in one of her tailored riding habits. It was obviously a Worth. No one else made female riding gear with such style. Her skirt and jacket were black. Her white blouse had high collar points and a stock tied in a waterfall. A tall black shako rested squarely on her head, adorned in front by a single white aigrette plume.

"What's this?" inquired Chartley, reining in. "Riding alone, Miss Taylor? Paden told Huxford you were trailed by a dashed cavalcade each morning. I've seen 'em m'self. Have they deserted you?"

Audrey was saved from answering by a shout. Mr. Eddington rode up, followed closely by Captain Ware. The captain was grinning.

"Miss Taylor!" he cried. "Please come down the path. I've been waiting . . . hoping to show you something."

They turned their mounts and followed Ware to the edge of the pond. The captain slid off his horse and helped Audrey dismount. Eddington got down too, but Chartley sat his saddle, leaning over the pommel to see what Captain Ware meant to show her.

"Here," said the captain. He thrust a small packet at Audrey. It was stale bread.

At a loss before Ware's laughing eyes, Audrey stared at him, puzzled.

He pointed to the water. On the pond was the most darling covey of freshly hatched ducklings, brown and ugly and adorable.

Audrey flushed with pleasure, her smile all the captain had hoped for. "Oh," she murmured, "how enchanting!"

Ware took her to the water's edge and she threw the crumbs to the greedy baby ducks, who gobbled them instantly.

"Thank you, Captain," Audrey said softly, as he threw her in her saddle. "That was a lovely gift."

At just that moment Lord Fawlkes and his fiancée came riding up a side path in the direction of the gate. Seeing them, Chartley excused himself before he could become enmeshed in small talk.

Leaning toward Audrey, he said, "You'll be all right now. Here's Miss Webster and Fawlkes to lend you countenance. I shall see you later."

Lifting his hand, Viscount Chartley rode away. Audrey could only conclude that he came to the park to make sure she had someone with whom to ride.

* * *

Audrey and Lady Marpleby were sitting in the long salon at Melbourne House in Whitehall that evening when Paden Offutt strolled in. It was something past ten o'clock.

"Just got back to town," he told them. "Where is everyone?"

"Egbertt is eating at Watiers with Captain Ware, Osgood Felcher, and Mr. Eddington," Lady M said. "I have no idea where Huxford is, and Chartley! Well, who knows where poor Chartley might be." Her ladyship shook her head and clacked her tongue.

"No," agreed Paden, shrugging. "Who does?" He lowered his voice. "I say, that Byron fellow hangs on Lady Melbourne's every word, don't he?" Dropping his volume still further, Paden added, "Plaguey man writes poems, don't he? Well, I know he does because I tried to read that Child something of his and—"

"Childe Harold?" inquired Audrey gravely.

"That's the one!" Mr. Offutt exclaimed. "Dashed thing doesn't make sense! I never got past four lines. Tell you what: The man's a poseur. Holds himself just so and presents his profile like he's a deuced picture. Pardon! Dashed picture. Hallo! Here's Chartley now. Oh, God! He's drunk!"

Kit came to a wavering halt before Lady Marpleby and Audrey and smiled engagingly. "Here you are!" he slurred. "I've found you at Melbourne House!"

He took Lady Marpleby's hand, and glancing sideways at Audrey, whispered loudly, "Thought I'd better look in."

"Sit down," commanded Audrey austerely.

Obediently, Chartley dropped to the sofa beside Lady M. "What's to do?" he asked amiably.

"What's to do?" hissed Audrey. "That's all you can say?"

"Say anything you wish, darling girl," Kit told her. His smile was gently vacuous.

Audrey, failing to gain Paden's attention, kicked him.

Paden grunted. "Here, I say, Miss Taylor! You kicked me!"

"Oh, no! Did I? So sorry. It's just that I think we should

make an effort to get Chartley away before anyone, especially our hostess, sees how drunk he is."

Kit lifted one lean hand and shook an admonitory finger. "Shouldn't say drunk, Miss Taylor. Should say foxed. No, not that, either! Lady should say disguised. No! Can't say that, either. Wait. Better not mention it at all! Ignore the whole thing, that's the girl. You are *so* pretty. Ain't she pretty, Lady M?"

Her ladyship, abstaining from hysterics only by the sheer force of her will, said, "Yes, dear boy, Audrey's very pretty. Now, do you want to make me very happy?" She spoke as one would to a child.

Kit's expression turned bleak. "Wish all—everyone— could be happy," he muttered sadly.

"Well, then," Lady Marpleby said brightly, "you may escort me to the door. And we shall forgo goodbyes because . . . I have a headache. That's it! A very bad headache."

They got Chartley in the carriage at last and he slumped in the seat next to Audrey, with Paden and Lady M opposite.

He laughed suddenly. "Should see your face, Miss Taylor. So prim and shocked! Think I've been to some damned orgy or other, don't you? Haven't though." He laid his head on the squabs and closed his eyes. "Had to check on you. Old Gideon gone; would have wanted me to stand by." He subsided into a gentle snore.

"Why," Audrey exploded, when she and her aunt arrived home, "is everyone determined to link me with Huxford?"

Lady Marpleby removed her pearls and laid them on her night table. "Do you mind?" she asked.

The corners of Audrey's mouth were drooping; she shrugged and grimaced. "Yes—certainly I mind."

Realizing that she was treading dangerous ground, her ladyship drew a long sigh. She was aware that everyone was beginning to link her niece's name with that of her godson.

"Audrey," she said gently, "you must realize Gideon has

never before shown a woman of your quality such distinguishing attention. And," she added with a smile, "I'm convinced you shall be receiving his proposal of marriage shortly."

Audrey laughed bitterly. "It's no such thing, Aunt Letty! Marriage does not enter Huxford's mind. He made that plain after we came from Holland House. He said he desired me but declined to form an *alliance*. He was kind enough to tell me that he wouldn't compromise his lifelong ideals of what or *who* was right for him!" So often had she reviewed that fatal exchange, Audrey was able to quote verbatim.

Lady Marpleby gave a muffled shriek. "What? How dared he?" Astonishment and anger chased across her face; it would have been almost comical, if Audrey had been in the mood to laugh.

"Oh, yes," she said, nodding. "Then he disappeared and Chartley appeared as some sort of self-appointed proxy. Chartley also comes to the park each morning to make certain I don't ride alone. And tonight he came to Melbourne House. You heard him say the marquis would want him there as a . . . a guardian or something! Not only that, but two days ago, when I was riding in Miss Webster's carriage, Lord Palmerston hailed us and asked me . . . *me*, mind you! . . . when Huxford was returning from the country. As if I should know! Why did he do that?"

Seeing Audrey so agitated, Lady M patted her hand. "Sit down, dearest, please! Shall I ring for some saloop tea or a glass of warm milk?"

Audrey shook her head and tried to smile. "No, Aunt Letty, thank you. It's just . . . it's all so infuriating! I wish I'd never left Boston." She sat on Lady M's bed, exhausted by her outburst.

"Oh, my love," her aunt said. "Can you feel nothing for Huxford? Perhaps you misunderstood what he said. I assure you he has an admirable character, in spite of what the gossips say. He was a good son to Madelaine and Hugo, and he takes exceedingly good care of his sister Victoria. It's true that he can be cold at times, but never to me. Nor to any of those he holds dear. And he's fond of Egbertt and Paden Offutt. Well, you must know he's the boy's trustee. As for Kit Hartwell: There are circumstances in Kit's life . . . Kit once told me that Gideon stood fast beside him all through . . . Kit is most unhappy."

"I gathered that, Aunt Letty, and I'm sorry for it. But Huxford! I'm beginning to hate that name. And you ask if I feel anything for him? Yes! The most profound dislike. The man is insufferable!"

"Oh, Audrey! Surely he's not that bad," protested her ladyship.

Audrey rose to leave. "It's only natural that you see him in a different light, Aunt Letty. He loves you; he doesn't persecute *your* every waking moment, nor look at you with such chilling hauteur."

Lady Marpleby gazed at her niece with shadowed eyes. *No, nor does he watch me with such warm approbation when he thinks himself unobserved,* she thought.

She said nothing more however, merely bundled Audrey off to bed, promising they should make a determined effort to forget the Marquis of Huxford on their sightseeing tour tomorrow.

Left alone, Letty rang for tea, her mind buzzing with conjecture. She wished she could discuss it with Egbertt. No, not Egbertt. She wasn't ready for the whole world to know.

When her tea came, Lady M sat huddled before the fire in her favorite old cap and gown, musing on her niece's revelation concerning Gideon St. Aubin. Her godson had been acting peculiar since he'd first clapped eyes on Audrey. She remembered how he had strolled about the room with her on his arm at the girl's come out ball. And not only once, but twice! And later, how furious he'd been at Holland House. He'd been livid to think that Audrey's reputation might be compromised. That must mean something. But why was he fighting it so hard? And why was he hiding in the country?

As for Audrey, she wasn't as impervious to Gideon's charms as her ladyship had thought. Lady M chuckled into her teacup. Audrey was a sly little actress. Or she had

been until tonight. But now her mask had cracked. Oh,
yes, and fallen off completely, if her aunt was any judge!

Lady Marpleby pursed her lips in a tiny smile. A bright
little hope was beginning to bloom in her heart.

7

Paden Offutt felt at home to a peg with Miss Audrey Soames-Taylor. He volunteered to escort her and Lady Marpleby on their sightseeing tour of London when he learned of it. "Ain't seen any of those places, m'self. Think I'd like to," he told them.

For two days Lady M tagged along, but the third morning she looked so wan Audrey took pity on her. "You look tired, Aunt Letty. Shall we cancel the British Museum? Except that I did want to see it. And Kew Gardens. And oh, yes! The Temple and London Bridge." Audrey was determined to keep herself busy.

Lady Marpleby couldn't quite repress a shudder upon hearing what a catalogue of treats was in store for her. Much as she loved having Audrey, her coming had jolted her ladyship out of her comfortable rut. Truth to tell, she liked nothing better than quiet evenings at home, playing at piquet with Egbertt and her cronies.

And the sad fact was that Egbertt could be depended on to say something in the course of the evening to set up someone's back, and in a voice that bounced from the rafters. Dinner parties were becoming impossible. He effectively drowned all attempts at conversation, so that one by one the other diners fell silent, and in the end her dear lord was declaiming another of his infamous monologues. No. It was better to keep poor Egbertt close and content within their own circle, where he was understood and tolerated.

Possibly her ladyship's thinking of Lord Higglesby conjured him up, for he came strolling into the back parlor where she and Audrey were sitting with Paden Offutt.

"Glad you're still home, m'love," Egbertt boomed, ambling into the room. "Have you got that *billet-doux* I sent round at breakfast? It had a list of things I planned on doing whilst you were jaunting about seeing the sights today. Forgot to tell Hazlit to copy it so's I'd know where to go. Where is it, m'dear?"

Lady Marpleby invited him to take his favorite chair. "I'll get it in a moment, Egbertt. But first help us decide something."

Higglesby smiled. "Name it, m'girl, and I'll see what can be dredged up from the old noggin."

"I have this scheme, Egbertt," Lady M began. "I am growing quite fatigued running about town with the children. I'm not interested in seeing all those things, but they are."

She touched Egbertt's sleeve. "Besides, I'd much rather have my breakfast late and wait for your letter and receive morning callers. But that's nothing to the point. What I'm trying to say, Egbertt, is that I don't want to go and they do."

Lady Marpleby sighed. "I thought of sending Agnes— you remember my abigail, Egbertt—but she's older than I am."

"No, don't do that!" snorted Lord H. "Fubsy-faced gabster if ever I saw one, Letty, and I've said that a thousand times!"

"Yes, but Egbertt, that scheme I had? The one I wanted your opinion on? Well, it's this: Why can't the children go and escort themselves? There would be nothing in it because Paden is so nearly one of the family. In addition, I was almost his godmother, but for the fact Matilda felt she should choose that second cousin of hers, Saraphonia Paden, instead. On account of the inheritance, you remember. But all these years, I've been his *honorary* godmother and loved every minute of it!" She smiled at Paden.

"Not only that, but if he were a cousin of even the smallest degree it would be unexceptional. And he has been acting as a substitute cousin to Audrey. Lately he has been here from sunrise to sunset. Yes, and back most evenings to go with us to the theater or parties or wherever we need an escort. I can't think what we'd have done without him."

Lady Marpleby smiled at Paden again, this time so meltingly that his ears turned bright red.

"Only too happy to have been of service, ma'am." Paden coughed behind his hand.

Lady M turned to Egbertt. "As for Audrey, she's no green girl. She's twenty-three, remember. I can't see where the hurt would be, can you?" She eyed Audrey and Paden uncertainly.

Egbertt took her hand. "No, my love, no harm at all. Good idea. And I'll tell you something. No one will see them because no one ever goes to those places. Well, *I've* never been. Have you?" He raised his brows at her.

"No. Oh! I don't know what to do! You're sure you won't take Agnes?" she implored the youngsters.

"No!" they chorused.

Audrey could imagine them pushing and pulling Lady Marpleby's antiquated abigail up and down all the steps.

It was settled then, but tacitly understood that the un-chaperoned tours were to be kept secret. The less said the better, Lady M advised them, sending the pair off in her closed carriage. She then turned to the task of so impressing the need for tact on Egbertt's brainpan that he would keep the cat in the bag.

Having exorcised Gideon St. Aubin in the long night watches, Audrey set out to enjoy the day. It was a beautiful morning and they went first to the British Museum.

Halfway through the Natural and Artificial Products, they established a first-name basis. "Though to be sure, Paden," Audrey warned, "we must remember to be more formal in company. But for you to always be saying 'Miss Taylor this, and Miss Taylor that' takes too long, and seems foolish, especially when we're alone."

This fell in exactly with Mr. Offutt's ideas of propriety, for although his mother was the daughter of an earl, she had raised him in an irregular manner, excusing herself on the grounds that his father was a simple baronette and Paden a younger son. To be setting the boy up in esteem of his own consequence would prove nothing short of fatal, Matilda Offutt claimed.

Paden was very ready to fall in with his companion's suggestion, and thereafter, she became Audrey to him.

Her resolution to forget the marquis served Audrey very well. She hadn't thought of him above twice an hour all day.

She and Paden started home enthused with future plans. In the carriage, Audrey said, "I think we should go back to the museum for another full day. There are two more sections I want to see, the British and Medieval Antiquities Exhibit and the Manuscript Room. I'm keen on history, you know."

Paden eyed her suspiciously. "Here," he said. "You ain't blue, are you?"

"If you're asking whether or not I'm some kind of scholar, possessed of an erudite nature, the answer is no. But if you are inquiring if I enjoy stories and myths from the olden days, then I must plead guilty," Audrey said firmly.

"I should think so!" agreed Paden, greatly taken with the idea. "I like history m'self, if that's what it means."

"It does. Which reminds me. I want to see the Magna Carta before I return to America."

"I know about that! It's a paper they made some king or other sign. You mean it's actually there at the museum?"

"Yes." Audrey had her finger in her guide book. "It says so right here."

"Good thing you bought that, Audrey. Book like that tells facts you'd never guess about this town."

"Um," agreed Audrey, busily turning the pages. "Now, if only I can find . . . Mr. Emmerhite said the Elgin Marbles were in a warehouse or a shed somewhere. Oh well, I'll ask Aunt Letty."

But her Aunt Letty confessed that she had no idea where Lord Elgin's infamous marbles were. Not did Lord Egbertt. Audrey was forced to abandon the marbles. The next day she and Paden went off to inspect the Tower of London and the Royal Exchange.

"I say," Paden ruminated on their way home. "Wasn't

that better than anything? I never knew they had such wild beasts in the Tower. Only imagine! Think how far the poor things had to travel. Then to be caged up all their lives! I wonder?" he mused and was silent so long Audrey had to nudge him.

"What do you wonder, Paden?" At twenty-three, she was only two years older than Paden, but there were times when Audrey felt much, much older. "What has thrown you into such a trance?"

"It's just that I got to thinking, Audrey. Could you set up a wild animal stud? Would they breed?" Paden stopped, aghast at what he'd said. Then he relaxed. Audrey was waiting for him to continue with a patient smile of inquiry.

No need to worry about what he said to Audrey, Paden assured himself. She was no dizzy society chit with cotton between her ears. Audrey had discussed with him, in such sensible terms as his mama might have, problems encountered on a horse-breeding farm, never hesitating to relate such earthy details as recalcitrant brood mares, their gestation periods, nor the interesting strains to be got by inbreeding, as well as crossbreeding. Unlike his mama, Audrey never mentioned such things in the beau monde. Lady Offutt and her fellow horse breeders might enjoy discussing traits of their stud's progeny, but other women were shocked.

So Paden, thankfully aware that Audrey wouldn't pretend to faint or something equally ridiculous, continued his speculations. *"Would* wild animals breed in captivity? Even in such domestic cattle as draft horses, the mares are sometimes barren. Simply never come into heat. Interesting problem, ain't it?"

"Yes, indeed!" responded Audrey sincerely. "I call to mind a filly Papa bought from a Mr. Ainsley down in South Carolina. They brought her up the coast by packet. The sea voyage must have scared her so badly she never fully recovered."

"What happened?" Paden asked.

"She never would stand for the stallion," divulged Audrey, sublimely unconscious that her aunt, or Lady Jer-

sey, or any of the other society dragons, would swoon
dead away to hear her. "The filly certainly came into
heat," Audrey said. "Time and time again. But she never
took."

Mr. Offutt, perfectly understanding how catastrophic
such an occurrence would be in a blood animal, was struck
speechless. He could only shake his head all the way back
to his lodgings in Pall Mall.

"Audrey," he begged, "don't fail to recite that tale to
m'mother when you meet her. Very downy, m'dam is. Lay
you a monkey she'd have that filly of yours breeding in no
time at all."

When the carriage stopped and he alighted in front of
his rooms, Paden stood on the sidewalk. "I'll see you at
the play tonight," he reminded her. "Save me a place in
your aunt's box."

That night, after the second act at Drury Lane, Audrey
strolled in the corridor on Paden's arm, followed by her
aunt with Lord Egbertt Higglesby. In the press of the
crowd, they were surprised to encounter the marquis of
Huxford.

"Hux," Paden said to his friend, "take Audrey while I
try for some punch. Never saw such a bunch of gabbling
people. Can't think why they're all here! I'll be right back,
as soon as I snab us something to drink."

He departed, leaving Audrey alone in the crowd with
the marquis.

Offering his arm, Huxford maneuvered them to a less
populated spot. At his first chill word, Audrey recoiled.

"Audrey? Is Offutt now made free with your Christian
name, Miss Taylor?" He stood very close; Audrey felt him
tower over her.

His tone was so critical that her cheeks flamed. *If he
raises that damnable glass and inspects me like a bug, I'll
kick his shins,* Audrey promised herself.

But the marquis obviously felt no need for his eyeglass.
He asked another question instead. "And you call him
Paden, I suppose?" His face was like a slab of stone.

Huxford clenched his jaw as Audrey raised blue-violet eyes directly to his. Her color fluctuated deliciously.

"Yes," she said shortly. She looked away and began fanning herself.

If only she knew how much she'd been in his thoughts these past few days, Huxford reflected. "I can only suppose this is one of your *charming* American customs." He heard the sneer in his own voice, but couldn't stop. "So refreshing to be on a first-name basis with Jack and all his kin. So *democratic*—such a *common* touch."

Audrey turned aside, but not before Huxford saw the glint of tears in her eyes.

And suddenly Chartley was there, squeezing past a gentleman in a hat adorned with silk flowers. He executed a bow and slipped one arm around Audrey—something he never would have done had he not been half bagged. "Family quarrel?" he asked, with a faintly slurred drawl. "I see you're at Miss Taylor again."

Gideon cast him a quelling look. "You're drunk, Kit."

"Ain't so drunk I'd pick a fight with a beautiful girl and make her cry in a public place," replied the viscount. He turned to Audrey. "Come, sweetheart. Let me take you back to Lady Marpleby's box. You don't want to talk to such a gudgeon. Go home, Gideon," he advised, and walked away with the trembling girl.

The rain came in sheets the next morning. The weather was cold and damp, a perfect reflection of Huxford's mood.

"I think you're falling in love with her." Kit Hartwell's caped driving coat dripped on the carpet as he kicked a booted foot against the fire fender.

"Do you, by God?" growled Gideon. He dropped the book he'd been trying to read and walked to the window.

"Can you deny it?" Kit asked. At his friend's angry shrug, he squared his chin.

"I won't be still, Hux. The whole of London is talking. You pay the girl marked attention and then slay her with your tongue. That display at the theater last night! Everyone was goggling, trying to crowd in to hear what you were saying. Had you taken leave of your senses?"

When the marquis shook his head and hunched his shoulders again, Chartley flung himself out the door in exasperation, leaving Huxford alone, staring at the rain.

8

Audrey didn't see the marquis for two days. On the third, Lady Marpleby exclaimed over a crested envelope at the breakfast table, "It's addressed to you, my love. From Huxford. What can he want?" Audrey felt her heart thud as her aunt handed over the missive. Breaking the seal with shaking hands, she read: "Miss Soames-Taylor: I shall call at ten today. Please drive out with me for the purpose of hearing an apology for my unwarrantable conduct at the theater two evenings past." The note was signed with one word. "Huxford."

Audrey stared at the scrawled name for so long that her aunt could not forbear a query.

"Pardon me?" Audrey asked, when she didn't understand.

"Your message from Gideon, love. What does it say?"

"Merely that he asks me to drive out at ten this morning," she murmured, nibbling at her lip.

"Ah!" exclaimed her aunt, obviously pleased. Then, glancing at the clock, she shrieked, "Audrey! It's twenty of the hour. You must hurry!"

Audrey had dreaded her next encounter with the marquis; now it was upon her. Clutching the envelope in trembling fingers, she went upstairs and dressed with even more than her usual care.

The sun was out, but the day was chilly. Audrey was glad she'd worn her sable cape. Glancing at Huxford's set face as they drove round the carriage path, she shivered. He'd greeted her repressively, his mouth a hard line, his

71

few words icily polite. Since they'd entered the park, he'd
been silent.

The least he could do, thought Audrey, was initiate
some sort of civil conversation. Digging her hands into her
muff, she decided she could be as stubborn as he, and said
nothing.

At last Huxford, perhaps to ease the constraint, said
something about the war despatches, an innocuous com-
ment one could hear at any polite gathering of the *ton*.
This was conversation such as he would engage in with a
stranger. Audrey felt dazed trying to listen. Wellington's
new thrust into Spain was going well. The Peninsular
Army was moving north-eastwards toward Salmanca and
Valladoid—names, Audrey thought, that were in all the
newspapers. She nodded politely, tried to respond, never
knew what she'd replied. She was aware that he glanced
at her searchingly from time to time.

They were driving along the east side of the park now;
she could see Kensington Palace across the way.

Hyde Park was almost deserted at the noon hour.
Audrey bit her lip when Huxford suddenly drew his racing
curricle to the side of the path, gave the reins to his tiger,
and invited her to walk by the Serpentine. His expression
as he helped her down was forbidding, almost frightening.

Taking her to the small bridge, Huxford held her elbow
as they stood and watched the ducks glide silently by. The
wind was cold. He moved behind her to stand close on her
left side. "There," he said. "Let me shield you from the
wind."

Kindness from Huxford? Audrey asked herself. When
she tried to thank him, he interrupted. "I seem to be
apologizing again, Miss Taylor."

A fleeting glance at his profile showed Audrey how
grim he looked. His manner was austere. She could sense
that he was caught in a tight coil of some unwelcome
emotion.

When she deliberately raised her eyes, staring up at him,
he seemed to bend toward her. She thought he was going
to touch her. Then his mouth tightened and he jerked erect,
moving slightly away.

"Miss Taylor, I hope you realize that I'm not in the habit of taking acquaintances to task. I can't imagine why you have such an effect on me." He paused. "Forgive me, if you can."

Audrey's knees felt weak. She swallowed. She'd never swooned in her life; she prayed she wouldn't start now.

"I . . ." Her voice trembled, and she tried again. "Please. Forget what passed between us, my lord. I have." This was a fabrication, of course. She said it for the sake of politeness.

His face held a look of savagery, his full-cut lips drawn in a tight line. "I'll take you home now," he said abruptly, then hesitated as if he were about to say something further. He remained silent, however, merely placing his hand on the small of her back to guide her off the end of the bridge. It was a small act, but intimate. Did he not realize what he was doing? Did touching her mean nothing to him?

As he took her to his curricle, Audrey thought his expression more implacable than ever. At the Lancaster ball he'd said he didn't like her. Why then did he always come to her? And when he'd indulged in one of his savage starts, why did he feel it necessary to apologize? How desperately she wanted to ask those questions of him.

Her nerves were drawn taut. She sat as far away from him as possible, but he was large and his muscular thigh crowded hers.

Audrey closed her eyes, then opened them to discover that he had glanced down at her, and looked away. There was a force about him that both mesmerized and repelled her. His lean body, his large size, his overtly masculine presence threatened her each time they came close. No, he didn't have to be near her. One look, from far across a room, and she still felt it. When he held her in the waltz, even when they danced a circumspect country set, his touch sent tremors through her body.

Never had a man affected Audrey the way Huxford did. Lately she'd taken to speculating on his kisses. Huxford's kisses—she knew instinctively—would leave her shaking for his embrace. She wanted those kisses, wanted his arms pulling her to him, wanted her body against his. None of that could ever happen, she thought. Huxford didn't even like her.

Audrey quickly brought her mind to the moment at hand. They had arrived at Marpleby House.

The marquis curtly handed her down, bowed her to the door and said, "No doubt we shall see each other again, Miss Taylor. Until then, goodbye."

Walking into her aunt's foyer, Audrey thought she'd never felt so desolate. Her ride with Huxford had been so distressing, she wished she'd refused.

She went straight to her chamber where she sat before her looking glass and stared at the unhappy face reflected there.

The image of that face was imprinted in Huxford's mind as he drove away from Marpleby House. He felt capable of cursing and committing unnamed acts of violence, all aimed at Audrey Taylor, all of which culminated in his imagination in his holding her and kissing her all over. He shook his head to dispel the unpleasant notion that kept creeping into his brain—the notion that he *had* to have her, even if it ruined his life and hers, too. The picture of deep violet eyes and pink lips, slightly parted, made him groan. Sweet nemesis, he thought. Sweet enemy mine.

Driving to an inch, the marquis did not slacken pace as he rounded the corner to the mews behind his town house. Jumping to the pavement, he threw the reins to his tiger. "Walk 'em, Tim, if I'm gone over five minutes," he ordered. "We're going down to Baddingly."

Victoria St. Aubin returned to London with her brother. They arrived in Brook Street long after noon. Gideon took her inside and told her to rest. "I'll take you to Marpleby House in the morning, Toria, but you must excuse me now. I'm going to the British Museum to deliver the 3rd marquis's papers. Should have brought them to town ages ago."

At the museum, Gideon saw the docent and was walking through the Manuscripts Room when he heard a shrill voice.

Lady Whitehead, leading her frizzy haired daughter, was confronting Audrey Soames-Taylor and Paden Offutt.

"But I don't understand, my dear," she said to Audrey in a falsely sweet tone. "Where is your aunt?"

Blanche Whitehead's eyes gleamed maliciously. Since the start of the season, the baroness had watched as the American girl took society by storm. Huxford suspected Blanche Whitehead could scarcely believe her good fortune in discovering Audrey alone and with no apparent escort other than Sir Paden Offutt. Paden had turned a bright beet color and the girl's face was ashen.

Audrey never knew what she might have answered, for at that moment Huxford's voice dropped into the lengthening silence.

Grasping Audrey's elbow, he pressed it slightly. "Now then," he stated briskly, "that is taken care of. Oh! How do you do, Lady Whitehead? And Miss Whitehead?" Gideon's bow was especially deep for the bewildered Whitehead daughter.

"Are you interested in antiquities, your ladyship?" Gideon asked the suddenly hopeful baroness. "We came to deliver a manuscript written by my great grandfather, the 3rd marquis. The board has been after me this age to bring it round."

Huxford bowed again. "So good to have seen you. Perhaps we shall have the pleasure of meeting you at the Duchess of Omsley's salon?" Without waiting for an answer, Huxford led them away, one hand clutching Paden's arm and the other biting into Audrey's elbow.

He dragged them down the wide corridor and finally released them in a secluded alcove beyond the Egyptian exhibit. "Where is your Aunt Marpleby, Miss Taylor, if I may ask?" His lordship's words were polite enough, but one brow quirked unpleasantly.

"We are here alone, my lord." Audrey was grateful her voice revealed nothing of what she was feeling. "Come, Paden. We must be going." She refused to thank his lordship. That would be admitting she and Paden were in the wrong. She elevated her chin at Huxford's frigid smile.

"I shall escort you home, Miss Taylor, just in case our friend Lady Whitehead is watching."

Audrey bit her lip. She couldn't refuse; it would be exactly like the old biddy to spy on them to see if they all left together. "Thank you," she murmured, her lashes brushing her flushed cheeks.

Audrey didn't see the unaccustomed softness in Huxford's eyes because she steadfastly refused to look at him as they left the museum.

Paden was silent the entire trip home, ignoring Audrey's valiant attempts at conversation. He felt sunk beyond reproach. Here he was in Huxford's black books again and only five days after enduring a sermon at the theater. Snatched into Huxford's box, he had been called on to explain—if he could!—why he had had the gross temerity to address Miss Soames-Taylor by her given name. It was only after he had apologized and promised to mend his ways that he was let off the hook, and here he was—back in the suds again!

At Marpleby House, Huxford surprised Audrey. Instead of ripping up at her, he sent her away to rest, saying they would discuss her transgression another time. He also advised her not to worry.

Pacing her room, Audrey stopped and pressed one hand to her brow. If only Huxford had ranted, she could have felt better! Now she was truly wretched.

Downstairs, the marquis was saying to his godmother, "It won't do, ma'am—letting Paden and your niece be seen about town unchaperoned."

Lady Marpleby had recourse to the thin wisp she called her handkerchief. "Oh, Gideon! I know! They never should have gone alone, but I was run ragged and Egbertt thought no one would see them. Who could imagine that nasty Blanche Whitehead would take it in her head to visit the British Museum?"

Her ladyship blinked her eyes rapidly. "Thank Goodness you came and could play propriety! Though heaven knows you're the last person I should have dreamed of seeing in that horrid place, and I didn't see you, yet you must have been there—"

"Exactly so, ma'am," Gideon interrupted gently. "I was there, fortunately, and able to bring it all about so there can be no unpleasant consequence, I think."

"Yes!" Lady M agreed fervently, dissolving into tears again.

From long experience, Huxford knew exactly what to do. He took his godmother into his arms and permitted her to enjoy a comfortable cry, ignoring the damage to his lapels. After a while, judging she had been indulged long enough, he shushed her, tipping her chin and drying her face with his own snowy handkerchief.

"Now give over, Godmama," he coaxed. "No more tears, if you please. No harm has been done, after all."

Lady Marpleby gave a weak sniff, striving to collect herself. "I'll do whatever you tell me, Gideon, from now on! I promise."

Gideon laughed. "I hope so, ma'am. You may safely put yourself in my hands, you know."

He kissed her and left, taking Paden with him.

Lady M sat thinking of her godson's face as he was discussing Audrey. She sighed, but refused to allow herself to repine. Everything was going very well, she thought, despite the inauspicious start they'd made.

In Brook Street, Huxford took Paden to his study. When they were settled in, and Twickem had brought some tea and a dozen of the little cakes the boy was fond of, he addressed his ward. "Paden," he said abruptly, "are you falling in love with Miss Soames-Taylor?"

Paden's cup rattled in his saucer and he stopped chewing his macaroon. Staring goggle-eyed at his host, he gasped and swallowed hastily. "I should think not, Hux! You know I ain't in the petticoat line. What gave you the idea that I . . . that we . . . ! It ain't like that at all!"

Paden set his teacup on a side table with a clatter. "Dash it, Gideon, Audrey—Miss Taylor, that is—she and I are friends, very good friends! Besides, she's more like a sister than anything. It's nice to squire her about like you do Toria, you know. Never had a sister. All I had was an older brother. Thing is, my brother Victor—he was always with you, Gideon. It was always Victor and Gideon. Later, it was Victor, Gideon, and Chartley. I was just a plaguey nuisance tagging along. Now Victor's dead and . . ."

Paden heaved a sigh and fell silent. When he roused himself, he said, "I was having a good time, being friends with her—with Miss Taylor. You notice I don't call her Audrey anymore, even though she laughed and pointed out that it was by her own invitation. She also said you had a bee in your bonnet! But that's neither here nor there. Thing is, I like her. If we want to laugh, we laugh. Want to disagree, we go at it tooth and tong. Fights like fury, Miss Taylor does, when she thinks she's right. Then we end up laughing again. She ain't one to pout or mope. Says things right out. I like her and you would too, Gideon, if you wouldn't be forever ripping up at her and giving her your bear garden jaw. Why do you do that?"

This ingenuous speech was all that saved Paden from the severe lecture Gideon had prepared for him. Ignoring the boy's question, he asked soberly, "Paden, would you want to see Miss Taylor injured in any way?"

Paden's eyes widened. "Certainly not! What can you mean? Told you how I feel about her. Love her like a sister. At least, I think I do. Who's trying to hurt her?"

"Gossip can do that," Huxford said.

"Oh, gossip!" Paden shrugged. "Never listen to it!"

"Yes, but other people do. And there will be gossip if it becomes known you and Miss Taylor are going about together, unescorted."

Paden dropped his head. "Should have asked you, Gideon. I know that," he muttered sheepishly. "Did ask Lord H. It didn't serve. Knew it was the wrong thing to do, only there seemed no harm in it." He raised anguished eyes to the marquis.

"Never mind that, halfling," Huxford said. "We have a decision to make. Think carefully, Paden. Do you believe you should take Miss Taylor about unchaperoned anymore?"

The boy blinked and swallowed. "If you don't think I should, Hux, then I don't think so. I'll go tell her." He rose from his chair, then hesitated. "Thing is, she wants to see the Muniments Room and Lady M doesn't like to go . . ."

"Victoria came up from Sussex today. She will be staying at Marpleby House. It's perfectly acceptable for you to escort the two of them anywhere they want to go."

As Paden was leaving, Huxford had one more thing to add: "Ah, about calling Miss Taylor by her first name," he said. "I think I must have had a bee in my bonnet when I came the ugly over you." His smile was self-mocking. "I'm sorry, Paden. Call her what you will. And remember, I'm not perfect. I *can* make mistakes, you know."

9

When Victoria St. Aubin came to Marpleby House, Audrey was surprised to find her so small. Huxford's sister had a very slender figure, was dressed in the first style of elegance, and wore her short black curls clustered all over her head. Audrey thought she'd never seen such great dark eyes.

The marquis presented her, saying they called her Toria.

Audrey held out her hand. "How do you do, Miss St. Aubin? I'm happy to meet you at last."

"And I you!" the girl cried. "But, please! You heard Gideon. Call me Toria. Or Victoria, at the least."

Without pausing for breath, Victoria spoke over her shoulder to her brother. "Gideon! She's everything you said!"

Audrey was trying to decipher this remark when she found herself being pulled toward the sofa. Victoria patted the cushion and said, "Do sit beside me so we may talk. May I call you Audrey?"

Reminded by Huxford of Lady M's other guests, Toria St. Aubin bounced up and said, "Oh! Yes! Miss Webster, how are you? And Lord Fawlkes? My best wishes on your betrothal. And Paden," she cried. "What a beautiful waistcoat!"

With one of her quick movements, Victoria ran to him and grasped Paden's arm, turning him this way and that, familiarly tucking his Belcher tie more securely into the buttonhole of his lapel. "I don't believe I've ever seen a spotted waistcoat with a riding jacket before!"

This was too much for the marquis, who shouted with laughter. "No, nor anyone else!"

80

Mr. Offutt, having been roasted in this quarter all his life, smiled but soon grew serious.

"I'll tell you what it is, Hux. I had my doubts when I put it on this morning. Admired it when I bought it, but if you don't like it . . ."

"Certainly I like it," lied Huxford kindly.

Turning, Paden asked, "What do you think, Audrey?"

"Wonderfully unique!" she replied at once, putting tact before taste. "I believe I've never seen such a combination of colors." Amused, her eyes sought Huxford's.

She found no laughter there. His steady gaze was hard and assessing. She looked away, cheeks gone suddenly pale.

Taking Audrey's statement as a high compliment, Paden thanked her, found a seat, and inquired whether or not the ladies would be wanting his escort that afternoon.

"Because if you don't, I plan to look in at Tatt's with Captain Ware. He's got his marching orders, you know. Needs a couple of mounts for Spain. Said he thought I might help with a hint or two. He didn't know you'd be back so soon, Hux. I'm sure he'd much better have your advice than mine. Care to come along?"

The marquis leaned back in his chair. "Certainly not. You've as good an eye for horseflesh as any man I know. Better. I'd trust your judgement implicitly. Wait up, I want to ask my sister something."

Politely interrupting the group around Lady Marpleby, he said, "Toria, Paden is going to Tatt's today. Do you want him to find you a hack, say a young mare? You'll be wanting to ride with Miss Taylor each morning."

"Oh, yes! Thank you, Gideon. Paden," Toria appealed with a smile, "you won't mind?"

"Mind? I should think not! Helped Audrey locate her bay, a beautiful five-year-old mare. Too big for you, Toria. Hux, what say to a little filly about fifteen hands high and . . ."

But Huxford was leaving. "Come along," he told the boy. "We can discuss it on the way. I have an appointment in the City at eleven."

"Yes, Gideon, I'll come, but first . . ." Paden paused, looking at Lady M. "You didn't say whether you wanted me today, ma'am." His expression was anxious.

Audrey hid her smile. It was plain that Paden was off like a shot when he found something more interesting than acting as escort.

Lady Marpleby cried that Paden must go, urging him to be off with Huxford at once. "We females are going to be vastly entertained." Counting on her fingers, she began enumerating all they were planning to do. "There's Hookum's Library and the Bazaar, and perhaps most important, we have an appointment with Madame Claudine to order Toria new frocks and a ballgown or two. She needs some town bronze."

When their company was gone, Lady M and the girls retired to the small parlor to lay plans for their shopping spree.

As they talked, Audrey thought that no one could help liking Toria St. Aubin. She was interested in everything and everyone around her. And Audrey received the impression that the girl possessed a rare quality of integrity found in only a few. Her forthright nature made Audrey feel they'd known one another for years.

Victoria was twenty-five, six years younger than Huxford. She looked much less. She was so small, she almost reminded Audrey of a child, in spite of her delicately rounded figure.

Although she was two years the junior, Audrey felt years older than Toria St. Aubin. It was because she was an American, she thought, raised in a less restricted society, and, perhaps, because she was a head taller. "Your brother is quite tall, yet you're so short," Audrey remarked. She bit her lip, hoping Toria wasn't self-conscious because of her lack of height.

It seemed that she was not. "Gideon has our papa's physique," she explained readily, "while I inherited mama's."

"Yes," declared Lady Marpleby. "And her beauty." Eyeing her old friend's daughter in a loving way, her ladyship shook her head and sighed. "Madelaine was the tiniest, most beautiful girl I ever saw. She was years younger than I, but we became the best of friends. How I've missed her since she's been gone!" Tears spurted from Lady M's eyes as Audrey and Victoria ran to comfort her.

"No, but here, Aunt Letty!" Toria cried bracingly. "Dry up, do. We can't have your eyes red when we reach Bond Street, now can we? We might meet any of your beaus on the toddle there! Sir Osgood, perhaps. Or Mr. Emmerhite. Even Lord Blaffington. Huxford tells me he has been buzzing around you all winter."

"Stuff!" snorted her ladyship. "Blaffington is a doddering fool and so I told Egbertt when the old fossil wanted to dance with me three times at Beakum House . . ."

Lady Marpleby suddenly stopped and smote herself on the forehead. "What are we about?" she demanded. "We have no time to waste like this! Run up and put on your prettiest bonnets while I order the carriage. I don't know what all we have to do this afternoon. And there's Vauxhall Gardens tonight, and tomorrow that rout party at Lady Brumley's. The Websters are having a musicale Thursday, and how I'm to get rid of Egbertt for it, I'll never know! He talks while the musicians are playing or singing, or whatever they're doing. Perhaps Cosmo could invite him for whist again. Never mind! We'll talk of that later."

Audrey had been afraid that having Huxford's sister living at Marpleby House might prove awkward. But shopping in the Bazaar that afternoon and visiting the libraries and bookstores reinforced her first feelings about Toria St. Aubin.

Audrey found that she enjoyed the girl's enthusiasm, her vitality, and her response to the moment. By the time their carriage turned into Bond Street, they were worn out from laughing and hunting for bargains.

The girls pleaded with Lady Marpleby to have the coachman head homeward instead of stopping at Madame Claudine's, but her ladyship was determined to herd them in to see the couturiere.

Good-naturedly shushing their protestations, she refused to listen to another word. "No, don't try and distract me. We must have some fittings, for it's my determination, Victoria, that you shall set the beau monde on its ear and end this season with an engagement ring on your finger."

The bright animation fled Toria's face. She stared stricken at Lady Marpleby.

It was such a startling reaction, and Audrey's attention was so fairly caught, that a moment or two passed before she realized someone was calling her name.

Pinky Tadburn and Lord Farquar Fulverton had been ambling along Bond Street when Lady M's barouche—its top folded to take advantage of the sunshine—pulled up to the curb.

"Miss Taylor! Lady Marpleby!" Pinky exclaimed. "And Miss St. Aubin! How do you do? Here you are, bringing the very person we've been wanting to see. Haven't we, Farq?"

Lord Fulverton blinked and bowed, and Audrey had her first good look at Mr. Tadburn. She'd never seen him in daylight. Now she could understand why he carried a nickname like Pinky. He had a high complexion, with delicate translucent skin, hair that was light blond, and his pale eyes seemed to have no lashes at all. He was prone to blush like a girl, and when he colored up—as he frequently did—even his hair seemed to take on a pink tinge. It was the strangest thing Audrey had ever seen.

Audrey soon found herself inside Madame Claudine's, secluded in a private nook and seated upon a Louis Quatorze settee. Lord Fulverton and Mr. Tadburn perched themselves on an overstuffed banquette, and Tadburn began telling Audrey all about the ongoing course of Tony's treatment.

Madame Claudine, wise to the ways of sporting men, knew horseflesh took precedence over fashion. She left them to their discussion, taking Lady Marpleby and Miss St. Aubin to the fitting rooms, promising Miss Taylor a tea tray.

"We had the first favorable sign yesterday," Pinky reported. "Farq thought it was taking too long, but I recollected you said your papa's treatment began slow and steadily increased. Stands to reason: such a tiny amount of arsenic in so large a horse. We gave Tony his second dose only last night and already his shoulder is better. Thought you might be anxious to know."

"Yes, indeed, Mr. Tadburn," Audrey assured him. "Which reminds me. I almost sent you a note last week but thought we should bump into one another sooner or later. What color is Tony?"

"Didn't I tell you?" Pinky spoke around the large teacake he was eating. "He's a piebald—whole team is. Beautiful matched set; wait'll you see it."

Audrey smiled. "That relieves me. You probably know this already, but the fact remains that if Tony has a solid coat, there is a danger that the healed place will show. They almost always grow back white cover hair."

"Told you so," Lord Fulverton said suddenly and subsided into confusion at speaking aloud.

Mr. Tadburn was regarding him proudly. "Farq! That's the first time you ever said anything in front of a girl." He fell silent, waiting. It was evident to Lord Fulverton's companions that another effusion was forthcoming.

His lordship's mouth opened and closed, and he nodded and blinked a time or two. With supreme effort he articulated two more words: "Violet eyes!" he croaked.

"Good God!" ejaculated Pinky, fixing a piercing gaze upon Audrey. "Takes a man in love to notice a thing like that!"

It was obvious Lord Fulverton felt he had paraded his eloquence sufficiently for one day. He leaned forward and whispered something in Pinky's ear.

Mr. Tadburn turned to the fascinated Audrey. "Lord Fulverton wished me to say this, Miss Taylor: He first fell in love with you because you knew so much about horses. Well," Pinky interpolated, "anybody would! But now he's seen you in daylight, he wants you to know he might have fallen in love with you even if you didn't know a horse from a billy goat. Might not!" Pinky warned, "but then again—might have!"

Lord Fulverton, eyes glued on Audrey, once again whispered instructions into his friend's ear.

Mr. Tadburn frowned. "Farq," he protested mildly, "I don't know about that."

His lordship took up his whispering again. Pinky shook his head doubtfully, but disclosed his friend's latest message.

"Farq says he ain't withdrawing his suit, Miss Taylor. He says if these plans of yours with the Marquis of Huxford should come to naught—this understanding between you, which Huxford spoke of when he hinted us off—Farq says to tell you he's still prepared to make you a formal offer."

In strangled tones Audrey managed to say, "No! I have no . . . I'm not . . . the marquis couldn't have . . ." She became so involved in a tangle of words that she stopped and didn't know how to start again. Fortunately there occurred an interruption.

"Here you are," Paden Offutt called as he entered Madame Claudine's lounge. "Saw Lady M's barouche parked outside. Hallo, Pinky. You and Farq here?"

Without waiting for an answer, he turned to Audrey. "Where's Toria? I've located her a bang-up hack."

Upon hearing this tidbit of information, Pinky and his lordship—quite forgetting a proposal of marriage in the face of superior news—fell to exclaiming and questioning their friend.

Amidst all this, Audrey tried to gather her wits. What had Huxford said to this pair and why had he said it? She became aware that Paden was asking her something and begged him to repeat his question.

"I was looking for Toria," he told her.

"The . . . the fitting room," Audrey murmured. She could hardly think.

"Oh, well!" Paden shrugged. "I say, Farq, would you and Pinky care to come to Tattersall's and see the mare?"

Assuring Paden they would like nothing better, they told Audrey goodbye.

She pressed her handkerchief against her lips to stop their trembling. Tonight she would see Huxford again. How she dreaded that encounter!

10

Vauxhall Gardens was situated across the river in Lambeth. They went in three carriages, Audrey and Paden Offutt riding with the marquis and his sister. Lady Webster's carriage came next, and at the rear of the cavalcade, in his ancient berlin, rode Lord Higglesby and Lady Marpleby. The teacup-shaped coachcar swayed so that Lady M swore she was going to be ill.

"No, now Letty, you ain't," Lord H assured her. "Remember how you always think you'll be, but never are. Here," Egbertt said, and rolled up the leather curtain. A blast of cold air hit Lady Marpleby, threatening her intricately coiffed hair. He chuckled when she screamed and clutched at it, pleading with him to lower the shade.

"Ha! Thought you'd forget being sick, m'love, when that beautiful hair was threatened. Never mind. Here we are, ready for the ferry to carry us across the river."

Their box was located on the main concourse, near the raised balcony where one of the lesser divettes was singing, accompanied by a small orchestra.

Throughout their supper of shaved ham, cheese, chilled gelatines and ices, Audrey was aware of how close her chair was to Huxford's. His sleeve continually brushed her bare arm. It was his party, and he had seated her and taken his place beside her. She couldn't imagine why; his face had settled in its usual haughty mold, and although he was gracious to all his guests, he paid her scant attention.

Audrey knew she should be grateful. Instead, she was perversely annoyed. All through the meal, she steadfastly ignored him. She was surprised and confused when the marquis stood, and taking her elbow, invited her to walk.

Victoria and Paden had already disappeared down one of the dimly lit paths with Lord Fawlkes and Miss Webster, and Audrey accompanied Huxford with numb knees and fluttering heart. They went, she couldn't help but notice, in the opposite direction to that taken by the other members of their party.

The evening was mellow with a large moon, and the shadowed walkway, studded here and there with stone benches and rustic settees in leafy bowers, led them farther and farther from the lights and music.

She must begin some sort of conversation, Audrey thought desperately. She forced her mind from Huxford's hand on her arm and opened her mouth.

"Why," she demanded to her dismay, "did you tell Mr. Tadburn and Lord Fulverton your interest was fixed on me, my lord?"

The marquis stopped them under the flickering light of a tall cresset. His face was all chert and shadow. "How did you learn that?" he drawled.

Her bosom swelled in indignation. "Then you don't deny it?"

He shrugged. "Why should I? It's true."

Audrey gasped, but Huxford wasn't finished. "I said it to deflect Fulverton's ill-judged proposal. Then I realized it was true; my interest *is* fixed on you, in a way. Having a monomania about someone certainly seems indicative of one's interest being fixed, wouldn't you say, Miss Taylor?"

Huxford had fought a hard-won battle for detachment since returning from Baddingly. He'd set out to prove to himself that Audrey was like all other beautiful women. It wasn't love he was feeling—he kept telling himself that over and over. No, he refused to call it love. In fact, he thought he was almost coming to hate how she made him feel. His response to her lightest touch set a fire raging inside him. Just to see her made him want her.

There was a tiny dimple at the right corner of her mouth. Huxford wanted to put his tongue just there and taste her. He stepped closer; he could smell the perfume she wore, the woman-scent of her. "Does it cater to your vanity when I admit that you're never out of my thoughts?" he asked harshly. "Don't let it flatter your conceit! You're most un-welcome there, or in my dreams, or in my life. However, you're not the first obsession I've suffered, and I've hit on a scheme to be rid of you."

His laugh was sardonic. "Yes—you have become an ob-session, Miss Taylor. Two or three times I've exhibited such pathological behavior, but the objects of my . . . desire were, fortunately, not *ladies*. Therefore, I was able to purge myself. That is scarcely possible with you."

The coldness of Huxford's smile pierced Audrey like splinters of ice. She had to concentrate with all her might to understand his relentless stream of words. He was so close, their bodies were almost touching. And he had hold of her wrists, making her look up at him. She was only too aware of a steamy heat that emanated from him. Ice and steam, she thought, and shivered. If he noticed, she couldn't tell.

He continued his diatribe. "My first intention was to avoid you. But I've decided against that. No, I shall com-mit myself to your company as often as I'm able. I'm cer-tain that before long you'll begin to bore me as the others did and I shall have effected my cure." He glanced down at his hands holding her wrists and opened them slowly, as he would a pair of manacles.

Throughout Huxford's vitriolic monologue, Audrey's anger had risen. Although her cheeks flamed, she was icy pale. Her eyes felt hot with unshed tears.

"What," she demanded immediately, in a low, furious tone, "does one reply to such an astonishing declaration? Should one beg pardon for arousing such unwelcome ar-dor? Should one offer heartfelt wishes for a speedy recov-ery? One could remember to speak in platitudes and promise to develop a giggle. Or no!—a squint. I confess, my lord: I'm at a loss how to alleviate your condition, or indeed, how to further this *delightful* conversation. I see no purpose in prolonging it. Please return me to my aunt."

Huxford bowed, and with a strange half-smile, offered his arm. Silently they walked, Audrey struggling to regain her composure.

As they neared the concourse, she became aware of a

couple by the pathway. The girl sat on a wooden bench staring at her hands, while the man leaned close as if irresistibly drawn. There was a brooding intensity about his attitude. Audrey caught her breath. It could not be, but it was—Victoria St. Aubin and Lord Chartley. They were directly under a flambeau, and when Victoria raised her eyes, staring blindly at Audrey and her brother, there was a well of unhappiness in her face.

Victoria stood and extended her hand to Audrey. Obviously striving to shed her mood of distress, she smiled a little and said, "Here you are. Aunt Letty told us you came this way. Kit and I have been waiting for you."

Chartley stood silently by, leaning against the bench. He reached for Victoria's hand and placed it in the crook of his arm as they made their way back to the others.

At their box, Chartley remained only a moment, and though he neither avoided Victoria's glance nor paid any particular attention to her, Audrey felt the pull between them, as if they were achingly aware of each other. When Kit left, Toria seemed more alone than ever.

Home in her bed, cuddling her pillow, Audrey tried to focus her thoughts on the obvious fascination between Chartley and Victoria, but her mind kept leaping to Huxford and what he'd said at Vauxhall. She did her best to revive the anger and indignation she'd felt. He had, after all, reverted to his chilling and sardonic manner for the rest of the evening, except for one moment when his amused eyes flew to hers at some ridiculous thing Lord Higglesby said. Try as she might, Audrey could do nothing to diminish her sense of satisfaction. Huxford might not love her, but he was—he kept saying it—*obsessed* with her. She couldn't help being thrilled at this evidence that he was fighting his feeling for her. Much, oh *much,* was answered regarding his behavior these past few weeks.

Before Gideon had left Marpleby House that night, Lady M had invited him into the small parlor where he sat without removing his overcoat, staring into the fire.

"I can't think you're indifferent to Audrey, my dear," Lady Marpleby had commented, gently and without prologue.

Gideon had not pretended to misunderstand what she meant. He nodded impatiently. "Certainly I'm not. Far from it. She occupies entirely too high a place in my senses for my peace of mind. But that's not wonderful, seeing how beautiful she is."

He closed his eyes for a moment, as if to wipe away some inner vision, and when he opened them, they held a hard gleam. "You must realize, Godmama, a man may look, and even desire, where he will not marry."

"You have no intention of offering for her?" Lady Marpleby asked.

"Certainly not. I refuse to marry anyone I'm infatuated with. Look at Melbourne. He loves Caroline Lamb to distraction—or did. That's his trouble. Now look what she's putting him through with Byron. It's killing him, but he can't let the beau monde see. And Chartley. He let his head be turned by a pretty face and coaxing manner. Now his and Toria's lives are ruined."

Her ladyship sighed and shook her head. "But what of your mother, Gideon? She loved your father and he loved her. That was a marriage made in heaven."

"Exactly so. And with that example in front of me, I have vowed to settle for nothing less. But I'm coming to realize that's a hopeless ambition."

"But Audrey . . ."

"Audrey," he said, "has never made a secret of the fact that she is not looking for a husband, nor that she is discontented in London and no admirer of Englishmen."

After a small pause, he continued. "No. When I am well into my forties, I shall marry some chit who cares for nothing except my title and wealth, someone who is perfectly comfortable in our London society, and I'll never bother my head with *love* again." Gideon's mouth held a twisted smile.

Lady Marpleby's heart had melted and she'd patted his arm tenderly. "We shall see, dear boy. We shall see."

Well after midnight, twenty-four hours after the ill-fated

trip to Vauxhall, in a dark, stuffy room in a flash house in St. Giles, Arnaud de Vinnay watched the Marquis of Huxford stoop and put his eye to a peephole. They had been waiting for their bumbling double-agent, old Lord Leland Arrington, to drop Brumley's false information to the French agent Daubray, who was seated in the next room.

Arnaud had just relinquished the peephole to Huxford, when the marquis stiffened and whispered, "Ah, it's Arrington, at last. Yes, Daubray is coming forward. Arrington gives him the folded paper—wait! A quarrel—something has gone wrong."

They heard Arrington shout, "No!"

"What has happened?" demanded Arnaud.

"Shush," cautioned Huxford. "The old man is grabbing the paper—trying to take it back."

Huxford motioned Arnaud to the lookout. "Keep watch," he murmured. "I believe there's going to be trouble."

Scarcely had the words left his mouth than a shot rang out. Huxford swore, dragged his pistol from his pocket and sprang for the door.

Only a step behind, Arnaud followed into the hall, his own gun cocked and ready. Huxford leaped forward just as Daubray wrenched the door open and tried to escape.

Eyes wild, Daubray backed into the room, pulling a second gun from his long coat tail.

Gideon, suddenly dead calm and dangerous, crouched, expertly squeezing off a shot, catching the spy in his right shoulder and knocking him to the floor.

Before Arnaud could react, the marquis was bent over Daubray, retrieving the discharged pistol and making sure his prisoner concealed no more loaded weapons.

"Watch him," Huxford said and turned Lord Arrington over. The old man was dead, a large bloody hole in his neck.

Gideon leveled a look at Daubray. The Frenchman cringed, shrinking back, holding his shoulder, his face a mixture of terror and pain.

"Were you Arrington's only contact?" Gideon asked. "Answer me," he said, between clenched teeth.

Daubray shook his head and Gideon laughed.

That laugh sent a chill up Arnaud's spine. He was glad he wasn't Daubray. He'd never heard a more menacing sound.

"Oh, you'll talk, Daubray," Huxford said. "Now, or to-morrow, or sometime within the next few days. You won't eat, drink, or sleep until you do. And don't worry, we'll have a doctor patch you up. You must live so we can hang you."

A loud knock sounded at the door and the proprietor—a large, slow, coarse-faced man—entered at Huxford's invitation. "Yes, Stahling, I've been expecting you. I'm going to need your help. Lord Arrington has just had a heart attack. I want a carriage called round to the back. This man Daubray is being detained by my friend on a matter of business. I shall require you to help me load his lordship into the carriage. You are not to trouble yourself over any of this. Do you understand me?"

Stahling, assessing all the blood and the gaping gunshot wound in the victim's neck, merely nodded. "Aye, Gov'ner. If you say it was a heart attack what killed 'is lordship, then that's what happened."

Gideon clapped Stahling on the back. "Good man. Now, order the carriage and send for a doctor."

To Arnaud, he said, "Tie Daubray's hands and take him into the next room. Stay there—I shall return within the hour. Our story is simple: We have been at my house most of the evening, playing cards. Now I must deliver Lord Arrington to his home in Liecester Square. Sad thing. His son went to school with me, you know. There must be no scandal."

A week later, Arnaud de Vinnay hunched his shoulders against the rain as the cab deposited him at the corner of King Street. The Kings Arms Tavern offered a welcome respite from the damp outside. De Vinnay entered and peered through the dimness of the smoke-filled taproom. Tom Cribb himself came forward. The ex-champion was past his prime, but he moved with the lightness and agility all boxers possess. He was surprisingly small, with delicate ankles and trim, sinewy hands.

He greeted the Frenchman politely and motioned toward the Parlor—that inner sanctum where the Fancy and the elite of the sporting world came to drink, lay bets, and visit others of similar ilk. On a nasty night such as this, Cribb could be sure of playing host to at least a dozen Corinthians, Bucks, and Swells who had deserted White's or Brook's for his more plebeian establishment.

De Vinnay tossed his greatcoat over a chair and sat at a sturdy table. The Marquis of Huxford, whom he'd come to meet, nodded and continued talking with Kit Hartwell and his friend, Lord Alvanley. The viscount suddenly drank off his brandy like ale and called for another. Then he resumed baiting Alvanley. The 2nd Lord Alvanley, a member of the prestigious quartet known as the Bow Window Set—the Unique Four—stood warming himself at the fire. His round cheeks were dusty with snuff.

"No!" Alvanley was heard protesting to Lord Chartley. "Can't do that!" He turned to Huxford. "Can't beat that time, damme. Can't be done! Gideon, tell this boy he can't beat the Regent's time to Brighton."

"That was a long time ago," the marquis said.

"Well," Chartley drawled, grinning up at Alvanley with a drunken glitter, "I could race *you*, my lord. How 'bout that?"

Alvanley looked at the younger man. "Can't go," he said kindly. "You'd probably beat me and I should be undone."

In the face of so blatant a falsehood—for Alvanley was a noted whip—even Kit had to laugh. "All right. I probably couldn't beat you anyway," he owned. "Only come. I'll take you to Watier's and beat you at écarté."

The two friends left, in excellent humor with one another, and Huxford went to sit with the Frenchman.

Arnaud watched Huxford come toward him. He hadn't seen him since the night of Lord Arrington's death.

"Ah, mon ami," he said softly, shaking the marquis's hand. "As you predicted, there was no scandal. So the old lord is safely buried, and Daubray—he is safely hung. What now?"

Huxford grinned and kept his voice low. "Brumley wants me to take you and Christine Jeffers to France in my yacht." He laughed at the Frenchman's pleased surprise.

Arnaud was, in fact, delighted. "We are going at last to rescue my young cousin? And I shall have the so charming Mrs. Jeffers for a companion. Lord Brumley speaks highly of her. She is an agent of the most excellent, *n'est-ce pas?*"

"Yes, indeed. But a trip into France is perilous. There are many details to arrange. We must discuss them all."

Gideon leaned his head toward Arnaud so they wouldn't be overheard. Perhaps if he could immerse himself in these spying affairs of Lord Brumley's he could get his mind off Audrey Taylor. Even a small distraction would help, for there were times when he thought his consuming preoccupation with her was driving him crazy.

It was with extreme reluctance that Victoria St. Aubin could be brought to speak of Kit Hartwell, and then only in answer to a direct question put by Audrey.

"I've known Kit since I was eighteen," Toria said. "Whitfeld is through the woods from Baddingly and was one of the Earl of Darley's holdings. The earl was Kit's grandfather on his mother's side. Whitfeld is opposite to Baddingly from Rosedale, which belongs to the Offutt's." Toria took a deep breath. "When Kit was twenty-two, he inherited the place. He grew to be great friends with my bother, and Victor and Paden Offutt. Kit was more often at Baddingly than his own home."

Victoria paused, tried to smile. Suddenly she rose from the sofa. "Audrey," she said brightly, "let's not recall old times just now." She was trembling and gripped her hands together to keep them from shaking. "Come," she said, "let's—let's see what you're wearing to Regina Selkirk's rout party tonight."

* * *

Soon or late those next few weeks, Chartley always came where they were. He appeared to be trailing Victoria. Unfailingly sober, he would look at his query, and Victoria would return his look with an anguish Audrey found trying, then exasperating. There was some tormented quality surrounding them that she couldn't account for.

Once Kit came to Almack's to waltz with Toria. When the dance was finished he handed her back to her seat between Audrey and Lady M with a savage, almost feral, expression. The girl seemed dazed, and Lady Marpleby took her hand and stroked it, talking all the while of their projected jaunts about town on the morrow.

At the sight of Toria's wretched face, Audrey could almost forget the way Huxford had just looked at her. She twisted the handkerchief in her lap. She never could tell what his attitude would be. At times he treated her almost casually—very nearly, Audrey thought, the way he treated Toria, laughing and relaxed. At other times, he was brusque, barely civil, and he seemed to avoid her. Once—at Lady Wrotham's musicale—he took her hand in a hard, quick grasp, squeezing her fingers. The blood had rushed to her cheeks. He laughed, and suddenly taking her wine glass, holding her eyes captive with his own, he deliberately turned the glass so that he drank from the rim where her lips had touched.

Tonight, striving to decipher the puzzle of Victoria St. Aubin and Kit Hartwell, she'd encountered a look she'd never seen before. Between them had passed an intimate look, knowing, one that took her breath and made it impossible for her to think of anything except how it would feel if Huxford held her in his arms and looked at her this way.

Audrey, greatly daring, raised her eyes at last. The marquis was gone. Almack's, never bright, seemed more lackluster than ever.

The season whirled on. Audrey, though plagued by her turmoil over Huxford, grew more concerned about his sister. Toria's vitality seemed sapped by some emotion.

Audrey knew where the blame lay: It was Kit Hartwell. His face wore a perpetual mask of hard bitterness, and he seemed more violent in his actions than ever. Rumor said he'd lately killed two men in a drunken brawl in St. Giles. Audrey became more troubled for him—and for Toria—than ever.

On a day when she could stand no more, she cornered Lady Marpleby in the library. "Aunt Letty, *what* is Chartley about?" she demanded. "It's abundantly clear that Victoria is in love with him, and he with her, but he is a married man! And is he trying to get himself killed?"

Lady M hesitated. "It's hard to explain, Audrey. The St. Aubin's took in a distant connection of theirs some years ago, the stepdaughter of a cousin of Madelaine's. Her name was Diane Haynes, and she was tiny and bright, with a halo of blonde curls.

"First she set her cap at Gideon. He would have nothing of her, so she turned to Kit Hartwell. Kit had been at Whitfeld for two years and Victoria was deeply in love with him. He hadn't declared himself, but had paid her an extraordinary amount of attention. So much so that in all our minds, and certainly in Toria's, their eventual marriage was a settled thing.

"Diane was older than Kit and seemed to exert some sort of spell over him. He was dazzled—captivated. He proposed and they were married. Soon it was apparent they had made a terrible mistake. It's been a tragedy all the way around. For everyone."

"Yes, but don't they have a child?" Audrey asked.

"A little boy, about a year and a half old."

"What went wrong with their marriage?" Audrey prodded when her aunt lapsed into silence.

"Diane is—she's nervous. Her moods are erratic and she is given to hysterical fits. At any rate, Kit must have realized at once what he had given up in Victoria." Lady Marpleby shook her head. "He has been disconsolate since the beginning of the marriage, never saying a word but plainly suffering. And Toria—you can see how it is with her."

Certainly Audrey could see. What she couldn't understand was Chartley. Now that he'd ruined his own life, why couldn't he stay away from Victoria and allow her to forget him? The distaste Audrey felt for Kit grew.

11

When he considered the matter, Paden Offutt was forced to conclude that Audrey Taylor did not like Kit Hartwell. She pokered up, became positively mackerel-backed, whenever he approached any group surrounding her and Toria St. Aubin. That her reactions furnished the viscount with a short of cynical amusement Paden understood; why he should insist on signing her dance card, or persist in seeking her out to engage her in conversation, was less easily explained.

It began to bother Paden. He grew troubled when people he liked were at loggerheads with one another. He tried to ignore the situation, then undertook to discuss it with Audrey, but got nowhere.

She could not admire Chartley's life style, she said. The viscount's attitude was to be deplored, as were some of his companions. Most of all, she couldn't approve of Huxford's allowing Kit to be constantly alone with Toria. When Paden tried to explain, realized he couldn't, and lost himself in a maze of evasions and declamations, they came near to quarreling.

He was miserable that evening and sought the marquis at Brook's. "Gideon, why can't Audrey Taylor be hinted off Kit?" he asked straitly.

"None of her business, Paden, and see you don't discuss it with her," he was adjured. Paden had to content himself with that.

At the Countess of Omsley's ball, from where she stood with Huxford in the conservatory overlooking the gardens, Audrey could see Chartley talking with Victoria.

Audrey looked up at Huxford's profile, sharply outlined against the brilliance of the ballroom. She closed her eyes, then said what she'd been wanting to say for days. "I wish Kit Hartwell were not so particular in his attentions to your sister."

Gideon moved toward her along the rail and stared down at the carp in the ornamental pond. "She'll come to no harm through Chartley." His voice was careless, as if he were thinking of other matters.

"I realize it's no business of mine," Audrey began.

"No. It's—you don't have all the facts." The marquis turned and held out his hand. "Come," he said. "Trust me."

Reflecting that there was little else she could do, Audrey allowed him to lead her back into the crowded ballroom. "Shall we find your aunt?" he asked.

She nodded. He was looking at her as he had all evening, as he had for days now. Lately, since that night at Almack's, there'd been a light of some kind glittering—burning coldly—in his eyes, giving them a strange silver gleam whenever he looked at her, sending keen shafts of warmth jetting everywhere inside her, making her shiver, then rage with heat. He seemed to be waiting, waiting for something to happen. But *what?* came the silent scream within her. What was Huxford waiting for, and how long before she broke? "Aunt Letty is in the card room. Will you take me there?" she asked.

His eyes on hers, the silver light glowing, Gideon murmured, "With all my heart."

Audrey lifted her head, tilting it proudly, trying to ignore the bright glances following them. What she couldn't ignore was the tumultuous pounding of her blood racing through her veins.

Sir Malcolm Motley had had a blazing for four weeks. It went beyond his wildest dreams that his golden run had lasted so long. His hoard grew larger each day, but one thing had eluded him. Not since the night of Lady Marpleby's ball had he been able to engage Gideon St.

Aubin in play. Now he looked up to see him approaching, the American girl in tow.

Paden Offutt had jumped up and was busily turning his coat wrong-side-out. Lady M watched in fascination as he put it on again with all the seams and lining showing.

"Change his luck," Lord Egbertt expounded loudly in her ear. "Might work, might not. Saw Charles James Fox wear his hat upside down at White's once for four hours. Didn't serve though. Lost anyway. Had the damnedest luck gambling, Fox did."

Motley arranged his features in a thin smile and bade Miss Soames-Taylor a good evening. Then he asked the marquis if he cared to sit in the game.

"Another time, Motley," Huxford said. "We've come to find Lady M."

Swallowing his disappointment, Sir Malcolm bowed and resumed his seat.

"Here," cried Paden to Audrey. "Come help me change my luck. See? I've got my coat turned all about. Surely that, plus the fact that *you* wish me to win—surely that must sway Lady Fortune my way!"

He was half-joking, for, not being inclined to deep play, he hadn't lost much. Audrey knew that Paden was a very rich young man, but he was a trifle close; he wasn't stingy, merely careful. "Now," he directed her. "Lay your hand on my shoulder and keep it there while I cut the cards."

For the next thirty minutes, Audrey stood with her hand glued to Paden's shoulder. "I say, just one more hand," he begged as Lady M, at a signal from Huxford, said they must go.

The marquis was adamant, however, and they left Paden to his own devices. These served him well enough, for it seemed Motley's run of luck had successfully been broken.

Over the next few weeks, at whatever club or hell he was losing in, Motley nursed his hatred for Huxford and his grievance for Miss Soames-Taylor. He believed that his change of luck and subsequent loss of chance-got gains could be laid squarely at her door. His fixation on the American girl grew into an irrational preoccupation, overshadowing all else, even his compulsion to gamble. Except for her intervention, Motley was convinced his golden run should still be flowing, and by now he could have enticed the Marquis of Huxford into gaming with him. Neither Huxford nor the girl would escape his vengeance! This Motley swore to himself, time and time again.

In Brook Street, Lord Chartley strode into Huxford's library. "I've got to run down to Whitfeld this morning. Tell Victoria, will you? And be nice to Miss Taylor while I'm gone."

"No—why?" asked the marquis.

"Everyone except she knows that you're in love with her." Kit grinned.

Gideon lazily took snuff. "One could almost think you were falling in love with her yourself, the way you were laughing together at Reggie Selkirk's party last week."

"Jealous, are you?" the viscount drawled.

"I'm not such a fool!"

"I should think you a fool indeed to be jealous of me," Chartley said. "You know where my needs lie." His voice grated on these last words.

At the Felbridge ball Audrey excused herself and sought refuge in a small back parlor half up the stairs.

There a single sconce of candles was lighted; this and the fire cast the only illumination. Tears blurred her sight as she made her way to the bay window facing the street. Water beaded the panes and occasionally lightning revealed the night-filled landscape as rain fell slowly, silently.

Audrey was tired. These weeks since Victoria St. Aubin's arrival in town had been trying. It was Huxford's fault. True to his word, he'd been constant in his attendance on the Marpleby House crowd.

Each morning the marquis arrived with Paden Offutt to ride beside Audrey in the park. He returned to Marpleby House and ate breakfast; afternoons he and Paden escorted Victoria, Lady M, and Audrey out shopping or on visits. These were commonly referred to as *morning* calls, although they occurred in the afternoon—ludicrous as that seemed to Audrey's logical American mind.

Wherever she was, whenever she chanced to look about, Audrey almost always discovered Huxford close beside her. Every evening he brought his carriage to convey them to rout parties, balls, even musicales, making his sister's presence his excuse.

If only Victoria had chosen to stay in Brook Street. Audrey brushed a wispy curl from her forehead, half-ashamed of such a thought. Victoria was the kind of friend it often takes a lifetime to find. In all the world, there were only two subjects they couldn't discuss: Huxford and Kit Hartwell. Audrey wished something could be done for Victoria, and she wished Chartley would refrain from looking at the girl with ravaged eyes. But what would *she* not give to have someone look at her in just such a way. Gideon St. Aubin's looks were silver cold. Not since the night at Lady Omsley's had he shown he was drawn to her. Frigidly polite, he talked or danced with her behind an unapproachable barrier. He had not indulged in another of his furies against her, but neither had he directed toward her even a hint of emotion of the more tender sort.

Audrey kept herself from revealing by word, deed, or expression what she was feeling. She stayed constantly on guard. Everything was colored by his presence.

But she'd been born with her father's pride. She would carry on as if all were well with her, hiding how she felt. Audrey decided the danger lay in exaggerating her contrived conviviality. When she laughed—and there were times when she did, because even low spirits could not suppress her sense of the ridiculous—she laughed moderately. And never, *ever,* did she cast one of those revealing side-glances at the marquis.

Audrey schooled herself severely; only those who knew her best recognized her unhappiness. This constant attrition was so wearing that her appetite and sleep suffered. She lost weight from an already slender frame and her cheekbones became more prominent.

The world kept turning no matter what her afflictions.

Audrey knew that. She felt she owed it to her aunt to appear in an agreeable and unexceptional light.

At times, she took to disappearing for a few minutes. Finding a sheltered spot, she would close her eyes, draw a deep breath and mentally gird herself. This enabled her to endure endless hours of chatter and to smile under the unrelenting scrutiny of the Marquis of Huxford.

Audrey knew he didn't like her, but did he still *want* her? Not by so much as the flicker of an eyelid did his lordship betray his desire, even when he claimed Audrey for his usual two dances. Not once, not for days, had he shown any effects such a desire might have upon him. The wall between them was higher each time they met. Audrey sighed, scorning her first faint hopes and laying them to rest.

Her solitude was shattered by the door being wrenched open. She turned, knowing with a precognitive certainty whom she would see.

Huxford slammed the door shut behind him and advanced upon her. "My sister asked me to ascertain whether or not you are well," he said. "I see that you are."

He was always so angry with her, Audrey thought.

He forcefully entered the room, his presence more potent than she remembered. "Are you hiding?" he asked. "Why don't you come back to the ballroom and flaunt yourself in that gown before everyone?"

Audrey stood transfixed at his brutal tone, realizing he was laboring under some violent emotion. She couldn't utter a sound, so stricken she could only stare.

Gideon stared back. A flash of lightning revealed the transparency of her skin, paler than usual, deepening the umber shadows under her violet eyes. Her beauty had taken on an ethereal quality these past few days, making her lovely in a way she never had been before. He took in her tear-bright eyes and tremulous mouth and bit back an oath.

"What a shame, Miss Taylor, that you're not married." He grasped her slender upper arm and held her facing him. "Why couldn't you be the wife of some red-faced American here on business? Then we could make love and have done with it. And when your husband removed to Boston in three months or six, I'd be satisfied to see you go. After I had my fill of you—of initiating you into delights such as your rustic spouse never dreamed of."

Huxford's grip increased. He loomed closer, his eyes, burning cold with those hot silver points, holding her in bondage. His voice roughened and dropped to a murmur. "And if we were lovers already, I'd take you now—here in this room, or another like it. Before the fire. With the rain and the night outside. And afterward I'd hold you."

Audrey, in violent reaction to the dangerously seductive picture he painted, was swept with a fiery anger of her own, white-hot, all consuming. Her retaliation was as swift as it was futile. She slapped him. Hard enough to make her hand sting.

Huxford reached for her with narrowed eyes. "But this is classic, my dear. You slap me, I kiss you. You knew that, of course."

Held locked against him, isolated against the window embrasure in the darkened room, they were caught in a fearful intimacy. He tangled his hand in her hair and pulled her head back.

"I'm going to kiss you, Audrey." He tightened his grip on her hair. "When you go away to America, you must forget it. The ocean should be wide enough to keep me from you; nothing else seems likely to."

Breathing raggedly, Audrey struggled to say something. As she started to speak, he brought his mouth down on hers, forcing her lips wide with a cruelty that betrayed his need.

She had wondered what it would be like to be kissed by Gideon St. Aubin, to know his taste, his mouth, his ruthless embrace. Now his tongue was invading her and she could picture a great fire wrapping them in sheaths of flame. A catalyst of heat seemed to consume and yet sustain them—nothing would ever be the same in either of their lives, Audrey thought. Suspended in time, she strained desperately closer, trying to get at him, to merge, to become part of him. Never had she known such a rapturous assault on her senses; never had she dared to contemplate such bright ecstasy.

She moaned low in her throat when he cast aside all restraint and crushed her even closer. She moaned again as he wrapped both arms fully around her, sliding his lips along her cheek and down the side of her throat.

Gideon put his tongue on the wildly throbbing pulse he found there, kissing it, feeling the force of her beating heart as he gently sucked the fragrant flesh of her throat, tasting her again and yet again as her hands clutched at him, and her body strained to mesh even more closely with his. He glimpsed her face, radiant with some inner joy, some thrill of discovery, her head thrown back, eyes closed, eyelashes fluttering, sweetly curved mouth open, waiting for his again.

She uttered small revealing cries of excitement and tiny muted gasps. "Gideon," she murmured entreatingly, over and over. "Gideon."

His name on her lips was all Gideon had ever imagined, spurring his passion, bringing him to a dangerous point of arousal. He doubted he could ever bring himself to put her from him, to push her pliant form away, to tear his lips from hers. "Beautiful," he groaned. "You're so damnably beautiful. I want you, Audrey—want you. Kiss me again."

It was Mr. Emmerhite's habit to find a secluded nook at every rout party, ball, or large gathering he attended. Here he could jot down such mots as they occurred to him and drink a glass of wine. These were his most enjoyable moments, with the house around him alive with people and the prospect of many more tidbits for his diary before the evening ended. When he took up his notes tomorrow, he knew he would be able to reconstruct the sights and sounds, the nuances of tone and expression he wanted to remember, to relive, and to record.

Mr. Emmerhite was assured of the perfect spot at Felbridge House. Lady Felbridge herself had called it to his attention. He was fumbling for his spectacles, juggling his wine and notebook, when he pushed open the door and beheld a sight he never thought he would see: Miss

Audrey Soames-Taylor being ardently kissed by the Marquis of Huxford. Mr. Emmerhite's wine glass shattered on the tesselated floor.

The marquis slowly raised his head, straightened, and released Audrey only partially. He swung about to face Mr. Emmerhite, his clenched jaw looking as hard as granite. Holding Audrey close with one arm still around her, his lordship languidly raised his quizzing glass and subjected the stupefied Mr. Emmerhite to a leisurely perusal. "Make you my compliments, sir. Nothing passes you by, does it? Secrets fairly leap out as you walk by."

Huxford's arm tightened painfully as Audrey, feeling as though she'd suddenly recovered from a fit of insanity, tried to move away. "It's no use, my love," the marquis said. "We must share our delightful news with Mr. Emmerhite."

Audrey, her face hot, opened her mouth to protest, but the marquis plunged in ahead of her.

"You, sir," he told Mr. Emmerhite, "have the honor to be the first to wish us joy. Miss Taylor has engaged herself to be my wife."

His arm tightened even more cruelly, warning Audrey to remain silent. "The announcement will be in the newspapers tomorrow. I must beg you, sir, to keep quiet about it until then."

Mr. Emmerhite, overwhelmingly sensible to the great good fortune that had befallen him, immediately offered felicitations. "Wish you happy, my lord and Miss Soames-Taylor. Only too delighted ... You mean ... no one knows?" He looked at Audrey. "Your dear aunt, I am persuaded ... But when did this come about? Yesterday! How very ... Well, I must say ... Can only assure you ... not a word! So happy, so very happy!" Mr. Emmerhite bowed himself out, blissfully closing the door. He left Felbridge House in a glow of euphoria. This was the ultimate, positively the most rewarding moment of his career.

Released at last, Audrey swayed back against a chair. Her mind was a whirl as she tried to think what had happened, and as she strove to understand what Huxford was saying.

"Brandy, I think, Miss Taylor. Or, rather—Audrey. Yes. First names definitely are in order. Brandy," he repeated, pouring from a cut glass decanter on the sideboard. "To celebrate this auspicious moment." His eyes were cool as he searched her face.

Audrey automatically reached for the snifter and walked to the fire, swirling the small glass in her cupped palm. After a token sip, she set it on the mantel. Then she placed her slim fingers together and raised them to her lips, falling into a brown study that lasted a full minute. Her mouth firmed.

Facing Huxford, her eyes a deeper violet than he'd ever seen, she burst out, "This is ridiculous! I thank you, my lord, for trying, indeed, for *saving,* my reputation. I'm all admiration for your instant response. But is it necessary to pretend to be engaged? And must there be an announcement in the papers? How uncomfortable to be caught up in a web of deceit, to be faced with all the congratulations and good wishes of a formal betrothal. Such a travesty!" She frowned. "I must say, it almost makes me wish you hadn't kissed me."

She jumped when his laughter exploded. It was the first he had offered her in many days. "I make you my compliments," he said. "Any society miss I know would be either drumming her heels on the carpet or scheming to turn this into a bona fide engagement. Oh—" his mouth twisted "—don't think I'm unaware of what a catch I am! I could be a bandy-legged, scrunch-faced gnome and still there would be—there *are*—ladies who are only too anxious to share my title and fortune."

Critically, Audrey eyed him. "Oh, no," she said in her politest tones. "Even *I* admit you're crushingly handsome, my lord." A gleam of amusement flashed in her eyes, and she raised her brows at him. "Surely there must be someone out there who could be brought to love you." The hopeful attitude of this speech was somewhat tarnished by her palpable air of doubt.

Huxford's eyes lit in response. "A hit, by God. Brutally

frank, that's what I call you!" His grin, wide and attractive, warmed her. "Still," he continued, "it's time for plain speaking."

He turned a little away, and when he faced her again, he was no longer smiling. "First of all, I make my apology. Not for the kiss. That I do not apologize for, and never will. No. I'm only sorry I didn't arrange it in a less—ah—vulnerable spot. Too careless, I'm sure. Now. The betrothal. Yes. It must go to the newspapers. The pressure on poor old Emmerhite would kill him if he couldn't vent this secret of ours to a few of his friends. And Emmerhite has friends. As for your aunt—my dear godmama is no dissembler! If she knows it's a hum, she could never be expected to keep her countenance in all the hubbub."

"Oh, no!" Audrey gasped. "She'd be bound to look distracted or sad when she was supposed to be happy. Or worse, dissolve in a puddle of tears at precisely the wrong moment."

"Exactly so," Huxford replied calmly. "And Paden, Chartley, Melbourne, all the others—they must be deceived now and ever more. The truth must remain hidden."

He fell silent, then continued. "We'll do the whirl, then you can cry off and get on back to America. Unless . . . I suppose you wouldn't care to make this betrothal genuine?" His expression was inscrutable.

Audrey's eyes widened, and she opened her mouth slightly, staring up at him.

Huxford tried to preserve his sangfroid, but his mind was anything except cool. That little curve of her upper lip, the cunningly wrought lift at the corners of her mouth—he had kissed those and wanted to again. He moved slightly, trying to deny the violent reaction of his body. Why must he always respond so quickly to Audrey's presence? Or even to the memory of her hand on his sleeve? It had been thus since he'd first laid eyes on her. He'd told her the simple truth. She was his sweet obsession, totally and for all time. All he could think of was lying with her stripped in a large white bed, the world far away and enchantment surrounding them.

Her eyes continued to regard him steadily. He couldn't imagine what her answer would be. Did he want her to say yes?

Audrey's voice was clear and firm when she spoke at last. "Let me understand you, my lord. In effect, you're asking me to marry you?"

"Yes. In effect, I am." A peculiar smile played across his mouth.

"Why?" Audrey asked. Her puzzlement was plain.

Gideon shrugged. "With no bark on it? Ultimately I must provide myself with an heir. It would bother me less to be leg-shackled to you than any woman I know. And I guarantee you complete freedom; you—you can do anything, go anywhere you wish, even back to Boston, so long as you cause no scandal. *After* you've given me a son."

A full three minutes passed before Audrey could trust herself to speak. She'd never been so angry. Her reply—uttered calmly and at total variance with the clamor of her heart—gave no hint of her fury.

"Truly, I'm most sensible of the honor you would do me, my lord. More especially your desiring to align my bloodline with that of your house. When this is all over, I must look back on that, at least, with satisfaction."

Audrey stopped and looked at him with a small smile. "I hope I'm not foolishly sentimental," she said. "Nor do I wish to appear provincial or old fashioned. But I'm a coward; I'm afraid I couldn't exist in one of your loveless marriages. Further, I refuse to give up a son of mine to be reared knowing his mother was held in such casual regard that she was allowed to wander thither and yon. I want to hold my son and kiss his little hurts, to watch him grow. I want to set an indelible pattern of womanhood in his mind, to make him know that if he searches far enough, and carefully enough, he will find one who will be true and cleave only unto him, making a home for him and the children they have together.

"That is what I want, my lord, that kind of love. And that is the kind of mother I aspire to be. If my destiny decrees otherwise, I will not love, nor will I bear sons."

Audrey's voice was low as she finished, and she fully expected to hear Huxford's cold laugh. When she forced herself to look at him, his harsh features were still and smooth.

He assessed her long and silently. Then he stirred, clearing his throat before he spoke. "What can I say, except that a man would be fortunate indeed to find such a love?" After a moment, he set his brandy glass aside.

"Come," he said. "Let us find your aunt and impart our tidings." His smile was almost kind when he touched his fingers to her cheek, lightly caressing her dimple with the hard ball of his thumb. "Don't repine, cherie. I make you my promise: This betrothal of ours won't be so very bad."

He grinned suddenly, and Audrey had no idea he was envisioning Kit's taunting laughter.

12

L ate on the morning after Mr. Emmerhite's discovery of their embrace in Lady Felbridge's back parlor, the marquis very naturally called upon his betrothed.

Audrey thought he looked the picture of composure until she realized his hands were clenched on the back of the chair he was leaning against.

"It's a delicate situation we find ourselves in," he began, then paused, as if weighing his words. He looked down, and when he raised his eyes, there was something very like warmth in them.

To Audrey's surprise, he came close and held out his hand. "Shall we cry pax . . . Audrey?"

She placed her hand in his. He looked down at her trembling fingers and grasped them more closely. "Audrey," he repeated, as if glad of the sound on his lips. "The name suits you."

Her hand felt warm in his clasp, and he was still holding it when he said, "I have your ring. Came from the jeweler's just now." He drew a box from his pocket, removed a diamond solitaire, and slipped it onto her finger.

Audrey stared at it, then at him. "I . . . I hadn't thought . . ." The ring was a perfect fit. Suddenly she shook her head. "I don't—"

"I know," he interrupted. "You don't want to wear my ring. Never mind. After all, it's no family heirloom such as I should give you if this were our real engagement. I didn't even pick it out; the clerk did. I'm sorry if you don't like it, but it's required, you know."

She nodded slowly. "I shall return it, of course."

Huxford shrugged. "As you wish." He drew another box

from his pocket and gave it to her. "Your engagement present."

Aware that he was watching her, she opened the plush box and discovered a particularly fine pair of diamond earrings. Audrey bit her lip. They were beautiful. "This affair has cost you a considerable amount of money, my lord. Were these necessary?"

"You don't like them?"

"They're splendid. Certainly I like them, but . . ."

"Then please me by wearing them," he said in his old, autocratic way.

"But later," she insisted, "they shall be returned with the ring."

"No, keep them. They may, in some small way, repay you for the trouble you've been through on my account."

Audrey gently closed the lid of the satin-lined box. "There's something I must tell you, my lord. I . . ." She stopped, then took the plunge. "My aunt and I gave it out that I had no money. That was a tale we concocted to save me from the marriage-go-round."

"I know," he said with perfect equanimity.

Startled, Audrey looked up. "You knew? How, my lord, did you know?"

"If you continually call me 'my lord,' people will think we're strangers. Can't you say 'Gideon?' "

"Very well." Audrey pointed her chin at him.

"Shall we begin now, in private?" He quirked one brow at her.

After an anger-sparked glance, her lashes swept her cheeks. "Gideon," she said, in unpromising tones.

"There." His smile was lazy. "That wasn't so difficult."

"No," Audrey said, then persevered in the face of his attractive grin. "G—Gideon?"

"Yes?"

"How did you know—how did you learn I'm not poor?" A tide of warmth spread across her cheeks as her words tangled.

Huxford laughed and tapped her chin with a careless finger. "You have a persistent mind, my love."

He saw that Audrey was determined not to acknowledge his endearment. She gazed steadily at him and waited.

Damn violet eyes! Gideon thought. "Very well, I'll tell you. You were at the bank some weeks past with your aunt and Lord Egbertt, remember?"

She nodded.

"I was making a detour through an anteroom, heard Egbertt prosing on, and discovered him and my godmama in an alcove. I said hello and they looked so self-conscious, my curiosity was roused. In fact, they became greatly alarmed when I chose—politely, I thought—to sit and chat awhile.

"Finally, Egbertt blurted that they were waiting for you. Naturally I inquired what business a young lady might have in Drummond's."

Huxford noticed that Audrey had stiffened, but paid no attention. He continued his tale.

"Egbertt then informed me that you were a very—ah—*warm* young woman. He said you didn't want it bruited about. Said he suggested you consult me concerning your financial management; though to be sure"—here Gideon thought he deflected an outraged explosion from his fiancée—"what business he thought it was of mine I can't imagine, for it was prior to our betrothal. Lord H said you fobbed him off when he made the suggestion. How did you accomplish that, my dear Audrey?"

"I've learned to be conciliatory, my lord."

When she smiled, her dimple flashed into play, and Gideon left her vowing to kiss her there and anywhere else she'd let him in the next few days.

Audrey wondered at Kit's behavior toward her. His attitude, always baffling where she was concerned, became even more peculiar when her engagement to Huxford was announced. He avoided her for several days, shunning all the festive occasions—the breakfasts, suppers, and drawing rooms—that ensued.

Finally, he appeared at the *intime* gathering held in their honor by the Countess of Omsley. He arrived just as the party was leaving the card tables and joined Audrey where

she sat blessedly alone for the moment, on a banquette in
the blue salon. It was the first time Audrey had seen him
drunk since Victoria came up to town.

In spite of his condition, Kit executed a flawless bow
and raised Audrey's hand to his lips. "So. We are to wish
you joy," he said. His tone was quarrelsome and he
swayed alarmingly.

"Sit beside me," Audrey begged. She patted the overstuffed seat. Reaching her other hand to him and glancing
about, she could only hope others hadn't noticed how very
foxed he was.

Kit sprawled beside her on the tufted banquette, retain-
ing her hand. He gazed musingly at it, seeming to contrast
its whiteness with that of his own hand, so lean and tan.

"You don't like me, do you?" he asked with a crooked
smile.

Audrey eyed him candidly. She would love to say she
didn't like him, but that would not be true. "No," she said.
"I find myself much in charity with you at times. There is
a sense of honor and integrity in you that one must admire.
Your profligacy cannot completely hide such qualities."

Kit looked piercingly at her. "Why did you become engaged to Gideon?" His eyes gleamed strangely. "I know
I'm drunk and shouldn't be saying this, but . . . will you be
kind to my friend?"

Audrey stiffened. "Why don't you ask Huxford about
our betrothal?"

Kit hadn't heard her question. "Why did God make
women so beautiful? So beautiful, and so necessary—and
some so deadly? Will you destroy Gideon, Miss Taylor?
You could, you know, if he loves you. A man can be
strong and powerful against the world. But inside, with the
woman he loves, he's vulnerable, soft. And she can reach
in and slash and wound in ways a man is incapable of,
dealing painful blows, lasting hurts, which bleed and never
heal." Chartley closed his eyes as if to shut out some
dreadful vision, then rubbed one hand slowly across his
brow.

Audrey glanced about her. They would be surrounded
by the others soon; she had only a moment. "Chartley, I

give you my word. I will deal in honor with the man I love."

"I believe you," Kit said, and carried her hand to his lips.

At the select dinner Lady Marpleby gave for Audrey and Huxford, it was obvious to their hostess that there was much constraint between them. The evening had been long, and Lady Marpleby felt it quite as keenly as the principles did. She couldn't be entirely happy about this unexpected turn of events. Not that she had the slightest objection to her niece marrying the marquis. It was what she'd hoped for from the beginning. That he had offered for Audrey was in the realm of dreams, especially after he'd said he wouldn't. But there was a tension between the pair that boded no good. Well, she must seem to believe that all was well and hope the best for her godson and niece. If only Gideon's mother Madelaine were here now! Standing beside him, Lady Marpleby expressed that sentiment.

His mask, the one he'd worn for days now, slipped. Setting his sights on Audrey, he murmured, "Yes, I wish my parents could see her." Something in his eyes made his godmother's heart easier.

Later, as Audrey sat talking with Miss Webster, she felt Huxford's stare and looked at him from across the room. She tried to tear her eyes away, but found herself trapped in the brooding intensity of his watchful gaze. Why did he not come to her? A wave of heat washed over her, beginning in the lower part of her stomach and flowing, flowing outward until she felt she would swoon. She'd never fainted in her life, but these dark currents coursing around her and Gideon St. Aubin were debilitating in their effects. In reaction, she felt a familiar lassitude sweep over her. Gideon had looked at her in just that way before he kissed her that fateful night of the Felbridge ball. Would he ever kiss her again? At last she was able to look away, her lashes hiding her thoughts as she concentrated on her fingers twisting her handkerchief into a knot.

The force of Audrey's look—plainly entreating—shot

through Gideon like one of Dr. Galvani's electrical shocks. There were times, he reflected, when even the most sincerely given promises did not hold true. Only ten days had passed since they had taken up their pretend betrothal. He had assured Audrey their ordeal wouldn't be so bad.

He shoved his drink into Paden's hand and went to her, wishing he could do something to erase the purple smudges under her eyes.

He bowed to her and Miss Webster. Addressing the latter, he said, "Will you excuse us, ma'am? Being newly engaged yourself, you can understand my wish to be private with my fiancée."

Miss Webster instantly yielded Audrey and he took her away, pulling her through the crowded rooms to the central hallway.

When they arrived up the second flight of stairs, Gideon took her into a small withdrawing room and locked the door. He had no intention of enduring another interruption by Emmerhite.

At his invitation, Audrey settled on the sofa. She leaned her head against the cushions. She closed her eyes, but almost immediately, they flew open. Gideon stood against the mantel, watching her. When he spoke, his voice was very low. "I'm afraid it's worse than we thought it was going to be."

He clenched his jaw as tears welled in Audrey's eyes and overflowed her cheeks. Gideon had never seen her weep before. He felt frustrated, helpless.

Audrey didn't sob; her face did not crumple; she simply looked at him with flooding eyes. The tears seemed to magnify and enhance their color. Careful not to touch her, Gideon gave her his handkerchief, then went to a side table to pour himself a brandy.

She refused his offer of a drink. "I'm sorry," she said, wiping her eyes.

"You're tired." He had returned to stand before the fire, and with his back to it, kept his face hidden in shadow.

She waited, and after a while he said, "Audrey, I have a scheme to make this easier for you. In a few days, we can give it out that we've decided to cut our season short, and go to my home in Sussex, to Castle Baddingly. Could you be content there with Victoria and my godmother? Lord Egbertt can be invited; I'm not sure your aunt would go without him. And Paden, like as not, will want to come to Rosedale. Everyone will assume that I'm staying in the country as well." He feigned an interest in swirling the brandy in his snifter.

"But you won't?" Audrey asked.

Gideon shrugged. "I'll escort you there and see you settled in. It might be more comfortable if I were to take myself off. There are things I can do . . . places I could go . . ." His words ground to a halt and he waited for a breath-taking moment for her to protest this plan, to say she wanted him to stay at Baddingly with her, but she simply looked at him.

Silently, Audrey measured the tall figure before her. *He's bothered with all the pretension,* she thought. An unpleasant notion hit her. *Perhaps—almost certainly—he has a mistress somewhere. He'll be spending his time with her.* She found her voice. "That would probably be best for all concerned."

As they left the withdrawing room, Audrey handed Gideon his handkerchief. She was no longer shedding tears, but that did not mean she wasn't crying inside.

Nothing would do Lord Egbertt except to give an intimate supper for the engaged couple. "Just a small dinner for twenty, m'dear," he told Lady Marpleby, who knew from experience upon whose shoulders the arrangements would fall. By the time he got through recollecting this one and that—"Wouldn't do to slight Amberdyne, m'love"—if they sat down less than a hundred covers in his lordship's formal dining room in Cavendish Square, Lady M would be surprised, and so she told Audrey and Victoria.

Since there was nothing she could do for Victoria and Kit Hartwell, Audrey determined to take as much of the work connected with Lord H's dinner party off her aunt as possible. It would keep her from thinking.

Strange as it seemed, her greatest comfort had been

Huxford himself. He had been all she could ask: supportive and kind, behaving as if she were actually his fiancée.

Chartley had left town two days before Egbertt's party. When he was gone, Victoria seemed a bit more relaxed, Audrey thought. Still, the girl's smile never reached her eyes and her shoulders drooped wearily. Audrey insisted on cosseting her, saying in stringent tones that Toria looked ready to drop. She advised her to get herself upstairs and into bed.

Giving Victoria a little shove, Audrey said, "Go. I have no intention of allowing you to fall ill so you can shirk your supporting role at Lord Higglesby's party."

Toria laughed and took herself away to bed, and Audrey left for Cavendish Square to supervise the thousand and one details of a large formal party.

She found it no easy task. First Egbert tried to invite everyone, then he wanted to omit Sir Cosmo Orphington, a great chum of his, simply because Sir Cosmo had slipped his arm around Lady M when she tripped at Beakum House the night before.

"But Egbertt," her ladyship protested, "I could have fallen."

"Fellow had no right grabbing you in his arms, Letty. You're a tiny thing; he should have taken your elbow," Egbertt fumed. "Don't know how I kept from calling the man out. Anyway, I'm not having him at my party. That rascal has been after you for years! You might as well admit it."

It took all of Audrey's considerable tact to persuade Lord Higglesby to invite Sir Cosmo. "Oh, but I think you should, sir. Because I know for a fact that my aunt doesn't care a bean for him. She never says he's her sole support, and she'd *never* take a Sunday nap with him. Surely you can afford to pity Sir Cosmo. You have my aunt's love. What does poor Mr. Orphington have except her friendship?"

"Well, well," he lordship commented expansively, "who can blame the fellow for making up to Letty? Any one would. He saw a chance to get her in his arms and made the most of it. I suppose I mustn't hold it against him."

* * *

Lord Higglesby's party was a huge success: at least the first part of the evening went smoothly enough. Audrey stood between her aunt and the marquis and accepted hundreds of good wishes. During the ball, Huxford appeared at regular intervals to claim her, and he seemed all right. But when the gentlemen joined the ladies after a late supper, he came and sat beside her in the long gallery, casting her a look so dark she wasn't sure she'd interpreted it correctly. After all, there were wells of shadow about the room, and she had chosen to sit by her aunt on a sofa away from the light and the crowd.

Lady M spoke a few words to Gideon, then excused herself and left them alone.

Audrey forced herself to look at Huxford and encountered such a glitter in his eyes that she flushed. Without realizing what she was doing, she allowed her gaze to drop to his mouth. She knew how it felt on hers—how hard it was and how it plundered her own. How it robbed without giving, and promised nothing in return.

She started when she heard him laugh.

Without a word, he grasped her arm in a vise of steel, pulling her with him, taking her up one staircase, then another, to a small book-lined room with a couch before the fire. He closed the door and Audrey heard the lock click.

Night and the silence held them as they stood close. When he swayed, Audrey laid her hand on his arm. "Gideon, are you perhaps ... just a trifle ... well to live?"

Gideon smiled grimly and made an effort to steady himself. "Yes, Love. I'm more than a little drunk, for which I apologize. But don't worry, you've nothing to fear. I wanted us away from the crowd."

"I'm not afraid." Something in his look made Audrey wonder if she'd spoken too quickly. A shiver of quicksilver shot up her spine.

"Shall I make a light?" he asked.

"No! No, this is very peaceful. I like it." *Here with you.* Naturally this last was left unsaid, but Audrey wondered if he might not sense the logical conclusion to her statement. Audrey looked about her. What she could see of the tiny chamber, she liked. Her father's study in Boston was much like this.

"Yes, a nice room." Huxford brushed her attempt at conversation aside when she told him of her comparison. "If you can be ready, Audrey, I'd like us to leave for Baddingly the day after tomorrow."

Her hand crept to her throat. "So soon?"

"Can you not leave then?"

"Certainly, my lord, but—"

"Don't say 'my lord,' dammit! You know my name. Why do you never use it?"

Color mounting her cheeks, Audrey murmured in a low voice, "Gideon."

He grasped her arm. "Yes, that's how I wanted to hear you say it." He looked at her slim wrist in his hand. Slowly he rubbed one thumb over the smooth skin where her pulse bounded. Then he released her and moved away.

"You've endured this ordeal very well," he told her. "I make you my compliments. You're all I suspected you to be. Through no fault of your own you've found yourself in an impossible situation and you've come through with flying colors. And, without being told what Toria's troubles are, you've proven a friend to her. You have managed to survive where many would have . . ."

He stopped. "Are you crying?"

"No," Audrey said, but she was. At first her eyes were only damp. Now they were streaming. She fought her emotions, angry at herself for her weakness, angry at him for making her weep. She turned half away to wipe her eyes.

Huxford muttered something and caught her up in his arms. He carried her to the divan and sat with her there on his lap in a corner filled with cushions. His arms, so strong, trembled a little as he held her, and with one hand he pushed her face into the side of his neck, forcing her to relax.

Held against Gideon's body, with her tears sliding across his flesh, Audrey rested. All the strain and tension, all the worry of the past few days drained away. She became aware that he was whispering to her.

"Sh—don't. Don't cry, Sweetheart. It's all right; everything will be all right."

Audrey felt comforted as never before, and she sighed, leaving her arm around his neck where she'd thrown it. Her tears dried, and still he held her. But gradually she felt a tension gathering in him, building, and he seemed to draw away. When she dropped her head back on his shoulder, he looked down at her. His mouth, so near her own, curved fiercely back against his teeth.

Gideon looked into her eyes. "I swore I wouldn't kiss you again."

"Not even if I slapped you?" she asked without thinking.

She felt his mirthless chuckle. "Not even then, cherie."

Insane to continue this, Audrey thought. "Well, I won't," she promised, then added almost as an afterthought, "but *I* could kiss *you.*"

Huxford's expression was obscure. "Do you want to?" he murmured.

"Yes."

"Very well."

"I've never done this before," Audrey warned.

"I know." Tightening his hold, Gideon bent so that his face was only an inch from her own.

Audrey screwed her eyes shut, laid her lips on his and pushed, but his mouth remained relaxed, unresponsive. She tried again. His arms supported her—actually he held her in his lap—and her lips pressed his. But something was wrong. Suddenly she punched his shoulder with her small fist. "Gideon," she cried, "do something! Open your mouth and let me inside. Kiss me back!"

His lips caught hers before she finished speaking, engulfing her in a blaze of desire. When he lifted his head, her arms tightened behind his neck, and he kissed her several times before he could stop. At last he put her aside. "This is madness!" he exclaimed and went to stand at the window.

Audrey sat up and shakily straightened her skirt. She was trying to smooth her hair when he returned and stood in front of her.

"Come, I'll take you to your aunt. Don't worry, you look fine." There was a need in his eyes to which Audrey couldn't help responding.

Taking her hand, Gideon turned her palm and laid his lips on it. "I beg your pardon; it won't happen again."

She looked her astonishment. "Gideon, *I* initiated this episode. You must know that!"

His laugh was a hard grunt of derision. "Don't be a little fool! Can't you imagine why I brought you here? I wanted to hold you, Audrey—to kiss you. I thought it might ease me." His winter-blue gaze glinted fire and ice.

"No, it hasn't helped," he said. "Only made it worse."

Audrey's heart thumped in her breast, and her hand crept to her throat to still the pulse leaping there. She left the room and descended the stairs numbly, thinking that she understood at last. She was deeply in love with the Marquis of Huxford.

13

The only person who questioned their move to the country was Kit Hartwell. He appeared in Brook Street the morning of their departure. As Gideon came down his front staircase, he found Kit leaning against the library door.

"What's this?" the viscount demanded. "Paden told me you are taking everyone down to Baddingly."

Gideon knew that along with Lady Marpleby Kit had doubts about his betrothal to Audrey Soames-Taylor.

"Yeas, we're going into Sussex," he said. "Leaving in a few minutes, as a matter of fact."

"Running to hide, are you?"

Huxford's lips tightened. "That's right."

"Because your betrothal is a fakery?" Kit challenged.

"As you say." The words were polite enough, but Huxford's tone discouraged further inquiry.

Ignoring the hint, Chartley demanded, "Then why the announcement?"

"Emmerhite caught me kissing her. It was all I could think of at the moment."

"Why *were* you kissing her?"

"She slapped me."

"Besides which, you'd been wanting to for days."

"Yes."

After a short silence, Kit said, "So you're going away to spare her what you can?"

Huxford's nod was curt. "Our plan is to escape the celebrations honoring our engagement. After a few weeks, we'll send an announcement to the papers saying the marriage if off, and Miss Soames-Taylor will return to America." His voice roughened as he finished the last sentence.

Chartley stared at his friend measuringly. "You say your engagement is counterfeit, but you offered her marriage—a genuine proposal—did you not?"

"I did."

"And her answer?"

Gideon pulled on his gloves. "That we would not suit. That she couldn't live in a loveless marriage." He raised bleak eyes to Kit's. "I had just assured her that the only reason I was offering for her was that I needed an heir."

Gray eyes locked with silver-blue. Kit uttered one word, and that softly. "Fool," he said, and Gideon nodded.

They left the house together. On the steps, Gideon paused. "I told you, I think, that I won't be remaining at Baddingly."

"No." Kit had no need to ask why.

"Will you come to Whitfeld while they're at the castle? Paden will be at Rosedale, but he's so young, and—"

"Can't decide on a damned thing without you," Kit finished. There was no rancor in his statement. "Yes," he said, and held out his hand. "I'll be down in a few days."

Huxford didn't thank Kit; the way he gripped his hand said it for him.

From the time the marquis informed Audrey they were escaping London, she had begun to think of Baddingly as sanctuary. The drive through Sussex—the rolling hills and green farms with their fields of hops, the orchards and sheep and cattle farms—these sights soothed her. The English countryside was unbelievably beautiful in the early summer.

Her first glimpse of the castle, just as the late afternoon sun was streaming through the avenue of oaks lining the long drive, made Audrey catch her breath. It was an ancient pile, massive and with formal gardens laid out in the enormous park fronting it. There were lesser gardens falling away to rows of shrubbery in the rear. Beyond could be glimpsed a long stretch of ornamental water.

Built of gray stone, the castle proper had a square tower

at each corner. Some early St. Aubin had added a fanciful touch in the form of two bartizans, creating twin turrets overhanging the front facade. As the three carriages rounded the circular drive, Audrey found herself wishing for a moat and drawbridge.

Victoria was the first to alight, and the marquis, who had ridden horseback from the city, was there to hand his sister and fiancée down. Lord Higglesby brushed aside his offer of help.

"No, no, m'boy. Lead your bride inside and show her your home. Make her welcome. No need to stand on ceremony, you know. Twickem will see us in, won't you, my good fellow?"

Gideon turned to Audrey and her look caused him to tighten his hold on her icy fingers. "You're very welcome, you know." His smile was enough to bring color to her cheeks.

Audrey realized he was merely striving to help her over an awkward moment. Her thanks were lost in her exclamation at the great hall with its three ascending staircases, its intricately carved strapwork, and the chiseled stone corbels supporting half-raised balconies. As she scanned the hall and upper walkways, her admiration was evident; when she turned, the animation lighting her face was genuine.

"Gideon!" she cried. "It *is* a castle! I love it! What a wonderful place to—" Her smile faltered; *to live,* she'd almost said, but *she* would never live here.

Audrey lifted her chin and said instead, "What a wonderful place to grow up." But her words were far from what she was thinking, and she paled at the look in Huxford's eyes.

She was relieved when Victoria said, "Tell us, Audrey. Do you really like it? Some don't, you know."

Grasping Victoria's hand, Audrey said, "It's marvelous. I don't know what to say, except I love it."

"You see?" Toria crowed at her brother. "I said you were being foolish when you kept worrying whether Audrey would like it or not."

The marquis said nothing, simply shook his head, and

Audrey went up the stairs with Victoria, confused at this evidence of his concern over her reaction to his home.

Dinner, served at six, was turned into a festive occasion by the staff after their formal presentation in the hall. Twickem—having informed Mrs. Pradle that with dispatch Miss Soames-Taylor had arranged a sit-down dinner for one hundred at Lord Higglesby's where, according to his friend Malden, she had juggled myriad details with perfect expedition—was on his mettle. For Baddingly's future marchioness, this first dinner must be memorable.

They dined in the great hall before one of the fireplaces. Each was large enough to roast an ox, which, Gideon informed Audrey, had been done in ages past. The heavy trestle table stood nearest the door leading to the kitchens.

"There were other tables set up in those times," he said. "Lord and lady, knights and guests ate here, as well as household retainers. The servants and lesser guests were seated below the salt, of course." His amusement was evident. "Do you think it's medieval, to be eating in the hall?"

"Oh, no." Audrey smiled. She fell silent as the first footman, under Twickem's direction, carried in a whole roast piglet, with an apple in its mouth.

He brought the huge platter directly to her, and she gave a tiny gasp of delight. The young servant dropped to one knee and held out the dish for her inspection. A glance at Huxford, lounging in his high backed chair, showed him watching with an unusual smile playing across his mouth.

She smiled at the boy kneeling before her. Sensible of the honor being shown her, she inspected the offering carefully. It smelled delicious. Before she thought, Audrey dabbed a finger at the succulent skin, transferring a taste of the glistening juice to her tongue. She looked at the butler. "Twickem! It's wonderful! Relay my compliments to the cook—Mrs. Molcombe?—and Mrs. Praddle, to your entire staff. Thank you! And—" She swung her eyes to the footman. "Jem, isn't it? Thank you, Jem. You must put it on the table now."

Jem turned bright red and blurted, "Think on it, mistress, you remembering me own name and me next nor the end on the line at introductions! Happen you'll make a fine lady for the castle." Audrey could not look at Huxford, but she knew he was watching her closely.

The bedchamber they'd given Audrey was, like most of the others, built into the great wall. It was so tiny there was barley room for her bed, a chair, and a dressing table. Her chair stood in front of the fireplace where a low fire burned constantly, even in summer. "That's to keep the dampness at bay," Toria told her. "Small as these chambers are, we're thankful in winter; their size makes them easier to heat. Much as we love Baddingly, there's no denying the stone walls hold the cold. Of course," she added, "that won't bother you, sleeping with Gideon." She broke off, staring at Audrey, who flushed.

"Audrey, you're not *missish!* What have I said? Only wait 'til I tell Gideon how I made you blush!"

"No! Please don't!" Audrey left off holding her cheeks to entreat Victoria not to mention the incident to her brother. "Usually, I'm not so foolish," she said. "But, all of a sudden, to hear you say . . ."

Victoria laughed and patted her shoulder. "Goose," she chided fondly. "Very well, I shan't tease you."

When Audrey met Huxford in the library, she colored in spite of herself. It was natural for him to ask what had put her in a taking.

"It's nothing," she said crossly. "If I told you, you'd only laugh, and I'm *not* missish, as I told your sister."

His lids drooped over his eyes. "What has the wretched girl said to you?" He sounded amused.

Audrey shook her head.

"Come. I insist." Huxford's voice was cool.

"It's nothing!"

"Audrey!" He took her shoulders, turning her so that she was facing him. "Tell me."

Shrugging out of his grip, Audrey walked to the window. She gazed down at the terrace for a moment, then turned. "Very well, I'll tell you and you'll say I'm silly. It's just—" She stopped, unable to go on.

One of Huxford's brows lifted in silent query and she forced herself to continue. "Victoria was explaining how cold the beds are in winter, and—and observed I need not worry, from having *you* to sleep with, and I—" Audrey ceased speaking when the marquis threw back his head and laughed.

Before she could turn away, he was beside her, pulling her into a bear hug of an embrace. Audrey closed her eyes as Gideon cradled her in his arms. He rested his chin on the crown of her head. "Funny one," he murmured. When she looked up to see his expression, he said, "No, don't raise your face to me. I'm not going to kiss you."

"Oh!" Toria spoke behind them. "I'm sorry to interrupt your lovemaking, but you must stop awhile. I promised the housekeeper I'd bring Audrey to tea. It's a great honor, you know, to be invited to Mrs. Praddle's apartment."

Huxford released her and she glanced up to find him watching her with narrowed eyes, as if he were weighing her, trying to read her thoughts. She hurried after Victoria.

There followed a period when Huxford was busy with his steward, Mr. Bole, riding out until dark, then receiving tenants in his study. Mannering, his agent, came also, and he and the marquis were closeted for hours. Finally they emerged, and Gideon came looking for Audrey. He found her in the east tower, where she, Lady Marpleby, and Victoria were engaged in mending the long tapestry from the chapel.

Dragging Audrey away, he took her to the billiard room where he proceeded to beat her three times in a row— which was no mean feat, and she told him so. She was used to besting all comers, she said. "Even my father. And he could put down nine out of ten at Brook's any afternoon of the week."

"Ah, but I am your tenth man, my love! Billiards is my particular game. Have you enjoyed riding with Victoria? Has she been showing you all our favorite trails?" he asked as he replaced his cue in the rack.

"Yes, my lord, she has."

Already close, Gideon moved even closer. He ran the tip

of his finger gently across her lips. "Say 'my lord,' if you will, but add 'my love.' " His voice was low and husky.

Audrey stepped hastily back; she couldn't bear this teasing. She spoke, eyes aglitter. "I think not! Don't forget this is make believe, my lord. I never do!" She clenched her hands, feeling the nails bite into her palms. "Believe me, I count the days, the hours, until I can quit this place."

She didn't trust herself to speak further. She didn't know what she might say if she allowed herself full rein! Casting him a sweeping glance—his expression was as unyielding as a rock—she fled.

In her room she found her dresser laying out her gown for dinner. It was thirty minutes before Matty could be got rid of. Audrey threw herself across the bed and lay with her arm over her burning eyes. She wouldn't cry—she *wouldn't!*

Paden Offutt brought his mother to dinner that night. No matter what Matilda Offutt wore, she looked as if she were dressed for riding. As tall as her son, she shook hands with Audrey, saying in her matter-of-fact way that she hadn't believed Paden when he told her how handsome Gideon's fiancée was, but didn't mean to prose on about that. She was certain Miss Soames-Taylor set no store by her looks—a chance thing in humans—for it was all in the breeding. Horses now, you could tell how they would look if the lines held true, but who knew how people might turn out? Be wonderful, now she came to think of it, if humans could be bred to type.

Tildy, as she insisted Audrey call her, was the daughter of an earl and had married beneath herself. Or so she casually told Audrey. But Gerald had been a horseman par excellence, a top-of-the-trees man with a team or on a hunter, and the only one for her.

"Short man," she said. "Came only to my chin. But we liked one another right off when he came to buy bloodstock from my papa's stud. He didn't say a word," she recalled, after the ladies had left the men to their brandy. "I looked at his face when he saw me mount up. He complimented me on my seat. Well, everyone did that, but they didn't say it with quite the gleam Gerald Offutt did. Couldn't ask me to marry him; was only a baronette, you see, and I could look high as I pleased. But I could ask him and I did. Wrote him a letter of proposal the week he went home. He came for me with a special license in his pocket and took me and two prize mares and the barb stallion Papa gave me for a marriage gift. Don't know which Gerald was prouder of—me or the blood cattle! No, that's not true. We loved each other 'til the day he died." Lady Offutt shook her head. "Ah, well," she sighed, "he was a man who never rushed his fences." Audrey knew this was the highest praise she could bestow on her husband.

Tildy roused herself and patted Audrey's hand. She had been holding it all the time she was telling her tale. "A good man, Gerald! I was sorry to see him go. But it was the way he would have wanted—riding after the pack. Young hunter named Rufus fell on him. Last thing he asked was if Rufus was all right. I lied, of course. Said the horse was already up and grazing. Gerald closed his eyes, smiled, and slipped away. Died in my arms. Then I had to shoot Rufus. He had two broken legs, you see. Worst day of my life, except when I got word Victor was killed at Badajoz." She smiled at Audrey and straightened. "Forgive me, my dear. Letty! Why did you allow me to prose on like an old woman?"

Lady M smiled. "Tildy, we *are* old women. We should be allowed to prose if we want to."

"Well," her ladyship said briskly, "I don't! Come now. Can't wait for the men to sip themselves silly. Who's for a game of billiards? I warn you," she told Audrey, "I play for blood!"

"Oh!" cried Toria. "Audrey is sharp with a billiard cue! You'll get scorched, Aunt Tildy!"

"Victoria St. Aubin!" Lady Marpleby gasped. She stared at Toria with a shocked expression.

"Er—as my brother would say," Victoria amended, grinning unrepentantly at Audrey.

"Vulgar cant expressions have no place in a lady's vocabulary," Lady M said severely, then bit her lip as Toria attempted to hug her. "Now don't, my girl, try to turn me up sweet!"

"No, how should I?" Victoria crooned. "You're a sugar lump, already!"

Smiling at this by-play between her old friend and Huxford's sister, Tildy said, "Come then. We'll see what kind of game Gideon's bride can give me."

Gideon's bride, with as pretty a run as Paden had ever seen—for the men had tracked them to the game room—vanquished his mother, much to that lady's delight.

"Ha!" her ladyship said, turning to Gideon. "I don't know where you got her, but this is some girl! Hang onto her."

Huxford, standing in a relaxed pose with his arms folded across his chest, merely smiled and said, "I shall."

In the library, Paden and Audrey, with Victoria looking on, played chess until the tea tray came. The others played whist, and each time Audrey looked up, the marquis seemed to be watching, lazily surveying her from across the room. Her head began to ache and Paden captured her knight, crowing so loudly she forced herself to concentrate.

The Offutts left at eleven. As the others took their night candles, Gideon said to Audrey, "Stay a moment." Bidding the party goodnight, she went with him to his study.

"Yes, yes!" she heard Egbertt say, as he puffed up the staircase. "Can understand that. They're young and in love, m'dear, and want to be alone," he told Lady Marpleby.

Audrey, pretending she hadn't heard, sat stiffly in the chair indicated by Huxford. There was nothing lover-like in his stance. He studied her, then said abruptly, "I'm going away tomorrow." When she merely stared, he continued. "I'll be gone a week or so. We'll say I have business to attend to."

Knowing she must reply, Audrey opened her mouth. "I see," she murmured. Never had two words seemed so inadequate.

"I will return," Huxford said, "and we'll quarrel. I'll go away again, stay another week. When I come home we'll have another fight. By then it should be plain to everyone we won't suit and you will cry off."

Before raising her eyes, Audrey finished pleating the fold in her handkerchief. *"Why* will we not suit," she asked, "and what shall we quarrel about?"

"About—oh—you don't like the castle."

"I do like it."

"You could *say* you don't."

"After rhapsodizing over it these last three days?" Audrey asked indignantly.

"You don't like country life," the marquis suggested.

"That's not true! I love the country. I'm bored in town and everyone knows it."

"You feel unable to learn to run the castle?"

Audrey jumped to her feet and snapped her fingers under Huxford's nose. "I could learn it like that!"

"You don't like England," Gideon produced in a helpful tone.

"I love England!" Audrey declared.

"You don't like Englishmen."

"I've changed my mind. Englishmen—some of them—are quite nice. I thought they had nothing in their heads, that they were all lazy. But look at you! You've run everywhere and done everything that was needed since we came home. Came *here,* I should say. Any fool can see you're a prodigious good landlord; your tenants love you. And the staff! No trouble is too great if they think they can teach their future marchioness something that will add to your comfort."

With a faint smile, Gideon played his trump card. "You've discovered you don't like me, neither my person nor my personality."

Audrey stared. She opened her mouth and closed it with a snap. The marquis watched as she executed a hasty circle about the room, up once, down and up again, stopping finally in front of him. "I will not be thought capricious, my lord." It was an adequate riposte, but she couldn't resist a parting admonition. "You'll have to think of another reason we won't suit."

"I don't believe I can."

Audrey's heart gave a great bounding thump. "Wh— what do you mean?"

He dropped his gaze to the snuffbox he held and remarked idly, "Perhaps we should marry, after all."

"No!" Audrey blurted. "I can't do that!" She had turned deathly white and began unconsciously to wring her hands in agitation.

Huxford's face assumed the glacial aspect he used to shield himself. Audrey wanted to explain but was unable to utter a sound. The wall he retreated behind was an unapproachable barrier. She could stand it if she wasn't in love with him. That was the trouble: She was. Oh, she knew he *wanted* her. But how long could that last if he wasn't willing to commit himself to loving her? A few days or weeks of bliss, and his desire—lust, he'd called it—would dissipate and he would wander. Then she'd be caught in another of those modern society marriages where husband and wife sought solace in others. She couldn't bear to lose him that way.

"No," she whispered.

He was taking snuff and his nod was a masterpiece of indifference. "I see. I'd thought—but no matter. We'll carry on with our original plan. And don't worry. I'll come up with something for us to quarrel about."

14

E gbertt had no opinion of the country. "Don't care where I am so long as Letty is there," he'd told Victoria before they left London.

Just as Victoria had predicted, their stay at Baddingly had worked out to Egbertt's supreme satisfaction. There was Letty at breakfast. Then they read the newspapers in the library. After luncheon they took a turn through the shrubbery and returned for a nap in the solar. Late afternoon found Lord H snugly ensconced in his favorite spot in the great hall. "You can say what you will, Letty, but the St. Aubins know how to please a fellow even in a great stone barn like this."

Lady Marpleby agreed, saying she was delighted to be at Baddingly and, from having visited numerous times in the past, felt quite at home. She looked about at what Madeline St. Aubin had accomplished with this cavernous hall.

The late marchioness had ingeniously arranged what she called conversation areas before each of the fireplaces with chairs and sofas. With screens in the winter, they were especially cozy. From two stories up, the windows on the west wall allowed streams of sunlight to pour in silver shafts on these agreeable places, so the hall was the favorite congregating point for the family, as well as for visitors. In the inglenook to the right of the main fireplace, Madeline had placed a game table with comfortable chairs, and it was here that Huxford and Audrey found Lady M and his lordship, playing piquet.

Politely declining an invitation to join their card game, Gideon addressed Lord Higglesby. "I have something to tell you, sir. I'm posting north for a few days on business. Would you keep an eye on things here?" he asked.

Higglesby raised astonished brows. "Only just got here, m'boy. Why do you want to leave?"

"It's not that I want to, sir, but rather, I must. Press of business, you see." Lady M did not miss the glance her godson threw her. Something was wrong, she thought, but what?

When Egbertt protested again, Lady Marpleby interposed. "We quite understand, don't we, Egbertt?" She laid a hand on his arm.

"Oh!" Egbertt grunted, receiving a sharp little pinch. "Uh—indeed! Only . . ."

"And we'll be delighted to stay and keep the girls company. Won't we, Egbertt?" The look she turned on him held a minatory gleam.

"Certainly, m'love, but . . ."

"When are you leaving, Gideon?" Lady M had already turned to her godson.

The marquis pulled his eyes from the sight of Audrey's hair in the afternoon sunlight and said, "In a few minutes, I'm afraid."

"Not," Lady Marpleby begged, "before dinner?"

"Yes. In half an hour." Gideon thought his level gaze must have precluded further questions from his godmama.

"I see," Lady M said slowly. "Well, come tell us goodbye when you're ready to go."

After promising to be downstairs shortly, he took Audrey away, saying there was something they must discuss. He left her in her bedchamber.

"I'll only be a few minutes," he said and went to his apartment in the south tower.

Audrey sat in the chair before her fire. She felt as if she couldn't breathe. She could hear the slow, painful thud of her heart pounding in her ears. This was the moment she'd dreaded. If things worked out as Gideon planned, this would be the first step toward ending their betrothal. In a few weeks it would be over.

She jumped when Gideon's rap fell on her door, and stood as he entered. "Now then," he said, "we're going down there and you will pretend you're sorry to see me leave." He glanced once at her mouth, then away. His jaw looked hard. "Can you do that?"

Audrey let her lashes brush her cheek. "Yes," she murmured, almost inaudibly.

"Good. Look at me," he directed sharply. "If you need anything, tell Manning. He's my agent, remember?"

Audrey nodded. He didn't touch her, simply held her with his gaze. After a pause, during which she tried to guess what he was feeling, he spoke. "Let's go down, then."

Everyone, including the higher servants, escorted Huxford to the foyer. An awful realization gripped Audrey as she walked in the circle of his arm. This was the last time she'd feel his body against hers.

He was throwing instructions to Bole, his steward, and to Twickem. "Oh, and Audrey. There's a note on my study desk for Manning. See that he gets it, please. It's about that terracing in the south section." He gripped her shoulder more tightly and she looked up at him. She'd been afraid to before; she couldn't bear to see him and know he was going away.

"I shall," she murmured.

Audrey was alone in the entry with him, the servants having disappeared or gone ahead to load the luggage in the boot of his traveling coach. After saying goodbye, Victoria had drawn Lady Marpleby and Lord Egbertt back into the hall. Huxford took Audrey's hand, holding it in his hard grasp.

"Yes, Letty, I know!" they heard Higglesby say as Victoria led him away. "Huxford wants us gone so he can kiss your niece goodbye. Don't blame the fellow—don't blame him at all!"

"Look up," Gideon rasped, more than a hint of anger in his words. "Why won't you look at me?"

"I can't," Audrey said before her voice failed. She lifted her head to view him through a glaze of tears. She tried to speak again, but shook her head mutely.

Gideon's grip hurt her shoulders. "I swear this will be

over soon." She sensed a barely restrained violence in him and thought he would say or do something more. He didn't, but passed quickly outside and entered his carriage. She was left staring at the oaken door that slammed behind him.

Within hours of Huxford's departure, it began to dawn on Audrey that the servants, the steward, and even Victoria, had begun deferring every decision concerning the running of the castle and lands surrounding it to her judgement. Her remonstrance to Victoria went unheeded.

"No, dear sister-to-be," Toria said, smiling. "You mustn't shirk your duties. This is your home now, and the sooner you grow accustomed, the better! We're obeying Gideon's orders, you know. You're in charge by his express command."

Toria laughed at Audrey's baffled expression and disappeared, riding out as she had the past two days.

Kit Hartwell joined Toria as soon as she reached the road. They rode past the home wood, past the tenant farms, up to a small rise. They said little, and when they reached the elevation, they dismounted and stood looking over the valley which held Baddingly, Rosedale, and Whitfeld.

"Whoever thought," Kit said, sweeping his hand over the view, "that there could be such misery in so beautiful a place?"

Victoria's eyes were deep wells of hurt. "Don't, Kit. Don't blame yourself so much. I've forgiven you, long ago, whatever there was to forgive. Let's not waste these precious moments in regret. Instead, tell me something."

"What?"

"Anything. Tell me . . . oh . . . say you like me."

"*Like* you?" Kit's laugh was harsh. "There's nothing of *like* in me, Toria. There are times when I think I hate you, if the truth be known." A flare of passion lit his eyes as he moved closer. "There's a burning inside me; I'm athirst for you, and one sip won't do. To drink deeply and forever—

only that will slake me." He didn't touch her, nor did he move to.

Victoria stood mesmerized, stroking her mare's neck. Kit's eyes were hard with need, utterly without pity.

"We could go away, where no one knows us," Toria said. "We could go to America, or even farther . . . to Australia."

"No. We'd hate each other after a few years; we don't want that." It was something Kit had thought about, something he'd rejected for both of them. When he threw Toria into her saddle, his hands were as hard as a stranger's.

Rain set in—not thunderous rains, but soggy spells that defied description. Each day brought opalescent mists that hung dull and gray, obscuring everything beyond fifty feet. Audrey took her cloak and walked the battlements, and it was a silent, lowering world she looked upon, with a lost, eerie quality. She shivered; Huxford seemed to have taken the sun away. Would the world stay dark while he was gone?

She had her answer the next morning. Audrey awoke with sunbeams across her face and jumped from bed to stand at the window, looking at the dazzling dew-sparkled grass.

Victoria scratched at her door and strode in. "Get dressed, lazybones! The sun is here and so is Chartley!" There was a vibrant gaiety beneath Toria's words, a jubilant tone that couldn't be suppressed. "We're going riding and you must come, too." Suddenly she flung her arms wide. "Ah, God, I've been so tired of the mist!"

"Toria, do you think this is wise?" Audrey was reluctant to force an issue that might best be left alone.

Victoria took Audrey's hands in her own and said, "Dearest friend, know this: I would go anywhere, do anything, to be with Kit Hartwell. His honor is what stands between us, not mine." There was a steadiness in her look which said she was done with social mores.

With an understanding gleaned from her own heart, Audrey hugged Victoria. "I won't intrude," she said. "I'll ride with you another time."

* * *

The wooded area beyond the lake had beckoned Audrey since her arrival at Baddingly. She was determined to explore it before she left. Dressed in her oldest riding habit and sturdy boots, she set out. She took the path past the lake until she reached the smallest of the ponds. Scrambling over the stone fence that separated Chartley's land from Huxford's, she went deeper into the area, the trees seeming to press more closely about her the farther she went. There was an abundance of undergrowth, with trailing vines and creepers which should have been pruned. Kit, in his nonchalant way, had said that she might walk on his land, but warned her not to get lost. "It's grown over. I haven't kept it trimmed—not these past three years."

As Audrey picked her way past a towering mass of grapevines, the stillness was broken by a loud thrashing in the underbrush. She looked back to see Bess, the spotted hound who had accompanied her on shorter strolls.

"Here you are, girl," Audrey called, and the intelligent dog came to her, panting and grinning and expecting to be petted. After being told she was a good dog, Bess wagged her tail and loped off through the trees.

Audrey followed and they broke into a tiny clearing which held a dark pool of water, smooth and deep. The place was in perpetual shade, so tightly was it bound 'round by the encroaching forest. A faint mist hung over the waters, making Audrey suspect it was fed by a warm spring. In spite of this, there was a dankness, a chill in the air, as if ancient shadows had won their battle with the sun eons past and now rejected admission into their presence any life form warmer than they.

The water drew her attention, and Audrey climbed a large flat rock. She stared down. The depths were murky. She looked more closely. The surface wasn't as still as she'd first thought. There was movement there, a roiling motion that seemed almost sinister.

With a shake of her head, Audrey knelt and dipped her hand in the water. It was warm and had an unpleasant mineral taste.

"No wonder you're not drinking, Bess." She grimaced, and sat on the rock beside the dog. Looking about, she decided it was the peculiar silence which gave the place its malevolent air. Not a sound could be heard, not even the rustle of a beetle. A chill gripped her. The pond, she thought, had been waiting for something, or someone, through untold ages.

Audrey realized she was being silly, but was grateful for the presence of the dog. She laid a hand on the smooth spotted head, and the hound, in appreciation of this closer, more distinguishing attention, flopped her ears up and down and thumped her tail on the rock. Then suddenly she ceased panting, closed her mouth, and assumed a rigid attitude of listening.

"Heard something, have you?" Audrey asked, and looked across the pond to where Bess had fixed her gaze. She drew in her breath. A girl stood there—her figure slight and insubstantial through mist. She was dressed in white, and in the muted gloom, she might have been an apparition. She clutched a large rag doll and stared across the pond at Audrey, standing stock-still, neither moving nor seeming to breathe.

After her shock subsided, Audrey waved and called a soft hello. Her voice across the water held a resonant, hollow sound, as if an echo had doubled back upon itself. "Are you lost?" she called, as she made her way carefully around the rocky edge of the pond.

The child hadn't moved, hadn't uttered a sound. "What is your name?" Audrey smiled, but her expression froze when she drew closer. The child was no child at all, but a woman dressed like a six-year-old.

It was her voice that was childlike. "I'm Dee," she said shyly and raised her face to Audrey's.

The thin countenance was delicate, the features fragile, with a pale, faded beauty. She eyed Audrey in an abstracted way, humming a toneless melody under her breath. There were fine lines about her eyes and mouth which revealed her age. *She's older than I am,* Audrey thought, *older by several years!* But it was the pale eyes—a strange colorless blue—which fascinated her.

There was a blank ingenuousness in them that must repel, considering how old she was.

Audrey swallowed. "Are you here alone?" she asked gently.

The girl—standing in the short, lacy dress, with her hair ribbon undone, stockings snagged and torn, one white slipper muddy—presented a woebegone appearance. For an instant, and so fleeting Audrey later wondered if she'd imagined it, there shone in her vacant eyes a cunning light.

Her voice became deeper, and she had assumed a dignified mien. "Excuse me, please," she said. "I'm not a *child,* you know. I have something to do now." She nodded regally, resumed her song, and stepped past Audrey to the very edge of the pond.

Suddenly, from the direction of the castle, came the sounds of running through the bush. Victoria St. Aubin pushed wildly through the tangle of vines and stopped short at the sight of the pair by the pool. She was white and trembling, breathing rapidly. She fastened her eyes on the girl. "Diane," she began urgently, then in a calmer, more compelling tone said, "Stay there, Diane."

"Hello, Victoria," she said in her most childlike way. "Diane . . ."

"I'm not Diane, Victoria. I'm Dee Dee. *Humm.*"

"Yes! Of course. Dee Dee. Well," Victoria drew a careful breath, "what are you doing beside the pool? Where is Mrs. Nestor?"

"Humm, humm. I ran away. Mrs. Nestor won't let me come here. My baby"—she half raised the rag doll—"is sick. I'm going to put it in the warm water and make it well. No! Stay there, Toria." She glanced past Victoria to where the two servants, Jem and Clarence, appeared, holding themselves ready for orders.

Dee Dee's voice rose, and she clutched her doll closer. "And make them stay back," she said, pointing at the men.

Without warning, evading Audrey's reaching hands, Dee Dee slipped feet first into the water. She didn't move her arms, but sank silently, holding her doll.

Victoria screamed and launched herself at the pool, disappearing under the black surface only to reappear drag-

ging a fighting Diane by her torn dress. With a slight
smile, the girl locked her arms about Victoria's neck and
drew her under the water with her. The footman, Jem, had
dived in immediately behind his mistress. He brought
them both up—Diane with her arms still clenched about
Victoria, still smiling, Victoria coughing and retching.

A large, angular woman loomed beside Audrey, and Jem
handed a suddenly passive Diane to this person, while
Clarence and Audrey got Toria onto the bank. She shook
and coughed, and her teeth began to chatter. Clarence
stripped off his jacket. "Here, miss. We'll wrap you in
this, and me and Jem will make a lady chair and have you
at the castle in no time."

Victoria, struggling to see past Audrey, said, "Is she all
right?"

"Yes," Audrey said. "That woman—who—?"

"Mrs. Nestor."

Audrey nodded. "Mrs. Nestor has her. See, she's wrapping Diane in her apron. And there, she is reaching in the
water for the doll."

This sodden article seemed all Diane cared for. She removed Mrs. Nestor's apron and wrapped the doll in it. She
started humming again, but broke off to say clearly, "See,
Nestor? Don't you think my baby is better?" They could
hear her chattering as she and Mrs. Nestor disappeared in
the direction of Whitfeld.

Audrey signed to the henchmen, and they crossed and
locked their arms between them. "Come," she told Toria.
"Jem and Clarence will take you home now. I'll be right
behind you."

By midnight, Victoria had a high fever, and Audrey and
Mrs. Praddle were afraid not to awaken Lady Marpleby.
By one o'clock, their patient was breathing more easily, although her temperature was still elevated and her pulse erratic.

In spite of their protests and after reminding Mrs.
Praddle to send for the doctor at first light, Audrey sent
the housekeeper and Aunt Letty off to bed, promising to
have them called at six in the morning.

Alone with Toria, Audrey got into bed with her, and arranging pillows about them, managed to prop up and hold the other girl in what was almost a sitting position.

"But whatever for, my love?" Aunt Letty asked, when she came to relieve Audrey at daybreak.

Audrey stretched tiredly and rubbed her neck. "So she won't take an inflammation of the lungs. It's an old American Indian treatment. Do keep her propped up, Aunt Letty." She started for her own room to try for some rest, but turned back. "Oh! I meant to tell you. If the doctor tries to bleed Victoria, don't allow it! If he insists, call me."

Audrey groaned and screwed her eyes more tightly shut. Someone was calling her name.

"Miss Audrey!" Audrey opened one eyelid. The tiny upstairs maid watched her, obviously reluctant to rouse someone whom she knew had been awake all night.

"What is it, Peggy?" Audrey murmured. Her eyes felt full of sand when she peeped at the clock. It pointed to ten. Suddenly awake, she grasped the girl's thin wrist. "Is Miss Toria worse, Peggy? Tell me!"

"No, miss," the girl said. "Mr. Twickem said as how I should wake you. It's that doctor, ma'am! He's here and a-fixing to go and bleed Miss Victoria, no matter who says 'im nay!"

Audrey's eyes took on a militant glint. Throwing back the covers, she swung out of bed. "Desire him, if you please, to await my presence. I'll be there in ten minutes! And Peggy. If he gives any trouble, come to me at once!"

The girl's eyes grew large and she sketched a curtsy. "Yes, ma'am!" she gasped, and left to do Audrey's bidding.

Audrey had not yet completed her toilet before the flustered maid was back, out of breath. Pegeen burst into the room just as Matty finished smoothing Audrey's braids.

"Oh, miss," she cried. "Mr. Twickem is a-standing between Miss Victoria and that doctor! Oud sawbones says he *will too* bleed her. Says as how it's needful!"

Audrey hurried out of the room and down the hallway.

When she pushed open the door to the sickroom, she found a tableau. Lady Marpleby, tears streaming down her face, was guarding Victoria on one side, while Mrs. Pradle stood watch on the other. Near the center of the room, the doctor—a tall, cadaverous individual dressed in black—was held at bay by Twickem, who gazed regally off into one corner. Contrary to Audrey's instructions, Toria had been placed flat on her back. Her eyes were closed, her cheeks flushed with fever, and she was dreadfully still.

Audrey swept in and advanced upon the doctor. Holding out her hand, she said, "How do you do, Doctor Shandy? How is—"

The doctor sniffed and took her hand in a loose, moist grasp. "Shandy's in London; I'm relieving him for a few days. I'm Doctor Moore."

"I see," Audrey said. "And how do you find Miss St. Aubin? I must tell you at once, sir. I won't have you bleeding her." Voice firm, she gazed coolly at the physician.

The doctor threw back his head and plunged into a rapid and elevated exposition which, Audrey felt sure, was designed to intimidate her, to point out how ridiculous she was to question his judgement or his treatment of her future sister-in-law.

"My dear Miss Soames-Taylor," he said, "in certain pathological conditions where febrile paroxysms, accompanied by severe rigors, are present, judicious cupping—bleeding, if you will—is quite the accepted norm, indeed the prescribed treatment. Any one of the four cardinal humors of the blood may have been thrown out of its delicate balance, especially in Miss St. Aubin's case, where the patient has been immersed in water. Certain noxious elements may incubate and multiply. Bleeding serves to drain away such poisons. In addition, by lessening the total volume of blood, the heart's work may be lightened for a time, affording further relief. If you have an aversion to the lancet and cup, I have no objection to employing venesection. The application of leeches, you know. Except in such a case, you would need a specially trained nurse around the clock to—"

Audrey held up her hand. "Pardon me, Dr. Moore," she interrupted. "Twickem, please call someone up—whomever you will; Bridey might serve—and have her help Mrs. Pradle and my aunt. I want Miss Victoria propped in an upright position again. And she is to be held that way unless she is arranged on her stomach."

"No!" exploded the doctor. "I protest most strenuously—"

"Certainly, Doctor," Audrey said in her most cordial tones, "you may be as strenuous as you please, only not here. Shall we go to the library? Twickem?" she said, signaling with her eyes that the butler was to accompany them.

In the book room, the doctor allowed his anger to overcome his civility; his blue-veined cheeks turned purple, and he rushed into speech before Audrey had a chance to say a word. "I will not allow my patient to be treated in this fashion," he declared indignantly. "I've prescribed a tonic, along with various inhalants, and she must be kept sedated as much as possible. I will bleed her, and then—"

"No, Doctor! You will not. But I thank you for the inhalants. Those should prove helpful. Now, if you will be so kind as to go with Twickem, he will show you out."

Dr. Moore drew himself up. "Young woman, permit me to inform you that the course of treatment you propose is dangerous in the extreme. If the patient dies, it shall be on your head. With *my* treatment, we may avert the pneumonitis which is attendant in so many of these cases."

"Pneumonitis? Is that not more commonly called inflammation of the lungs? Yes, I thought so. With *your* treatment, Doctor, she will be too weak to fight it!" Audrey nodded and tried to pass him. "Good day, sir." It was a clear dismissal.

When Moore went so far as to lay a restraining hand on her arm, Audrey looked up in surprise and raised her brows.

The doctor's mottled cheeks went bloodless. He dropped his hand and stepped back. "You leave me no alternative," he said in an arctic tone. "I must withdraw from the case." With the smallest of bows, he went away with Twickem.

The butler returned from escorting Dr. Moore out, and Audrey at once desired him to send for Dr. Shandy, begging his immediate attendance on Miss St. Aubin. She further requested that someone get in touch with Huxford, advising him of his sister's illness.

Twickem coughed and said both messages had already been sent, prayed that Miss Audrey would not judge him or the staff too harshly for taking, as it were, the liberty of doing so without her orders, and directed her attention to the breakfast tray Mrs. Pradle sent. Just a bite of toast and marmalade, he suggested, would serve to strengthen her before she went up to sleep awhile.

Audrey thought sleep beyond her, but was grateful for the food. Twickem went off with her thanks in his ears and she sipped her tea, wondering how long it would take the doctor—and Huxford—to arrive. Dr. Shandy could easily be found, but the marquis might be anywhere.

Doubt swamped Audrey. Was she doing the proper thing, sending Dr. Moore away? But she couldn't let him bleed Victoria! It was all too much, she thought, and buried her face in her hands.

Lady Offutt arrived, took one look at Audrey, and ordered her to bed. "I have no doubt you were up all night," she declared. "A pretty bear-jawing we'll get if Gideon comes home and you're sick, too! Sleep will restore the roses to those cheeks, my girl."

"I couldn't," Audrey protested.

"A drive then; that will relax you. Twickem! Order a carriage for Miss Soames-Taylor. She's going for a breath of air. And don't send a gabby maid with her. She needs rest, not conversation." She patted Audrey on the shoulder. "With a coachman and footman up behind, you'll be safe enough. I'm going to Victoria now. Where's Letty? I suppose she's tired herself completely over this?"

"Yes, she's resting at the moment." Audrey smiled. "Thank you, Lady Offutt—dearest Tildy."

"Oh, pooh!" Tildy waved the thanks away. "It's no

bother. I enjoy ordering people about." Her horsey smile flashed as she mounted the stairs.

Audrey was waiting for the carriage when the porter handed her a letter. On the front of the envelope was written: "To Baddingly." When she unfolded the smudged and spotty note, Audrey found this much underscored message: "Please come, dearest Toria, please I must see you. And I wish you will bring Miss Soames-Taylor and Lady Marpleby and anyone else who happens to be in your house party. We shall drink tea and have such fun! Don't fail me, I am desperate. Please, please come! I shall be waiting. Love, Diane Hartwell."

Audrey stared at the note. There was something peculiar about it—it sounded hysterical. She remembered how her aunt had described Diane: *Erratic and highly unstable,* Aunt Letty said.

Audrey drew a deep breath. She had tried not to think about that poor, mad creature at the pond. That girl—woman—was Kit Hartwell's wife. And *she* had written this note. Audrey read it again and straightened. She was going to Whitfeld. After all, she'd been invited. When the porter said her carriage was ready, she didn't hesitate. She stuck her head in the library and spied Lord Higglesby. When she told him she was riding over to Whitfeld, he waved and bade her be careful.

Completely hidden by a dense thicket of oaks, Whitfeld was located a mile or so from Baddingly. Audrey was shown in and met by a flustered butler who tried to say madame wasn't receiving today.

"Oh yes, Peters! Yes, I am!" a high voice exclaimed. Audrey turned to locate its source. Half down the stairs stood the girl of the pond, dressed in a blue, partially buttoned morning dress. An attempt to put her pale hair up had failed; one side was straggling over her ear. She wore long gloves and an old fashioned court necklace. On her head perched a tiny straw bonnet. She was barefoot.

Advancing down the stairs, she extended her hand. "How do you do? Have you come to tea? I'm Diane

Hartwell." There was no indication that she remembered Audrey or the incident at the pond.

Trying not to stare at the garish rouge Diane had applied to her lips and cheeks, Audrey took her hand and stammered, "Hello. I'm Audrey Soames-Taylor, and I—"

She was interrupted by a commotion at the door. Kit Hartwell strode into the hall with his riding coat open, still wearing his hat. Diane stood motionless and seemed to hide behind her visitor.

Chartley raked his wife with an appraising glance and settled his gaze on Audrey. "Why are you here, Miss Soames-Taylor?" There was ice in the viscount's question.

Audrey produced the note, her hands shaking. "I received this not thirty minutes ago. Victoria is ill and my aunt had just gone to nap. It sounded urgent. I didn't know what to do." She elevated her chin. "I came at your wife's invitation to have tea."

"Then by all means, we shall have it." Kit swung savagely around. "This is my wife Diane, Miss Soames-Taylor. Diane, this is St. Aubin's fiancée." There was weariness and irony in his tone. "She has come for tea."

"Oh, yes!" Diane's face was eager. "It's ready. Come this way, Miss Soames-Taylor," she said and led them into the parlor.

Diane poured a cup for her guest and one for herself, then hesitated. "Do you want any?" she asked her husband, never once looking directly at him.

Kit, leaning back in his chair, declined and watched Audrey trying to drink the tea. Diane sipped hers, ignoring the fact that it was cold and that she was spilling it on her gloves. Her conversation, carried on in the manner of a small girl conducting a tea party for her dolls, consisted of commonplace comments on the weather and questions concerning the state of Lady Marpleby's health. Then she spoke of her acquaintance with Lord Higglesby. "I haven't seen him for the longest time. Nor Victoria, come to think of it. Did you say she was ill?" Diane shook her head sadly. "That's too bad," she said, then her face brightened. "I know! I'll drop over tomorrow with a little present for her. That should make her feel better."

Audrey murmured a vague reply and said she must be going.

"No!" Diane jumped from her chair, dropping her cup and saucer onto the carpet, splashing tea everywhere. "Stay some more! *Please*—I like you!"

Audrey turned to Kit, but his eyes were on his wife. "But Miss Soames-Taylor must go, Diane," he said gently. "Perhaps she can come another time," he suggested.

"No!" Diane Hartwell screamed. Sudden tears gushed from her eyes, flooding her cheeks, smearing the rouge into a grotesque mask. "No!" she screamed again. "She's only going because *you* came. You ruin everything." She whirled to face her guest in frantic agitation. "Miss Soames-Taylor! Audrey. May I call you Audrey? I like you! Don't go," she pleaded and swiped at her face to dry it. "I know—I know! Let me show you my baby! Please?"

Audrey sought Chartley's gaze. His expression was resigned. "All right, Diane. We'll go upstairs and she can see our baby, then Miss Soames-Taylor must go."

Diane seemed to crouch. "Not *your* baby," she spat at Kit. There was a feral gleam in her eyes. "Not yours. He's mine! Only mine!"

Turning smoothly to Audrey, her face held only an entreating smile. "Come up to the nursery, Audrey, and I'll show him to you." Diane began to hum. It was the formless melody she'd been singing at the pond yesterday. She hummed all the way to the nursery.

Mrs. Nestor, at a motion from Chartley, stood away from the door as Diane took Audrey across to a larger-than-usual crib. In it lay a limp, white, vacant-eyed child about two years old. It was perfectly formed but seemed boneless, somehow. It made no movement, nor was there any sign it knew they were there.

Audrey realized Diane's song had words now. "Water baby," Diane crooned, fitting the words to the vague tune. "Mama's little water-water baby. He will be . . . better-better soon, when we find . . . the water."

Gently, Kit took hold of the girl's shoulders. "Come, Dee Dee," he said. "Go with Mrs. Nestor. I'll show our guest out."

Diane stopped singing and lifted her arms. "Kit! Let me kiss you, Kit. Please?"

After a moment, eyes watchful, Chartley slowly lowered his head, and then flinched away. Diane flashed an insanely brilliant smile at Audrey. Blood glistened on her mouth where she had bitten her husband. She uttered a low laugh which rose to a shriek. "Water and blood; water and blood! Sparkling and shiny, water and blood!" Then she forgot they were there and sat on the floor. Rocking back and forth, she picked at her toes, humming again.

Holding a handkerchief to his torn mouth, Kit took Audrey down to the library. He gave her a glass of wine and poured a brandy for himself.

Audrey sipped her wine. After a moment she said, "Kit, I'm so sorry. I didn't know."

He shook his head and smiled tiredly. "No, how could you?" He was silent for a long while, then stirred to say, "Everything is my fault. There never was a fool like I am, Andrey. I threw my life away, and Victoria's as well." He sipped his brandy and continued.

"Diane is the step-daughter of a cousin of Lady St. Aubin's, you know. She came to Baddingly and soon had me convinced that Toria thought of me as a brother. And she lied to Toria, claiming that I'd said I loved her and wanted to marry her. When Toria began to shun me, I turned to Diane. Before I knew it, we were engaged.

"After our wedding, I learned Diane had no idea what the physical side of marriage meant. It was two months before I consummated our vows. I—I was drunk, and insisted. Rather forcibly, I'm afraid. She couldn't bear my touch after that." Kit patted his bleeding lip and continued. "Diane was made pregnant as the result of our one connection and it stabilized her somewhat. But when she went into labor, and her water broke—her mind snapped. She began to scream, 'Water and blood' and beg for Victoria. Then the baby was born. You've seen the baby . . . We've had all the best doctors."

Eyes brimming, Audrey said, "Oh, Kit—"

Chartley's smile was gentle. "I never wanted you to know; never wanted you to be burdened with the knowledge." He paused, then sighed. "Will you do something for me, Audrey? Look after Toria? I'm going away next week. To Spain. I can't stay here or in town. It's too close to Baddingly, too close to Victoria. I'll take her if I don't go. If I do that, all honor will be lost. Don't tell her I'm leaving. I'll tell her myself."

Grasping her hand, Kit forced Audrey to look at him. "When Gideon gets home," he said, "take Toria up to town. Marry her to someone who will love and cherish her." His voice turned low and husky. "If she can be happy, I could bear it, I think."

Audrey squeezed the firm hand holding hers. "Yes, my lord. I promise. I shall do everything within my power to help Victoria."

Chartley raised her hand and laid it against his lips. "Lucky Gideon," he murmured. "And he deserves you. They don't make a better friend than he is." His sudden smile lit his features. "And now! How is it 'my lord?' Surely it must be 'Kit' from now on?" He cocked his eyebrow at her in his old, familiar way.

Audrey blinked away her tears. "Kit it is, and I'm Audrey, you know."

"But, my sweet, so you've been anytime this last half-hour. And Gideon *be damned* if he's jealous."

They smiled, and he asked "How is Toria? Mrs. Nestor sent me word what had happened."

"I think she'll be all right if I can keep the chill from settling on her lungs. Lady Matilda is with her now. We've sent for Huxford and Dr. Shandy."

"Shall I take you home?" he asked.

Audrey shook her head. "No, but you're coming later, aren't you?"

"Certainly. I must know how she is before I return to London."

15

The carriage ride back to Baddingly passed in a blur for Audrey. A series of images filled her mind: Diane's tea party, the pitiful baby, Chartley's eyes when he spoke of their lives. Audrey had every intention of saving her tears for the privacy of her bedchamber, but of their own accord, they flowed.

A job-chaise was standing at the end of the drive when she arrived at the castle. Audrey was met by Twickem, who informed her that it belonged to Dr. Shandy. "And a good thing he got here when he did, miss!" Twickem added.

Audrey stopped and faced him. "Oh?" she asked, alarmed. "Is Miss Victoria worse?"

"No, miss. She's as well as might be expected. That was what the doctor was reporting to her ladyship when it happened," Twickem said elliptically.

"When what happened?"

"The accident, miss."

"There's been an accident?" Audrey asked.

"Yes, miss."

"Twickem," Audrey said, "you will please tell me what happened, and to whom."

"Lady Marpleby slipped on the stairs and broke her anklebone, miss, not twenty minutes ago."

"Oh, my God!" exclaimed Audrey blankly.

"Yes, miss. And that's why I said it was a good thing Dr. Shandy got here in such good time."

When Audrey arrived at her aunt's bedchamber, she found a short, bald man bending over the bed. Matilda

Offutt stood by, holding a brown bottle. "That's the girl, Tildy," the doctor was saying to her ladyship.

Dr. Shandy glanced over his spectacles at Audrey and smiled. "And this must be the termagant who spooked my colleague. Oh, yes!" he nodded when Audrey flushed, "I met the good doctor just as I turned into my drive as I arrived from London. He recounted every blow. Now don't," Dr. Shandy begged, "mind what happened. Moore is a damned prig. He was wrong into the bargain. Bleeding Victoria could only have weakened her. Rest assured you did exactly right in stopping him."

Audrey's smile was tremulous. "Thank you, Doctor. But my aunt! How is she?"

Lady Marpleby's eyes were closed, and Audrey peered at her fearfully. Her ladyship uttered a tiny snore, and the doctor laughed. "Feeling no pain at the moment. Tildy just administered enough laudanum to fell a horse!"

"Oh, no!" Lady Offutt snorted. "You prescribed the dosage, my dear Regis. Don't let him quiz you, my dear. Your aunt is about to have her ankle set and plastered. I'm here to help, along with Pegeen." Her ladyship nodded at the white-faced servant girl who held a roll of bandages. "Now then: I want *you* out! Mrs. Pradle is with Victoria. What you must do is go down and prevent Lord Higglesby from falling into a fit of apoplexy. Run along, now. That's a good girl."

Audrey peeked in on Victoria and found her asleep. She told Mrs. Pradle she would be in the library with Lord Higglesby and descended the stairs.

Lord H was pathetically glad to see someone, anyone, and after commenting four or five times on how it could have happened, and reminding Miss Soames-Taylor that he always told Letty to be careful on stairs, plus recalling exactly where he was when the footman brought him the news and recounting what his first, second, and third reactions were, Egbertt fell to ruminating on what his life would be worth without Letty.

"Told you once, didn't I, how we—Jasper and I—both wanted her? You remember that, don't you, Miss Soames-Taylor? We flipped my coin and Jasper won." Lord H sighed heavily. "Ah well, it's too bad she couldn't have married the both of us."

"But my lord," Audrey said, grasping the bull firmly by the horns, "she can."

"Eh?" Higglesby cocked his brow and regarded her with faded blue eyes. "Couldn't have heard you right, m'dear. Thought you said Jasper and me . . . that the both of us . . . Letty . . . What *did* you say, m'girl?" he demanded.

Audrey went pale at her own audacity. "I said that Aunt Letty could marry both of you."

Lord Higglesby stared at Audrey in fascination. "Don't see that," he said at last. "Don't see it at all."

"You could marry her *now*, Lord H."

"Now?" Egbertt echoed vacantly.

"Now!" Audrey's voice was determined.

"But Jasper won the toss! He married her."

"Yes, my lord, but Uncle Marpleby is dead," Audrey pointed out.

"Dead? Well, I know that! Attended his funeral three years ago. Was three years in January." Lord H shook his head. "Sad thing that. Just Letty and me—left all alone." Egbertt heaved another sigh. "Been lonely without him, Letty and I."

Audrey felt like rolling on the floor in hysterics. She tried another tack. "Was my uncle ill for very long before he died?"

Egbertt nodded. "Was sick for months."

"What did he say to you?" Audrey held her breath.

"About what, m'dear?"

"About dying and leaving Aunt Letty." Audrey spoke slowly and enunciated each word carefully.

"Oh, that!" Egbertt frowned, obviously trying to recall. "Said, 'Been better if you had won the toss, Egbertt.' And then I asked him; I said, 'Why, Jasper?' And he thought it wasn't fair to Letty to be left without a husband. Said if I'd won the toss, Letty would still have me, and it wouldn't matter if he died. Would have though. Would have mattered to me and Letty, even if he wasn't her husband. We didn't want to lose him, you see."

"Yes, well," Audrey cleared her throat, "but did he not say something else?"

"About what?" Lord Higglesby looked puzzled.

"About Aunt Letty. Did he ask you to take care of her?"

"No need, m'dear. He knew I would."

"But did he not *say* something?" Audrey asked insistently.

Lord H squinted thoughtfully, then simply shook his head again.

Audrey straightened. Stern measures were clearly called for here. Aunt Letty had reported Uncle Marpleby's last words verbatim, and she had them down pat. "Perhaps Uncle Jasper said, 'Egbertt, I leave Letty in your hands?' "

His lordship opened his eyes ar her. "How did you deduce that, my dear Miss Soames-Taylor? That is exactly what he said!" He stared at Audrey in wonderment.

"A lucky guess?" Audrey ventured.

"Must have been!" Egbertt shook his head.

"I'm trying to imagine what he meant by it," Audrey mused.

"Plain as a pikestaff! Meant he left Letty in my keeping!"

"Yes but . . ."

"What else could it mean?" Egbertt rasped. It made his lordship nervous when a conversation went too deep.

"Hand!" Audrey suddenly exclaimed.

"Hand?" He looked dazed, as if she'd lost him completely.

"I see it now!" Audrey cried triumphantly. "Uncle Jasper left you Aunt Letty's hand."

"Eh?"

"My uncle gave you Aunt Letty's hand! He gave you her *hand* in *marriage!*"

"Eh?" Egbertt ejaculated again.

"Lord Higglesby," Audrey began in her most reasonable tone, "wouldn't you have done the same? Only think! If you'd won the toss and married Aunt Letty and had died, wouldn't you have wanted Unc—wanted Jasper to marry her later?"

Lord H blinked, then turned to Audrey, his stays creaking. "You have a point, m'girl, damned if you don't. You're a sly little puss, aren't you?" he asked.

"My lord?"

Egbertt pinched her cheek. "Figured all that in that pretty little noggin of yours, didn't you?" He shook his head and smiled fondly. Then he frowned.

"Now don't," he cautioned, "say a word of this to Letty. Wouldn't do just to spring it on her out of the blue. If I suddenly asked her to marry me, it might be too much of a shock to her system. I'll hint her about; give her some time to get accustomed to the idea, you know."

There seemed no safe answer to this; Audrey remained silent.

Egbertt chuckled again. "Well, m'dear, you did a fair piece of work here today."

"Me?" Audrey asked.

"Got yourself a new uncle. Never thought of that, now did you?"

Audrey had to admit she hadn't thought of it in that light at all.

By late afternoon her aunt was resting with a cast on her ankle, and Audrey was so lightheaded from lack of sleep she barely remembered Chartley's arrival. He scooped her up in his arms and walked steadily up the stairs with Audrey protesting all the way.

"Be still," Kit told her. "Which way to your room?"

He placed her on her bed and covered her with a light blanket. "Sleep," he ordered. "I'll be with Victoria all night."

Audrey nodded and tried to smile, but her foolish eyes teared up.

Going down on one knee, Kit grasped her hand and kissed her on the cheek. "Don't worry, Gideon will be here when you wake up."

But Gideon wasn't. Two days and two nights passed, nights Victoria spent sleeping propped in Kit's arms, waking to rub her cheek on his ruffled shirt front and smile sleepily.

* * *

Twickem's messenger tracked Huxford to Southampton where he was fitting up his yacht, getting it ready to carry the two government agents, Arnaud de Vinnay and Mrs. Jeffers, to France.

As they turned into the long drive leading to Baddingly Castle, it was so dark in the carriage that Gideon could barely see the young woman sitting beside Arnaud de Vinnay on the seat opposite.

Christina Jeffers was extremely unhappy. Not five miles past she'd remonstrated with him again, saying she thought it unkind in Gideon to thrust his apparent bit 'o muslin into his fiancée's presence.

"No, she'll be happy and will seize on your appearance as an excuse to break our engagement," he said in a rough way. He's explained to Mrs. Jeffers, not once, but several times, exactly what the situation was.

When he'd received the information that his sister was ill, Gideon left the yacht in the capable hands of his first mate and returned to London posthaste. He and de Vinnay had ridden round to Mrs. Jeffer's lodgings, and he'd expanded on the part he wanted her to play at Baddingly.

Now he looked at her with something close to exasperation. This was a role she'd have no trouble with, consummate actress that she was. It was a unique talent in a country-reared vicar's daughter—one she employed with great finesse, serving her country in her dead soldier-husband's stead.

"I can't imagine why I've let you talk me into this," Christine said. Her anger was evident in her words and in her stiffened posture in the dark corner of the coach. "It's true that I am unacquainted with Lady Marpleby and Lord Higglesby, but I do not relish the idea of their regarding me as a light skirt. They will think we're lovers!"

Necessity made Huxford harsh. "You're traveling in France as Arnaud's lover. I see no difference."

Christina's laugh was scornful. "Don't or won't, Gideon? In France no one knows me. When I'm no longer a spy, I'll be living in England—retired deep in Somerset, it's true, but I don't want to spend the rest of my life wondering if someone is going to spot me as one of your discarded mistresses. I'd appreciate being left with some shred of a reputation. Already there are those who look askance at me, though I have striven for discretion, I assure you. I do not move in the first circles of society and do not aspire to, but I should love to be able to hold my head up in that country circle wherein I plan to live."

"Dammit, Christina, no one will know! I see what it is. You feel sorry for Audrey, but if only you can be brought to believe it, she has no need for your pity. She doesn't care for me."

Gideon gestured with a curt chopping motion of his hand. "Very well, I can't force you." His words were ungracious and he tightened his lips and gazed out at the moon-dappled trees speeding past the carriage window.

Christina looked at Arnaud de Vinnay, her brows raised in query.

Arnaud cleared his throat and began to suggest that his friends go softly, that perhaps some compromise could be worked, *non?*

"No." Gideon shrugged his shoulders. "My plan was to introduce Christina as my traveling companion. They weren't to know she was working with you. Everyone would assume the worst and Audrey would have a valid excuse for breaking off."

The Frenchman appeared to consider for a moment. "Couldn't we simply appear and have you introduce Christina as a friend and let them draw their own conclusions?"

Gideon looked at Christina. It might serve, if she'd go along with that much, at least.

Reluctantly, she nodded. It was plain she couldn't like any part of it.

A few minutes later, as the carriage halted in front of the castle entry, Gideon caught a glimpse of Christina's face in the light cast by one of the tall lamps mounted by the steps. He could read nothing amiss in her expression, but the way she held her head revealed her distaste for the situation.

Inside, after assuring the marquis that Miss Victoria felt much better and was fast asleep, Twickem explained as briefly as possible Lady Marpleby's mishap on the stairs and added that Dr. Shandy had lately left the castle, pronouncing himself pleased with both his patients' progress.

Twickem then bowed and said, "I shall go up and inform Miss Soames-Taylor that your lordship is home."

Audrey entered the library prepared to be severely formal in accordance with the plans she and Gideon had made to end their betrothal. She found Paden Offutt and Lord Higglesby there, still playing whist.

She saw that Arnaud de Vinnay, whom she knew slightly, had accompanied Gideon. The marquis stood squarely in the middle of the room, looking as dark and ominous as a thunder cloud, waiting, apparently, to introduce another person.

This was a young woman of about thirty, tall and willowy. The chill of the spring night showed in the high color of her cheeks. Her hood was thrown back, and being lined with some kind of white fur, reflected the pale tones of her beautiful skin. Her hair was heavy and black, and her brows—over long slanting eyes of a peculiar amber color—swept back in well-defined arches.

There was a depth in the glance she gave Audrey, a hidden meaning that could only by guessed at. When Huxford introduced the stranger as a Mrs. Jeffers, and described her as his "friend," Audrey promptly forgot all his instructions. A perverse little demon clicked in her brain, and she smiled. "How do you do, Mrs. Jeffers?" she asked. She was remote, but very polite.

Then, as everyone watched, Audrey turned to the marquis and exclaimed breathlessly, "Hello, Gideon. Welcome home." And she went on tiptoe and locked her mouth on his.

In reflex, Gideon wrapped his arms around her. Sweeping her close, he opened his mouth wide to taste as much of her as he could before raising his head. He looked down into her face.

Audrey held onto his neck while he examined her upturned countenance. One corner of his wide mouth turned down in a satirical grin. "Come, my love. We must excuse ourselves. I believe there's something we should discuss."

Propelled into the chill dining room, Audrey hugged herself while Gideon directed Twickem to light a branch of candles.

"Don't you have something to explain to me?" he demanded, when the butler was gone. "No, dammit, don't look at me like that. Bringing Christina Jeffers here was the perfect opportunity for you to cry off. From her unexplained presence, everyone naturally would think she's my inamorata."

"And is she?" Audrey asked. Her violet eyes were guarded.

"No! Merely a friend. The widow of one of my fellow officers in the 95th. She and de Vinnay are on their way to France to bring out a young cousin of Arnaud's. Christina Jeffers works for Lord Brumley and is in love only with her dead husband. I'm taking them across the channel in my yacht."

Her lashes fringed her cheeks as Audrey studied the pattern in the carpet. She didn't know what to say but was keenly aware of a vast, shaking relief. Had she really dared to kiss him? Could she ever forget his flashing response? What must he think?

Breaking the strained silence, Gideon said, "Tell me how my sister is. And what about Lady M?"

Audrey tried to describe Victoria's condition, and her voice steadied as she told him all that had happened. When she finished, she said, "I—I understand about Toria and Kit now, Gideon, and about Diane and the baby." After a long silence, she looked up to find him watching her.

Behind his silver eyes, a banked fire looked ready to blaze. "Thank you," he said. "You've managed beautifully."

Audrey felt the sting of treacherous tears and jumped to her feet. "I want to be gone from this place as soon as Victoria is well."

She flushed when he raised his brows. "Oh, really? After that ... uh ... warm, and ... particularly *seductive* welcome?" When she didn't speak, he seemed to take pity on her and said, "Never mind. These next two days, when we're so cold to one another, everyone will be convinced my interests lie in another direction."

True to his word, from that moment, Huxford ignored Audrey and was assiduous in his attentions to Mrs. Jeffers. He seemed impervious to the sorrowful aspect of his godmother. Luckily, Egbertt didn't notice, but Tildy Offutt shook her head, told Audrey that Gideon was playing deep, and vowed to keep Paden away from Baddingly to spare him confusion.

It was a bad two days. Supper that last night was an ordeal. At last, at ten o'clock, Audrey excused herself from the distressed and silent company. When she did, Gideon said abruptly, "I must speak to you, Audrey. There'll be no chance in the morning. We're leaving very early."

Audrey nodded, said goodnight, and went off to her bedchamber to sit by her fire and wait for him to send for her. Would Gideon ask her to stage a scene as he was leaving tomorrow? Would he want her to repudiate their engagement at that time? She shrank from such a public denouement. She sat a long time listening as the wind rose and thunder crashed about the chimneys. Flashes of lightning showed the rain gusting against the window.

It was twelve midnight before the footman came to escort her to Gideon's suite in the south tower. The low pitched chamber was dark, lit only by the glow of embers on the hearth, and Audrey hesitated just inside the open door.

Gideon stood against the window frame, gazing into the night. He must have heard something; perhaps he sensed her presence, for he turned. Crossing the room, he shut the door—locking it, she thought. She started to speak, but he stopped her.

"Hush," he said. "Come here." He took her arm and guided her to the window. It was huge and bowed and ran from floor to ceiling.

Standing close to the panes, they seemed in an island of storm. Audrey couldn't speak—the sensation was overwhelming. She felt exposed and vulnerable.

When she could bear no more, she turned to Gideon,

but he wasn't looking outside. He had his eyes on her and stood so close she could feel the heat of his body. She smelled him, his warm and welcome scent, compounded of the earth and the sun and the brandy he'd been drinking. His black hair fell in a wanton tangle over his forehead, and he was in his shirtsleeves, his cravat having been cast aside. The collar and the front of his shirt were unbuttoned so that she saw for the first time the smooth tanned skin of his throat, strong and muscular, the thick hair matting his chest. Audrey felt a rush of her senses, a keen yearning for him to touch her.

"I wish," he said in a low growl, "that I could take you here by the fire. We would love one another, thinking only of ourselves, and the others—the whole world—would be forever and far away." Grasping her shoulders, he pulled her to him, and when he slid his arms around her body, he held her hard, his fingers biting into her tender flesh, never caring, it seemed, if he hurt her.

Audrey felt him tremble. Without thinking, she put her open mouth against the bare skin of his throat.

Gideon gasped and buried his hand in her hair, pulling her head sharply back, as if he couldn't bear the intimacy of her kisses. "You're warm, so warm," he murmured. "I want to feel you, to hold you like this whenever I see you. No! Not like this. I want you with your hair down and in a loose robe." He began pulling the pins from her chignon. "Help me, Audrey. Take down your hair. I want to remember it that way when I'm gone."

Slowly, slowly, Audrey raised her arms. In seconds her hair was falling to her hips, veiling her in twisting, red-gold strands.

Gideon gathered a handful and pressed it to his mouth. Then he had both hands in her hair, pulling her face to his. "Kiss me goodbye, Audrey—a true lover's kiss. And I want to kiss you the way I do in dreams when I lie down at night, holding nothing back. You will return my kiss like the sweet lover you could be—would be—after we'd made love half a lifetime."

With tears in her eyes, Audrey opened her lips for him,

turning as Gideon meshed his mouth deeply with hers, then deeper still, until all reality dissolved.

This was it, Audrey thought, lost in the wonder of his mouth, his hands, his embrace. This was the answer to the man-woman mystery she'd wondered about since she was a small girl. She felt that she was on the verge of some great discovery, standing on the precipice of a deep, burning abyss. And now she was falling. Only Gideon could save her.

Gideon raised his head at last, and with unsteady hands put Audrey from him. She swayed, and he grasped her shoulders.

"Go," he said in a hoarse whisper. "Get away from me, Audrey. Get out of this room, or I swear—go now!"

Audrey found herself running through the halls, stumbling, her long hair streaming behind her. She didn't dare stop, for each step was a fight against going back.

More than anything, she wanted to return to Gideon's room and throw herself into his arms, to desperately seek the bright promise implicit in his last, alluring threat. When she reached her room, she locked the door. Throwing back her counterpane, she lay huddled under the covers, a small, shivering figure in the huge bed. A storm of weeping overtook her, and when finally she dried her tears, she lay listening to the rain beat against the window.

Tonight, she'd tasted ecstasy, or its prelude. For a moment, when they shared those searing kisses, her soul had flown out and joined Gideon St. Aubin's. Never again would she be whole without him. She was only half a person now, and here in this bed, separated from him by walls of stone and misunderstanding, Audrey had never in her life felt more alone.

After Audrey fled, Gideon stood inside the bow window and watched the storm.

He couldn't fight loving Audrey any longer. It wasn't merely her body he wanted. No, he had to have all of her, and for all time. When he returned from France, he'd make her love him. She trembled in his arms, she opened her mouth to his kisses. He wanted more—her laughter, her sweet sighs of surrender, her body clinging to his, her every wanton dream.

At long last he was ready to lay aside the foolish battle he'd waged against loving her. Exactly when his desire to possess her had turned into love, Gideon didn't know. That was far gone in time, beyond memory. Now it seemed he'd always loved her. He would marry her if he could persuade her; he only prayed his senseless fight hadn't cost him Audrey's love.

16

When Sir Malcolm Motley fled London, he left behind a flood of debts and a disgruntled mistress.

His scheme for revenging himself on the Marquis of Huxford was vague. Sir Malcolm gambled that a plan would present itself to him once he was on the scene in Sussex. He established himself at a small country inn called the Red Bull, not five miles from Baddingly Castle. He knew how to ingratiate himself with yokel innkeeper's wives, and impressed this one with his faded style and smooth address. A manufactured air of sadness, punctuated by long sighs, further intrigued and disarmed his hostess. Mrs. Simpkins seemed gratified to find her lordly guest so pleased with the rustic inn.

As luck would have it, the Red Bull was precisely what Motley needed. He grew expansive, assuring his doting landlady of his pleasure in her house. The Red Bull's charm of setting, its quiet country air, even the simple fare, he said, would suit him exactly, after the rigors of the London season.

Sir Malcolm, as he insisted she call him, told Mrs. Simpkins that he had some acquaintances in the neighborhood. "But first I must seek peace and solitude until such a time as I feel myself capable of even a morning visit."

Motley sighed. "For a while," he said, "I shall desire only peace and a book or two, and possibly a stroll in the late afternoon sun. Or, if I feel up to it, my team may be brought around and my henchman Stubbs and I shall tool along between the hedgerows, going nowhere in particular, coming home late to this house and a good supper."

167

Motley, enjoying the sympathetic expression on the simple country woman's face, asked, "Mrs. Simpkins, do you—or perhaps your worthy husband—know where I might wet my angle rod?"

All this happened to suit Mrs. Simpkins' notion of how members of the *ton* must spend their time in rustication, and so she informed Simpkins when she sent him to give his lordship some hints on where to fish.

Heavy-eyed from lack of sleep, Audrey came to breakfast the morning after Huxford and his party had left Baddingly.

Twickem handed her a note, saying, "From his lordship, miss."

Slipping it into her pocket to be read at a later time, she drank her tea and ate her toast, declining the coddled eggs and marmalade Twickem urged on her.

She went to check on Victoria and found Peggy McGuire moving quietly about the freshened room.

"How is she, Pegeen?" Audrey kept her voice low when she saw that the patient was sleeping.

"Oh, *very* well, miss," the Irish girl whispered. "She had a good night, or so Mrs. Pradle reported, and ate a rare breakfast. I believe she's nearly recovered. After her bath, she wanted to rest again and now—as you see—she's sleeping like a babe. 'Twill do 'er a world 'o good," the small redhead nodded sagely.

"That's wonderful," Audrey told her. "Leave her alone to rest."

Entering Aunt Letty's suite, Audrey discovered a most memorable scene. An extremely red-faced Lord Higglesby sat on the edge of Lady Marpleby's bed. In his arms he held a weeping Letty, and—as he patted and consoled her—he became aware by gradual degrees that they were no longer alone, but were being watched with considerable astonishment by Miss Soames-Taylor.

"Here, Letty! Hold up, m'girl. Your niece will think I'm strangling you." His eyes beseeched Audrey's help. "I only asked your aunt to marry me as you suggested, Miss

Soames-Taylor, and now she has fallen into this fit. Letty Girl!—Stop it!"

Lady Marpleby, gaining a measure of control, turned her teary phiz to Audrey and quivered, "Oh, I'm so happy. Egbertt and I are to be married, Audrey. I'm the luckiest woman in the world."

Audrey smiled, genuinely happy for them, and went forward to drop kisses on her aunt and to shake hands with her uncle-to-be. Then she left to read her letter from Gideon.

There was no date and no salutation, only two short lines and his signature. "I shall be back in a week—ten days at the most. We'll talk then. Gideon."

No matter how often she read it, and Audrey perused it many times in the week to come, the cryptic message came off the page the same way. What the marquis hadn't written was more important than what he had. There was no reference to what had happened between them—no word of love, as she'd permitted herself to hope he was beginning to feel.

Audrey's shoulders slumped. It was finished, then. Final. There remained only the last scene to be played. She must act her part for the benefit of the others: for Victoria, who seemed to have made a remarkable recovery, for her Aunt Marpleby, for Lord Higglesby. Somehow, she must manage to survive until Huxford returned.

By morning, Audrey's resilient nature had reasserted itself. Finding that everyone insisted upon her making the everyday decisions around the castle and home farm, Audrey fell to with a will.

She instituted Huxford's plan for terracing the two fields south of the Hambly Ridge. Behind the castle, beyond the summer house, Audrey laid out beds of roses. She recruited a small army of helpers for the aged head gardener, who was in high gig at having so many strong hands to command. Within two days, she had the beds dug out, had replaced old soil with new, and had designed an herb garden in rocky tiers. She planted sage and mint and lavender, added parsley, fennel and thyme, and set in a border of shallots and leek.

Each time Audrey put her hands in the rich loam, she realized she was creating a living memorial to what might have been.

In this fashion, a week passed. Audrey existed in a blur of days, falling each night into a well of sleep filled with spectral scenes where she searched for Gideon.

She couldn't help feeling a sort of muted joy when she saw her plants valiantly breaking through the soil she must leave. She was full of unshed tears but remained calm. In less than a week, she thought, Gideon would return and this . . . ordeal would be over.

Far to the south, Gideon St. Aubin stood on a French headland and squinted at the sky over the Bay of Biscay. The dark clouds hung low; the seas were running high. Seven days had passed since he'd left Audrey at Baddingly, seven days of torment in which he'd lived with the knowledge that he loved her. But it was fear that was driving him: Would he be able to make her love him? He relived every hurtful word he'd said to her, every hateful thing he'd done since he'd realized what a strong hold she had on his emotions. He grunted a laugh. There's no fool like the fool who will not love, he thought.

Gideon paced the boulder-strewn path, trying to contain his impatience. If de Vinnay and the two women were delayed, the weather would prevent their crossing the bay and reaching Southhampton on the schedule he'd projected to Audrey.

For two days he and his crew had hidden off the coast of Cornwall, in inlets and behind river mouths. Now, a few miles down the shore from Bordeaux, he was laying to in a natural channel, placing his reliance on a group of French citizens who were hostile to Napolean. But he felt closed in, trapped, and he wanted to be away and home to England and Audrey. For the hundredth time, Gideon thought of how she'd looked that last night at Baddingly. He gazed northward and tried to imagine what she was doing.

* * *

Fresh from the potting sheds, Audrey found the servants whispering in clusters. They fell silent as she entered the kitchen, staring at her with solemn eyes. She realized, even before she noticed tears in the eyes of one of the maids, that something was amiss.

Fear shot through her like a bullet. "What's wrong?" Her query was sharp. *Had something happened to Gideon?* She'd tried to keep her mind off the danger he was in, while dedicating her prayers to his safety.

She stood still as a path opened for Mrs. Pradle. The housekeeper said quietly, "It's Lady Chartley, miss. They found her and her poor baby drowned in the Stepney Pond a short time ago."

Audrey frowned. "Diane?" She was shaking, and allowed Mrs. Pradle to put her in a chair. She stared dazedly about at the concerned faces, then found her voice. "But how—?"

"It was late last night. Lady Chartley took her baby and slipped out of the house. She went through the woods and drowned herself, and the child, too, poor thing. Word came from Whitfeld just this minute."

"I must go to Victoria," Audrey murmured. After thanking them all, she went to see what might be required of her.

Lady Matilda Offutt, from neighboring Rosedale, was the only one of the women who attended the funeral. "Perhaps Kit will feel better if I'm there," she told Audrey.

Lady Offutt was pleasantly surprised to see Sir Malcolm Motley, a mere acquaintance, at the cemetery, and driving his grays. She took him home for lunch, along with Pinky Tadburn and Lord Farquar Fulverton, who had driven down from London for the sad occasion, extending the hospitality of Rosedale for a few days. Pinky and Lord F were only too pleased to accept, but Motley declined, saying he was situated at the Red Bull and would, if he might, drive over again in the near future.

Paden was relieved when Motley refused. "Never liked that man," he confided to his mama and two friends. "What's more, Gideon don't like him, either."

Pinky Tadburn nodded agreement. "Man's a dashed card shuffler; can't leave 'em alone. Have no use for him, m'self. Should be fair, though. It was good of him to come to the funeral." Pinky became aware that Lord Fulverton was blinking, a sure sign he wanted to say something. "What is it, Farq?" he asked kindly.

"Good judge of horses," his lordship screeched in a voice rusty from disuse. He rolled his eyes at Lady Offutt, as if begging her pardon for speaking in her presence. Actually, he was quite at ease in her company; it was with young women his own age that Farquar was rendered mute.

Matilda smiled fondly at the young man. "You're right," she said. "No one is a better judge of horseflesh than Motley. Not since my Gerald died." Her son opened his mouth to protest, and she threw up her hand. "Very well, Paden, not counting Gideon St. Aubin. But even you must admit that Motley knows horses."

The afternoon of the funeral, the sky was dark and a cold drizzle made the trees drip. A fog came through the woods as night fell, and Victoria waited by the fire with Audrey.

Audrey couldn't help noticing the tiny crease that came and went in the middle of Toria's forehead. The strain of waiting—for surely Chartley would come—showed in the way the girl clasped her hands together.

They hadn't spoken what was loudest in their minds: Kit Hartwell was free now, and soon he would come, and something would be settled. At last they heard sounds of arrival in the hall, and their waiting was ended, for Kit stood in the doorway.

He removed his hat and stared at Victoria without smiling. "No, Audrey, don't go," he murmured. "I just wanted to say goodbye to Victoria before I left for London. I wasn't going to stop, but found myself unable to resist the gateposts of Baddingly." He smiled then, a tired little grimace, and a dry sob broke from Victoria.

"Don't cry, Toria," Kit said, and her name was a caress in his mouth. "Don't you see that there is nothing we can say *now*, except goodbye?"

If Victoria heard his faint emphasis on the "now," she gave no sign, but stood frozen, gazing at Kit as he did her, with Audrey watching them both. Then Kit wrenched himself out of the room and was gone, the door slamming behind him. Victoria collapsed sobbing on the sofa.

Audrey ran to her. "Toria! Don't cry. Chartley will return. He *can't* say anything—it's too soon."

Victoria grabbed Audrey's hands. "Don't you see? He feels guilty. *As I do!* Oh, the times I've wished Diane dead. Never in so many words, but the thought was there. I've asked myself over and over why I didn't let her drown that day."

Toria shook her head when Audrey would have spoken. "Diane has taken him from me again and this time it's forever!" She arose and walked across the room to gaze out at the stormy night.

Almost at once she turned violently. "Kit will never come to me now. It's his damned honor again. How I hate that word. No!" Her voice rose. "Don't touch me! What do you know, Audrey? Everything's fine for you. Gideon loves you; you'll marry him and live happily here at Baddingly." Her tears broke at last, and when Audrey embraced her, Victoria allowed herself to be held while she shook with sobs.

As Audrey hugged the girl, she closed her eyes. How little Toria knew. *Nothing* was fine between herself and Gideon. This present moment, however, was not the time for such a disclosure. She escorted Victoria up the stairs and popped her into bed, preparing a small dosage of laudanum. Victoria refused it, saying she'd take it later, if she needed to.

After reporting to her aunt that Victoria was resting at last, Audrey laid herself in her own bed and watched the moving shadows cast on the ceiling by the dying fire. When she blew out the night candle, it was as if her every chance at happiness had been extinguished as completely as that small, flickering flame.

17

At the Red Bull, just as Sir Malcolm finished changing for an early dinner, Mrs. Simpkins brought news of a strange arrival at the country inn.

It was, the landlady reported, Miss Victoria St. Aubin, along with her maid, seeking shelter while the smith fixed her broken carriage wheel. Miss St. Aubin was hiding in her room, fearful, apparently, of being recognized.

Motley schooled his face to polite interest and begged Mrs. Simpkins to tell him more. Inside his head, thoughts spun round and round. Here was Gideon St. Aubin's sister. Should he make some excuse to see her? Could he use her in his scheme against Huxford? No, it was the marquis himself whom he planned to lure into a trap when he returned from France. That was—according to Lady Holland—where Huxford had gone. It was an open secret that he was taking two British agents across the channel.

Retrieving a freshly ironed handkerchief from the pile brought by Mrs. Simpkins, Motley affected extreme boredom and encouraged his hostess to tell him about Miss St. Aubin's arrival at the Red Bull.

"The young lady," she divulged, just as Jeremy Stubbs walked into the room, "is evidently embarked on an elopement. According to what Bridget Neely, her maid, told me, Miss St. Aubin is headed for London to convince Mr. Christopher Hartwell, Viscount Chartley, to marry her out of hand and only hours after the man has buried his wife and child."

"Interesting," Motley said. "But I shall honor the young lady's wishes and keep out of sight. I certainly don't wish to embarrass her. Let my presence here remain a secret.

Ah—Jeremy, I need nothing more. You may seek your dinner. As for mine—" He turned to Mrs. Simpkins once more. "Do you suppose, good lady, that I might have mine served here in my room?"

Assured that his dinner would be forthcoming, Motley turned to gaze out the windows. He'd thought of abducting Miss St. Aubin, but only for a moment. No, it was Audrey Soames-Taylor he wanted. She would be the perfect lure to bring Gideon St. Aubin to the cottage in Madsen Lane. He would eat and then make his play. Just about dark would be right. He knew that Miss Taylor always walked in the back paths of the home wood between Baddingly Castle and Rosedale. Motley knew because, twice before, he'd spied on her. Yes, this was going to work. The blood raced through his veins like warm wine. This was the biggest gamble of his life.

It was Audrey's habit to work on her petit point every day just before tea. Discovering a note next to her embroidery frame, she picked it up, saw her name, and hurriedly perused it.

"Dearest Audrey," Victoria had written. "I won't be joining you and Aunt Letty at tea, nor for dinner this evening. I'm taking the carriage, as I've decided to spend a day or two with Lady Matilda. Please forgive the unkind things I said last evening. Love, Victoria. P.S. I know things will work out very soon for Kit and me. P. P. S. I'm taking Bridget."

Telling herself nothing could be better for Victoria than the congenial atmosphere of Rosedale, Audrey drew a breath of relief and went to sit with her aunt.

"Why don't you drive over to Rosedale, too, Audrey dear?" Lady Marpleby suggested. "It would do you a world of good. Don't worry about me. I have Egbertt to keep me company."

At Audrey's smile, Letty's face softened and she reached for her niece's hand. "I know, my dear, that I have you to thank for bringing poor Higglesby up to scratch. Yes, I'm very content to marry him, and I'm happy for you and Gideon. Kit will return to Victoria in a few weeks." Gradually, Lady M's face fell into a sorrowful mold and she sighed. "It's not something one would want to say aloud, and I wouldn't except to you, my love. Poor Diane's death—yes, and the baby's—can only be a blessing." There were tears in her eyes, but she hurriedly wiped them away. "Now," she said. "Get yourself over to Rosedale. Take the governess cart if you don't want to walk."

Audrey allowed herself to be persuaded. "No, I'll walk," she said. "However, I don't like to leave you sentenced to your bedchamber," she said.

"Pooh! Egbertt and I won't miss you. You'll only be in the way."

Shaking her head and smiling, Audrey kissed her aunt and left, charged with messages for the Offutts.

Dusk gathered in the trees and night shadows loomed as Audrey hurried through the back woods, headed for Rosedale. Not usually fanciful, she jumped and cringed when a late-homing sparrow-hawk swooped directly in front of her face. It was nerves, nothing more, she told herself, resisting the urge to look back over her shoulder, imagining headless horsemen, eyes in the trees, blue-painted druids lurking all around her. She smiled but couldn't help increasing her pace. She was almost running now.

She gasped when Sir Malcolm Motley stepped out of the undergrowth before her, blocking the path. Audrey's heart almost stopped and she threw up her head. "What are you doing here, Sir Malcolm?" she asked.

She could see the strange glitter in his eyes. For once Motley wasn't hiding behind a gambler's mask.

"I'm afraid I must ask you to come with me, Miss Soames-Taylor. My curricle is hidden in the next grove of trees."

Anger suffused Audrey, almost swamping her fear. "And why should I do that?"

Sir Malcolm smiled. "Because if you don't, I shall make it very uncomfortable for you. As you can see, it will be dark soon. I might knock you over the head and tie your

wrists and ankles and hide you in the floor of my curricle."

Audrey swallowed. "To—to what purpose, may I ask?"

Motley straightened. Audrey thought she'd never seen
anyone with a more menacing aspect. "You are my bait for
Gideon St. Aubin. I'd laid careful plans, but the marquis
left sooner than I expected. I've rented a small house just
over in Kent. It's not far. Less than an hour's drive—some
twelve miles. I'll hold you there, and Huxford will come
to rescue you, bringing the twenty thousand pounds ransom I shall demand in my note. Come!" He grasped her
arm and tried to drag her down the path.

Audrey screamed, jerked away, and ran as fast as she
could. Before she could escape, Motley gave chase and
grabbed her. She fought, slapping, kicking, scratching, furious that he would lay hands on her. Cursing, he cuffed
her on the side of the head and shoved her roughly to the
ground. She lay stunned, not really hurt but unbelieving.
This couldn't be happening to her!

Breathing heavily, Motley bent over her. "Miss Taylor,
don't resist me. I'm a desperate man. Give me trouble and
I will kill Gideon St. Aubin when he delivers my twenty
thousand pounds."

Something twisted inside Audrey. She clamped her teeth
shut and mutely allowed herself to be pulled upright. An
ugly violence was evident in Motley's manner: witness the
ringing in her head. If she'd been afraid before, she was
terrified now.

"Will you come quietly, or shall I tie your hands and
feet?" Motley asked.

"I—I will go with you," Audrey said.

Motley's lips thinned. "Yes, I thought that threat to your
fiancé would ensure your cooperation."

Sir Malcolm urged her into the waiting carriage and
climbed in beside her, untied the reins, lowered his hands
to give his grays the office, and they were off. Within five
minutes they'd gained the highroad. Flying past the
wrought-iron gates of Rosedale, Audrey gasped as she
caught sight of three riders coming down the tree-lined avenue to the road. Paden Offutt, Pinky Tadburn, and Lord

Fulverton! She shot an agonized glance at her captor. Had he noticed them?

He had, for he said, "You must pray that your young friends did not recognize us, Miss Taylor. I wouldn't care to have them meddle in my affairs. It might prove dangerous for them." He laughed then, the first time Audrey had ever heard him do so, and the high raspy sound sent a shiver up her spine.

Lord Farquar Fulverton was cantering out of Rosedale's gates with his friends Pinky and Paden on his way to the local pub, when a passing carriage caught his attention. As loquacious with his male companions as he was silent in the presence of females, he exclaimed, "Those were Motley's grays! And Miss Soames-Taylor was riding beside him in his curricle!"

"No, Farq," Pinky said. "Couldn't have been!" By the merest chance, Pinky had been speaking to Paden and hadn't seen the curricle, its team, or its passenger when it passed the gate.

"Yes, it was," Fulverton insisted. "I'd know that team anywhere. Motley's rig, too. Has yellow wheels."

"Lots of curricles have yellow wheels, old man," argued Pinky patiently.

"You're sure?" inquired his lordship. "Did you see it, Paden?"

"Yes, I did," Paden said slowly. "And do you know what I think?"

"What?" they chorused.

"Abduction."

"Abduction?"

Paden tightened his lips and nodded.

"Why?" Fulverton and Pinky asked in unison.

Paden thought long and hard. "Revenge," he pronounced, squinting one eye.

"Revenge?" Pinky was shocked. "Explain," he demanded.

This conversation might have continued for some time had not Lord Fulverton intervened. "Pinky!" he cried. "No time now! Don't you think we should follow?"

Nothing could have suited Paden and Pinky better than

the idea of rescuing Audrey Taylor from the clutches of an abductor. "Get going!" Paden yelled at his two friends. "Don't let them out of your sight." He pointed to a solitary worker still scything grass in the home park. "See that gardener over there? I'll give him a message for m'mother— say she's not to worry, that we'll be back in a day or two. Then I'll follow you."

Pinky Tadburn was horrified. "You're never going to say where we're going!" he exclaimed.

"No!" Paden laughed. "My mother would insist on helping us. I'll fob her off with some story. She'll think we've gone to a mill."

Pinky and Lord Farquar whirled their mounts in pursuit of Sir Malcolm's curricle, while Paden rode along the stone fence and shouted his message to the surprised gardener. He then raced to catch up with his friends.

Almost an hour later, just as the moon rose and the last streak of the westerly sunset disappeared behind them, Motley looked back, still watching for Paden Offutt and his friends. Driving his curricle with consummate skill, Audrey Taylor beside him on the narrow seat, Motley wondered if Jeremy Stubbs had reached Madsen Lane yet. Surely he had.

He looked down at the American girl as she roused herself to ask, "How far is this place you're taking me?"

Motley saw no reason not to tell her the truth. "Another mile or so. We're a little way down from Maidenstone. Are you acquainted with the district, Miss Taylor?"

"No."

Motley slapped the reins against his team's haunches. "We'll be there very soon," he said, feeling satisfied with himself. Huxford would come to rescue Miss Taylor, all right, bringing the twenty thousand pounds ransom, but *he* would be the one who left for France. And who could tell? Huxford might never live to see him go. His impetuous threat to kill the marquis had raised an intriguing notion in his brain.

* * *

Victoria St. Aubin sighed and leaned her elbows on the window casement of her bedchamber at the Red Bull Inn, staring at the stars in the still, cool night. She was glad the clouds had been blown away. The moon was very bright.

By now, she reckoned, Audrey and Aunt Letty thought she was with the Offutts, while Lady Offutt had no idea that she was supposed to be entertaining Victoria.

In spite of her broken wheel, Victoria found her cares dropping away. After learning her carriage wheel wouldn't be ready until morning, she'd resigned herself to a night's sojourn at the Red Bull. Throwing off her worries, Victoria ordered a nice dinner for herself and Bridget. She ate with an appetite she hadn't enjoyed in months, lost in dreams of being with Kit at last.

Now she and Bridget had retired to an early bed. Her maid was sleeping, but Victoria was unable to close her eyes. Since she'd impetuously left home this afternoon, there'd been no time for rational thought. Victoria was having doubts. Even without Audrey's reassuring words, she'd known in her heart that Kit would return for her. Now she realized she couldn't forge ahead with her scheme to follow him to London. She must return to Baddingly and wait. But first . . .

Having decided what to do, Victoria went in search of Mrs. Simpkins and asked for writing materials, inquiring where she might hire a messenger to take a letter to Baddingly. "The castle is near Deaking, Mrs. Simpkins. Perhaps you've heard of it."

"Oh, yes, miss," Mrs. Simpkins assured her. "My sister Sarah is married to Farmer Perkins not three miles beyond the castle. Happens her boy Sidney is here and leaving for home early tomorrow. I'm sure he'd be glad to deliver a letter for you."

Called from his supper, Sidney Perkins said he was delighted to be of service, and stuck the letter Victoria gave him in one pocket and the bright new guinea in the other.

"Now, Sidney," Victoria adjured the tow-headed farm boy, "take this letter to the servant's entrance tomorrow, and tell whoever is there it's not to be given to *anyone* except Miss Audrey. Can you remember that?" she asked.

Assuring miss he could remember anything for a guinea, Sidney rehearsed Audrey's name all the way to Baddingly the next morning. He reached the castle shortly before eight and gave the letter to Annie, the new between-stairs maid.

Annie knew Miss Audrey had left the castle the evening before, but she obeyed Sidney's urgently repeated instructions: The letter must be delivered *only* to her as it was addressed to. Annie carried it straight to Miss Audrey's room and propped the sealed envelope on the bedside table to await the girl's return.

The three riders following Motley's curricle held a hurried consultation when at last, soon after dark, the vehicle entered a narrow country lane, plainly visible in the bright moonlight. Paden and Lord Fulverton dismounted and went forward to skulk behind some bushes, peering around them to spy on Sir Malcolm and Audrey Taylor.

Much to his disgust, Pinky Tadburn had been elected to stay behind and hold the horses. He was about ready to holler his friends up when they came scrambling around the bend, their faces furious.

Upon being questioned, Paden assured Pinky that it was just as they'd thought. Miss Taylor had been constrained by Sir Malcolm to enter the cottage at the end of the lane, and it made no difference what Pinky might say, and even if there was a very respectable looking country woman there, as well as a little old crone in a mobcap, something was damned smoky!

Pinky had not the least desire to say otherwise and was endeavoring to convince Paden that instead of disagreeing, he felt much the same way, when Lord Farquar Fulverton was heard to inquire if either of them had thought to bring a pistol.

This naturally gave Mr. Offutt and Mr. Tadburn pause, as neither was in the habit of carrying a horse pistol, and certainly not on a jaunt to visit the pub in Deaking.

"For you must know," Lord Fulverton said apologetically, "I don't have one, either, and I'll go odds Motley does."

"Yes, by God!" Paden ejaculated, thunderstruck. It seemed as though they were helpless to effect Miss Taylor's escape. First of all, there was Sir Malcolm, then his man, and third, that great hulk of a farm boy. Without weapons, they had no chance of rescuing Audrey Taylor at all.

"Know what I think?" Paden asked and didn't bother to wait for an answer. "One of us must go up to London for Chartley. Other two remain here on watch. Can't call the local constable. Huxford wouldn't want this abduction noised about."

Lord Fulverton had been nodding his head. "You or Pinky go. I'm staying to look out for Miss Taylor."

Neither Paden nor Pinky wanted to resign in favor of his lordship. "You stay here?" demanded Paden. This was seconded by Pinky's indignant protest. But Paden wasn't through. "Why you? I'm more nearly acquainted with Audrey Taylor than you! As for Gideon—I've known him forever."

"Then remain here with me and send Pinky," Lord F advised calmly. "I'm staying. I was nearly engaged to the girl. I discovered her violet eyes! Man don't get over a thing like that in just a minute!"

18

Dragged roughly inside the cottage, Audrey was shown to the large overhead loft by the widow who owned the place.

Thankful she was relieved of Motley's company at last, she drew a deep breath and said, "Mrs. Flammock, you make a terrible mistake when you believe anything Sir Malcolm Motley says. He forced me into his curricle, to what nefarious purpose beyond ransom I can only guess. I can't imagine what the man has told you in order to gain your cooperation, since it's obvious that your are a respectable woman. What did he tell you? Surely you must know he was lying."

Rose listened quietly enough as Audrey pleaded for her help. Her lips were set in a straight line and she shook her head.

"It's no good trying to cozen me, miss. Sir Malcolm said you'd try to persuade me; said you was a good actress and I must keep up my guard. But I hope I'm a loyal Englishwoman. I refuse to listen to some French spy. Or to help one. No, not ever, and neither will Mr. Stubbs nor my poor son Roscoe. So leave off, miss, do."

Audrey was almost speechless. "I? A spy for the French? Never! Why would I do that? Motley is mad! A French spy, indeed!"

Rose said repressively, "Yes, and that marquis of yours, too. Sir Malcolm said as how the foreign office had him on this case to capture the two of you when your future husband comes back from France."

"That's ludicrous! It's my fiancé who works for the for-

184

eign office, not Motley. Oh, how can I make you believe me?" Audrey cried.

"Well, miss, you can't." Rose put her hands on her hips. It was plain that she was unconvinced. "You're an American after all, and England is at war with your country. Don't my sister Betty have a son across the waters at this very moment, afighting for his country and flag? Yes, and poor Louie may be dead this instant, my very own nephew, and me with a French spy in my house!" Rose left the loft, refusing to listen any longer.

Audrey sat in a chair, drained and exhausted, barely able to think. She'd heard Motley's orders to Jeremy Stubbs; she'd seen the ransom note handed over.

Now Jeremy was on his way to Castle Baddingly. When Gideon arrived from France, that note would be delivered, and sooner or later it would bring her fiancé to this trap in Madsen Lane.

Audrey shuddered and stifled a sob, trying to control her fear. Gideon mustn't die! What should she do? she asked herself numbly. What *could* she do?

Audrey's small candle had burned half down by the time she was summoned downstairs to share Motley's dinner. She forced herself to eat, trying to reply to the man's conversation, thinking all the while of the scheme she'd hatched.

She knew Gideon would come as soon as he returned from France and learned of her plight. Her terror had previously diminished; now it returned in full force. She was certain that Motley planned to kill the man she loved.

There was the menacing way he spoke Gideon's name, his gloating air. Once, he choked with laughter—that erie, high-pitched laughter—murmuring, "What I'd give to see his face when Stubbs hands him the note I wrote."

Recalled to himself by the way Audrey was staring, he curled his lip and added, "But I shall see him myself when he brings the money, won't I?" He laughed again harshly and sipped his wine. "What do I care how he looks? I'll have his twenty thousand!"

Audrey remained silent while Mrs. Flammock poured

her tea. Steeling herself, she said, "You don't know it, Sir Malcolm, but I'm a very rich woman. Let's you and I strike a bargain. Leave Huxford out of this. Who knows how soon he will come? In the meantime, I have no desire to spend that time waiting in your upper room. I'll give you my note of hand and a letter to Drummond, my English banker. You can cash it and be out of the country in hours."

Something in the way she made the offer, a sense of certainty, perhaps her flat, businesslike tone, seemed to convince Motley that she was sincere, that she actually had the money. He looked at her with an avaricious glitter.

Audrey waited, allowing her captor to assimilate her proposal. Then delicately, when she felt the timing was right, she sweetened the pot. "And instead of twenty thousand pounds, shall we say thirty?" Her voice was perfectly even, her eyes steady on his.

Motley prided himself on his poker face. There was nothing in his gaze or his manner that might reveal how seductive he found the notion of taking money from Gideon St. Aubin's fiancée. And such a sum! Before the silence dragged out too long, he drawled, "Just how rich are you, Miss Soames-Taylor?"

Only a slight lift of her chin betrayed what Audrey thought of such a question. She set her eyes on his and replied in one succinct word. "Very." This was punctuated by the elevation of one curved brow.

Motley had no reason to doubt the girl. He hadn't previously considered whether or not Miss Soames-Taylor was possessed of a fortune. An unpleasant quirk drew one corner of his mouth downward. Trust Huxford to discover an heiress who was rich and beautiful into the bargain. She must care a great deal about him, to offer so much. Thirty thousand pounds was a staggering sum. Motley leaned back in his chair to relish the situation. How much would this girl pay in order to avoid a confrontation—quite possibly fraught with danger—between Huxford and himself?

"Why," he asked idly, "should I settle for thirty thousand when I could have it and you, too?"

Startled eyes the color of plums—the girl really was

beautiful—flew to his, and Motley knew she had anticipated the question.

"Yes," Sir Malcolm continued smoothly. "I see you've
guessed what I mean." Abruptly he laid down his bluff. "If
I refrain from ambushing Huxford, will you come away
with me? Live under my protection? To what lengths will
you go to protect Gideon St Aubin? . . . To avoid this—
meeting I've set up?"

The girl turned pale and looked away. Motley was content to leave Audrey to her thoughts for a while. He
sprawled in his seat and reflected on the dilemma she was
in. A sudden thrill, an ecstatic chill mixed with flashes of
danger took possession of him, and once again he experienced the sense of release that came when he staked all,
everything, on one turn of the cards. Even though this
wasn't a real gamble, the American girl thought it was.
She thought she was being asked to wager herself and her
fortune to ensure the safety of the man she loved.

A glint of admiration crept into Motley's gaze. She was
hiding her feelings very well. Instinctively she had
dropped her eyes to conceal her thoughts from him. How
many times had he shielded himself in just that way? She
was in perfect control and preserving her composure, too.
For an amateur, she was doing splendidly.

It didn't occur to Audrey that Motley had ascribed her
equanimity to control. She wasn't controlled; she was par-
alyzed. She kept her eyes averted. She didn't want him to
see the revulsion she felt, or the fear—the wrenching,
twisting, all-pervasive fear. There was no question, she
could never let Motley touch her. And Gideon would
rather be dead—she knew he would. Perhaps he didn't
love her, but he would never countenance such a sacrifice
to save his life.

But, she thought, she could lie to Motley. She could *say*
she'd go with him. She didn't mind lying to a man of Motley's stamp.

She straightened and met Motley's gaze. "Agreed," she
said in a strong, tight voice.

Motley threw up his head. *Called,* by God! The chit had
called him!

Before Sir Malcolm could speak, Audrey had changed the stakes. "Wait," she told him, "there are stipulations."

A light of pure amusement glimmered behind Motley's smile. He was delighted with her. How well, how *very* well, she'd played this hand. What a little gambler she would have made, under his tutelage! What a swath they could have cut across Europe in the gambling salons. Her money and his expertise, an unbeatable combination. It was tempting. He saw himself at a crowded table overflowing with his winnings, Audrey dressed in a Parisian gown, her hand placed on his shoulder, lending support and encouragement, joining her luck to his as she had once done for Paden Offutt. Yes—tempting.

"What are they—these stipulations of yours?" he asked lazily. Not that it mattered. This hand was almost over. He only half listened while Audrey said he must agree to leave England for good.

"And this must be an—an arrangement of—*convenience* in the strictest sense of the word," she said. "Until we are out of the country."

Motley cocked an amused eye at her. What an innocent she was! What man would resist taking her once she was at his mercy? But this was merely a hypothetical situation. Motley had a strong disinclination to invite anyone—even Audrey Soames-Taylor—to share in his dream no matter how briefly. No. Shining schemes of breaking casino banks paled alongside the cherished dream he had of a confrontation between Gideon St. Aubin and himself. If he agreed to take the girl and her money, he knew he'd always regret being cheated of that final resolution. After all, it was St. Aubin's money he wanted. And more and more he was coming to believe that nothing would satisfy him like taking St. Aubin's life. He fingered the trigger of the small pistol he carried in his pocket.

Abruptly he said, "No, my dear. It is with sincere regret that I find I must decline both of your attractive offers—that of your money and your charming self." He watched as Audrey unsuccessfully tried to hide her relief.

"And now, my dear, please allow Mrs. Rose to escort you back upstairs . . . Hold up. What's that noise?"

There came to their ears, just outside the dining room window, several scuffling sounds, accompanied by grunts and a bitten-back oath.

"Ah, excuse me, Miss Soames-Taylor. I believe there's a disturbance of some sort outside. Can it be that young Paden Offutt and his friends saw us passing Rosedale, after all? You won't try to escape, will you?" This last question was academic, for Audrey had a guard.

At a gesture from Motley, the large figure of Roscoe Flammock emerged from the shadows beyond the fireplace. He stood and stared at Audrey. "Guard!" said Sir Malcolm, as if to a dog. He patted the farm boy on the shoulder and left the cottage.

Roscoe fixed such a suspicious gaze on Audrey that she was sure he'd throttle her if she moved an inch. She had no intention of doing so, but strained to hear what was going on through the walls of the cottage. There was a curse, a muffled shout, a deafening gunshot, and then silence.

Audrey caught her breath, and when her lungs were about to explode, the door was flung wide, and Lord Farquar Fulverton came through it, supporting a white-faced Paden Offutt. She saw blood on Paden's upper leg, seeping through his fingers where he gripped his wound.

"Paden!" Audrey exclaimed. Rising from her chair, she would have gone to him had not a low whistle reached her ears. Her eyes flew to Roscoe, who shook his head watchfully.

Sir Malcolm, who had entered the house in his prisoners' wake, snapped his fingers, and Roscoe subsided.

"So!" Motley smiled, holding them under his pistol. "Here we have two brave knights to the rescue. No, Fulverton! Don't put Offutt down. Take him upstairs. You can tend to his wound there. Miss Soames-Taylor, it seems you shall have company in your lonely chamber tonight."

Rose Flammock, wringing her hands, rushed forward from the kitchen. "Let me help the poor wounded young man up the stairs," she cried.

Motley refused to allow it. "No, Rose. Miss Soames-Taylor can care for him. Get her some bandages and soap and water. You stay belowstairs."

"But he's bleeding that bad, sir!" Rose protested.

A flash of anger exploded behind Motley's eyes. "No!" he said, then, with what seemed a supreme effort, he controlled himself enough to smile at her again.

At the foot of the stairs, Audrey and Lord Fulverton were supporting a half-swooning Paden between them.

As she handed Audrey the supplies, Rose called her attention to the small jar of basillicum powder she'd included. "Here, miss. I think it's only a flesh wound. Clean it, sprinkle the powder on, and bind it up tight."

Audrey thought the woman seemed to be trying, by an expressive look, to indicate that she'd come to believe her story. Was it possible, she wondered, that she now had a friend belowstairs? Smiling gratefully at Rose, she turned to help Lord Fulverton get Paden up the steep staircase. The last thing Audrey heard from below was Sir Malcolm telling Rose to lock the loft door.

Paden had now swooned and was bleeding profusely. They quickly laid him on the narrow cot, which, along with a straight chair, comprised the only furniture in the loft.

The long room where Audrey had already spent a solitary hour had no windows. The area was not partitioned, being one large space. At each end of the house were placed horizontal slits for ventilation, for which she was thankful.

Asking Lord Fulverton to hold the candle, Audrey slit Paden's pant leg and studied the wound. The ball had plowed a furrow across the outside flesh of Paden's right thigh. As she applied wet compresses, Audrey could see the bleeding was about stopped. After sprinkling the wound liberally with the medicine, she bound a dry compress against it with strips of cloth.

As she tended Paden's wound, Audrey was thankful for Lord Fulverton's help. Silently, and with alacrity, he obeyed her every command, handing her the scissors, moving the candle closer, or tearing cloth as she needed more bandages. Now, as Paden seemed to slip into a restful sleep, Audrey sat back exhausted on the chair by the narrow bed. She sighed, raised warm violet eyes to Lord Fulverton, and smiled. "Thank you," she said.

Lord F blinked, drew several deep breaths, hyperventilated, and fainted dead away at Audrey's feet.

His lordship came to his senses with his head in his idol's lap. Audrey was seated on the floor, bathing his forehead with a damp cloth. Each time Lord Fulverton opened his eyes and gazed up at her, he began hyperventilating again.

Audrey soothed him, begging him to keep his eyes closed. Fulverton lay quietly awhile, then gingerly sat up as Audrey directed, carefully keeping his eyelids shuttered.

When he seemed calmer, Audrey suggested softly, "Now keep your eyes shut, your lordship."

Lord F nodded and Audrey saw that he had relaxed. It was actually quite pleasant, she thought, sitting here on the floor, taking time to breathe. Paden slept peacefully close by.

After a moment, she said, "Tell me, my lord, why does it disturb you to look at me?"

Immediately, Farquar began gasping and breathing heavily.

"No, no," Audrey cried. "Don't do that, I beg you." She handed him the damp cloth, which he clapped hurriedly against his forehead.

When he seemed stable once more, Audrey tried again. "Remember, keep your eyes closed," she cautioned. "We shall play a little game."

Lord Fulverton liked games. He had six sisters, most of whom were older than he, and he'd always played games with them. Unlike most men closely surrounded by women, his lordship enjoyed being the center of attention. His father had died when Farquar was five, and he was reared by an adoring set of females who cosseted him, while at the same time professing to place the greatest reliance upon his masculine guidance, always asking in the most flattering way for his advice and even, on occasion, taking it.

Farquar motioned that he understood Audrey's instructions. He would keep his eyes closed.

Audrey drew a relieved breath. She must do something if Fulverton was going to faint every time he looked at her. That wouldn't do if he was to help her nurse Paden for—for *however* long they might be here.

"Now, then," Audrey soothed, and inspired by her good fairy, uttered the magic word. "Why do we not pretend I am your *sister,* Lord Fulverton? You have sisters, do you not?" Audrey prayed a kind Providence had granted his lordship sisters.

"Yes," came the strangled reply. His lordship, ever prudent, was careful to keep his eyes tightly closed.

"Good!" declared Audrey. "That's wonderful! Now, perhaps you might tell me why, before I was your sister, you couldn't bear to look at me?"

"Too—too beautiful!" came his lordship's strained response.

Audrey bit her lip. Then, in a bracing and sisterly tone, she said, "Oh, but that is nonsense! Are none of your sisters beautiful?"

Lord Fulverton opened his eyes—slowly and experimentally—and after only four or five false starts was able to look directly at Audrey. He nodded. "Yes," came his answer at last. "Cecily and Margaret are especially beautiful, though not, I think, quite as beautiful as you."

Lord F leaned close and gazed dispassionately and quite objectively into Miss Taylor's countenance, which she was striving to preserve in some semblance of gravity. Suddenly he half-closed one eye and pursed his lips in thought. "I have it!" he said. "You would be my sister between those two, or possibly between Margaret and Saraphonia? No! You'd come between Cecily and Margaret, all right. Three years between them—you'd fit nicely there. Strange," he mused.

Audrey swallowed her mirth. "Strange, Lord Fulverton?"

"Strange how you affected me so strongly before. Can't usually talk to girls. But I never fainted before."

Audrey nodded. Words had failed her, but not, it seemed, Lord F. After a moment's cogitation, he nodded wisely and fixed her with an imperative stare. "Won't do!

Won't do at all," his lordship told Audrey in a tone any of his sisters would have recognized on the instant.

"What will not do, Lord Fulverton?"

"Now, see? There you go again! Can't call me *Lord Fulverton*! Man's sister don't call him *Lord Fulverton*! Call me Fumbo."

"F . . . F . . . ?"

"Fumbo! Family name. All m'sisters call me Fumbo! Got six y'know." His lordship put a hand under Audrey's arm and hauled her unceremoniously to her feet. "I'll call you Audrey. Always liked that name. Don't think I ever heard it before, but if I did, I liked it."

"Th—thank you," Audrey murmured, biting her lip to stop the quiver in her voice.

His lordship turned lively eyes upon her, smiled, and raised an admonishing finger. "Thank you, *Fumbo!*" he corrected.

"Yes, of course. F . . . Fumbo," Audrey managed, and watched as her new-found brother went to thump on the door of their prison.

"Mrs. Rose!" he yelled. "Oh, there you are! Do you suppose I could have some bread and cheese, Mrs. Rose?" he called through the door. He grinned over his shoulder at Audrey. "Devilish hungry, y'know. Missed m'supper," he added, by way of explanation.

19

The night had been most frustrating for Mr. Pinky Tadburn. Attempting a short cut after leaving Madsen Lane, he'd lost his way and wandered about the Kentish hedgerows until he was sure he'd never see civilization again.

Seven miles short of London, his horse cast a shoe, and Mr. Tadburn was forced to dismount and lead him to the next posting house, which he reached at daybreak.

The horse they hired him was short in the wind, but Pinky was able to reach town shortly after seven. Only then did it occur to him that he had no idea of Chartley's direction. He rode to his own chambers after remembering that never yet had he asked his man Limping a question he couldn't answer. Having no occasion to believe Limping would fail him now, he heard without surprise the man's precise instructions for reaching his lordship's rooms in Albermarle Street.

Sooner than he'd expected, Pinky was confronting an impatient Kit Hartwell. "What the devil do you mean by telling my man it's a matter of life or death and concerns Huxford's fiancée?" demanded the viscount, coming down the stairs half-dressed and looking like he'd been out late and drinking. "Where is she? Where is Audrey Taylor?"

Pinky whipped out a lavender handkerchief and, mopping his delicate brow, uttered in stricken accents, "Oh, how can I tell you? It's too dreadful for words. There's no time to lose." Then, to Chartley's horror, he burst into tears.

In Chartley's parlor, overcoming his emotional outburst with a cup of strong tea, Pinky Tadburn completed his re-

cital of Miss Soames-Taylor's abduction. "So Paden said I
was to lope off and find you, Chartley, since Huxford was
out of the country. He and Fulverton are watching the cottage to see they don't take the girl away." Pinky fell silent,
gazing expectantly at the viscount who had lapsed into a
brown study.

"You say this henchman of Motley's rode away last
night?" Kit asked. "He's probably creeping about Baddingly Castle now, waiting for Gideon's return."

Kit surged to his feet and decisively smacked his fist
into his other palm. "Pinky, we're going to Baddingly ourselves. And don't I wish we'll find Gideon has arrived in
the night? I know! We'll take the ransom money with us.
We can ride round to Drummond's and get it on our way
out of town. Come! There's no time to lose."

The Drummond bankers were only too happy to accom-
modate Chartley's request for the twenty thousand, and he
and Pinky were able to arrive at Baddingly Castle shortly
before ten.

Lady Marpleby, evidently ignorant of Audrey and Victoria's whereabouts, said the girls were visiting Rosedale.
"Now you must have some breakfast in the hall. I shall order something substantial," she said.

Observing that Pinky had opened his mouth, Kit trod on
his toe, telling him on the way downstairs that they'd better withhold the news of Audrey's abduction until Gideon
arrived. "He can tell Lady M if he wants to," Kit said.

Jeremy Stubbs had wrestled with his doubts all the way
to Baddingly. Even after he made certain that the Marquis
of Huxford hadn't yet returned home, Jeremy couldn't rid
himself of the notion that he was delivering a genuine ransom note and that Huxford was no more a French spy than
he was. Learning of the marquis's absence had been a simple matter of knocking on the door at daybreak, asking for
Lord Huxford, and allowing the porter to ring a peal over
his head for his impudence in coming to the front of the
castle instead of the back. "It's the servant's entrance for
you, my man," the porter huffed. "And when the master
returns it's still a question of *if* 'e will receive yer. W'ich

I doubt he will, you being who you are and 'im a markis and that. When he does come, you can apply for a h'interview at the back door like the rest of us." And so saying, he slammed the door in Jeremy's face.

Jeremy retired to the high road and spent the rest of the morning watching for the marquis. It wasn't until ten o'clock that a rider came into view who matched the description he had of Huxford. Having made up his mind what to do, Jeremy followed his lordship right into the stables at Baddingly, prepared to carry out the plan he'd worked out during the night. Jeremy only hoped the marquis was a reasonable man.

The marquis walked into the castle just as Lord Chartley and Pinky Tadburn finished eating. He was accompanied by a small man dressed in black who was obviously a servant.

Kit hurried forward to grip the hand offered by his friend, crying, "Huxford! Thank God you've come. Wait 'til you hear—"

"I have heard, and I don't think you can know the whole," Huxford told him grimly, handing his coat and hat to Twickem. These small, customary actions calmed him somewhat. Panic had gripped him when Jeremy Stubbs had given him Motley's ransom note and revealed the great danger his beloved was in. He pushed his fear back. He must *think* if he was going to rescue Audrey.

Huxford turned his attention to the young man by Kit's side. Pinky, crimson faced and highly agitated, was plucking wildly at the viscount's sleeve. "Pinky," he demanded, "what do you know about this affair?"

Pinky found his voice. Pointing a finger at Jeremy Stubbs, he croaked, "It's him! *He* was at Madsen Cottage. He's Motley's creature!"

"Here, now!" came Jeremy's indignant rejoinder. "I'm not nobody's *creature!* I *was* working for Sir Malcolm Motley, who tricked me into helping him abduct the marquis's promised. But no more! Too much smoke, I tells myself, and there's bound to be fire! And there was. Smoke, I mean. So whilst I was riding to give my employer's note to the marquis here, I did me some thinking. I decided Sir Malcolm weren't no British agent trying, as he tells me and Rose Flammock—her as owns Madsen Cottage—to capture two French spies. That's what Motley claimed his lordship and Miss Soames-Taylor was. So, when the marquis arrived just now, I walks into his stables bold as brass, gives him the note, and tells him what I suspect. Lord Huxford convinced me as how I was right to trust him. So now, I'm going to help him rescue Miss Soames-Taylor, and Rose Flammock and her family, for I know Motley is dangerous and on his last legs."

Gideon had taken the plate of food Twickem handed him and, standing by the sideboard, wolfed down kippers and eggs, observing the effect of Jeremy's speech on Kit and Pinky as he ate. He swallowed and said to Pinky, "So you brought Chartley the news of my fiancée's abduction? How did you learn of it?"

Pinky very willingly launched into an account of how he and Paden, along with Farquar Fulverton, had trailed Sir Malcolm and Miss Taylor into Kent. "And I left them there, sir, keeping watch on the house. I only hope they haven't been discovered."

"Yes—so do I," the marquis replied. He laid aside his plate and turned to Chartley. "I've got to ride to London for the ransom," he said.

Kit hefted his saddlebags. "Got it right here."

Huxford clapped his friend on the shoulder. "Good man!" he exclaimed. "That will save several hours. Now then: Kit, I wish we could all go into Kent, but I'm afraid I must ask you to undertake another mission."

At Chartley's questioning look, Huxford hurriedly recounted what he knew—intelligence he'd gleaned from Jeremy Stubbs—of his sister's stay at the Red Bull and her destination.

"Victoria was coming to London? But why? I thought she was at Rosedale!" Kit exclaimed.

"No. It seems she had a notion she could persuade you to elope." Amusement at his sister's unmaidenly determination caused Gideon's mouth to quirk in a brief smile.

Kit was dumbfounded. "Persuade me to elope? What

for? I was coming to Baddingly in a few days with a special license—"

"Did you tell her so?" interrupted the marquis, reaching for his riding coat and shrugging into it.

"No! Not the same day I buried my wife and child! What girl would want a marriage proposal at a time like that?"

"My sister, apparently," Gideon said dryly, jamming his hat on his head. He headed for the front of the great hall, the others trailing him.

"And she's on her way to London?" Kit demanded. "Now?"

"Evidently." Gideon glanced back at Jeremy Stubbs for confirmation.

"Little gudgeon!" muttered Kit fiercely. "To come all that way alone! Oh, won't I *shake* her when I get my hands on her." He looked at Gideon. "You're right—I wish I could go with you, but until I know where Toria is—"

"Quite right. You'll see my sister restored to Lady M here, and then—"

Kit pulled on his gloves. "Then I'll come to Madsen Lane."

Huxford nodded agreement and departed, taking Pinky Tadburn and Jeremy Stubbs, and leaving Chartley to search for Victoria.

At Madsen Cottage, Audrey had new worries. Her relief at learning that Pinky Tadburn had ridden to London to bring Chartley was tempered by the restraints she found necessary to place on Lord Fulverton and Paden Offutt. Paden had awakened almost free of fever, clear headed, and delighted to be one of a party where abductions, captures, shootings, imprisonment, and the threat of imminent death were the order of the day.

"It's beyond anything great!" he kept exclaiming, until Audrey wanted to strangle him. What was worse, Paden had infected his lordship with a full measure of his misguided enthusiasm.

"To think," Paden said thickly around a huge bite of ham, "we'd have missed all this if we hadn't decided to go

to the pub in Deaking!" He took another bite of his roll.
Rose had been so thankful he wasn't dying of his gunshot
wound that she'd prepared them a sumptuous breakfast.
"Only think how fortunate the timing was," Paden said.

His lordship nodded agreement. "Yes, and I'm not sure
but what it's a lucky thing you fell against the house and
got us caught, Paden. Sleeping in those bushes without
blankets would have been devilish uncomfortable."

They looked at Audrey in surprise when she was no
longer able to smother the rather hysterical laughter rising
in her throat. She lifted her handkerchief to her mouth as
Lord Fulverton reached to thump her heartily on the back.
"There, there, m'dear. You must have swallowed wrong.
Alicia—you remember my youngest sister, Paden. Alicia
is always choking. Take a sip of tea, Audrey," he advised
kindly.

"Here," Paden said. He looked suspiciously from one to
the other, only now becoming aware of his friend's altered
attitude toward Miss Taylor. "That's the second time
you've called her that!"

"And she calls me Fumbo," his lordship imparted, lav-
ishly buttering one of Rose Flammock's flaky rolls.

"But ain't that what your sisters call you?" Paden demanded. "Oh, never mind all that! I'm just glad you can
say two words in front of her; would have been awkward
locked up together if we couldn't talk. Spoiled our fun.
Only I can't think what happened."

"Ain't in love with her anymore," his lordship said simply.

"Oh!" Paden looked blank, then shrugged, eager to get
back to business. "What shall we do first?"

A small flutter of alarm snuffed Audrey's amusement.
She proceeded to deliver a pithy little sermon on the mer-
its of prudence and patience, which found no favor at all
with her auditors.

"Not *do* anything? You're the last person in the world
I'd have thought pudding-hearted," Paden told her.

"Thank you," Audrey uttered faintly.

But Lord Fulverton intervened. "She ain't afraid." He
seemed unable to countenance aspersions cast upon the

courage of someone whom he now perceived to have a place among his nearest and dearest.

"Oh, she ain't, huh? Well, I think she is, else why should she try to persuade us not to plot an escape?"

Paden turned to Audrey and said cajolingly, "You must see how tame it would be to sit here and do nothing?"

Audrey sighed and shook her head.

Paden tried again. He took her hand and said, "I wish you wouldn't try to make me think you'd find it any fun to sit about twiddling our thumbs waiting to be rescued. If only we put our heads together, we can come up with a scheme to confound Motley and gain our freedom. And only think, Audrey, how famous it would be if Chartley came and found us—er—in possession of the field, with the tables turned and Motley locked up here in our stead."

Audrey snatched her hand from his grasp and jumped to her feet, staring at Paden in dismay. "How can you possibly derive any enjoyment from this situation?"

Seeing Paden's astonishment, Lord Fulverton plunged into the breech. "He's right, m'dear. Opportunity like this don't come along all that often."

Tossing aside her napkin, Audrey commenced pacing back and forth between the bed and chair. Once or twice she stopped as if to say something; each time, words failed her, and she resumed pacing. What could she say? What could she do to keep these two from getting themselves killed?

Finally she faced them. "I'm firmly convinced Huxford would say you should wait until Chartley arrives and not attempt this escape by yourselves."

Paden's shoulders slumped and he sank back against the pillows they'd piled on the floor. Miserably, he looked at Audrey. "You're right, of course. I've been trying to ignore the voice in the back of my head telling me Gideon would think it rash—if not completely scatterbrained—to go against Motley's gun when we're unarmed." He shook his head. "But surely there's something we can do."

"Yes," Audrey said. "We can wait."

* * *

Huxford's expression was stern as they left Baddingly. He set his horse into a mile-eating trot. Pinky Tadburn and Jeremy Stubbs followed silently. "We'll come about," he told them, praying they would. "I hope Paden and Fulverton haven't thrown everything into confusion in their attempt to help." He fully expected to arrive and find his young friends captured and locked away with Audrey. But he couldn't worry about Paden and Fulverton. It was Audrey who filled his mind.

For the first time, Gideon had time to think about actually losing her. Terror clutched at him, blinded him, threatening his reason. No, he *couldn't* lose her—couldn't bear it—not after he'd discovered how much he needed her. From the moment he'd seen her, Audrey had captured his soul. He'd thought it nothing more than desire, the strongest he'd ever felt. Now, his highest ambition was to hold her safe, tell her he loved her, wanted to marry her, to hear from her own lips that she loved him. He eased back on the reins, finding it almost impossible not to rush. If Motley had left, taking Audrey—

Gideon shook himself. He must analyze the situation. He didn't think the gambler would leave. The hand wasn't played out yet, and Motley was the type to wait for the last turn of the cards. Madsen Lane was where it would happen, where Gideon would manage to rescue Audrey, or die trying.

Shortly after noon, from behind the concealing screen of a heavy stand of trees, Gideon studied the thatched cottage of Madsen Farm through his field glass. Pinky crouched beside him.

Jeremy had just returned from scouting the barns and outer buildings. He pointed to the steeply pitched roof. "There," he said. "Your young lady is being held in Rose's loft."

The marquis grunted and asked if there were any windows on that floor.

"No, Governor. No windows and only one door," Jeremy said. "I couldn't find your friends. Likely the young gentlemen are being held in the loft, as well. I couldn't see anything of their horses, except some tracks leading to the stable. I think you're in the right of it, m'lord. They've been captured, too."

Gideon nodded. "It's just as we thought," he said, and in a low voice began, once again, to go over their plan. "Pinky, you stay here. Yes, I know that's an unexciting part to play, but you'll help me most by doing that. Can I count on you?" he asked.

Pinky flushed and nodded and Gideon continued his instructions.

"We'll walk in," he told Jeremy, "you holding me under your gun, and carrying what you'll *say* is my only weapon. Motley trusts you; he thinks you still believe he's a British agent. He won't suspect that I've got this handgun in my side pocket." He took out the small, serviceable pistol, thinking of more than one occasion on which he'd used it. As he inspected its priming, he asked, "Jeremy, do you think you could shoot Motley if it became necessary to save my fiancée's life?"

"Oh, aye, Governor, to save her life, or yours, either. Or any of them what lives at Madsen Cottage. I ain't without experience, you see. When I was in the Royal Navy, didn't I follow Captain Wade aboard that Barbary pirate ship off Madagascar? And how about them times in the Indies? I can shoot, Governor, and I will. Don't make no mistake about that."

Gideon smiled and clapped Jeremy on the shoulder. "Good man! Let's go. We're as ready as we'll ever be."

In the cottage loft, Paden had fallen into a heavy sleep after they ate the lunch Rose sent up.

Lord Fulverton laid a spread close to one of the ventilation slits. "Lie down and rest," he told Audrey. "When our rescue comes, we want to be up to anything."

It was a long time before she slept, dreaming she was on a deserted shore where she stood and listened as Huxford called across the dark water. Then she realized Paden was shaking her and the dream was true. She was hearing her fiancé's voice.

A hurried conference took place. The situation had come to a head. Frightened to hear Paden's jumbled schemes, Audrey knew they must be squashed, and she knew exactly how to do it.

"Paden," Audrey said, "you and Fulverton stay here until Gideon needs you. I'm certain that's what he wants you to do. I'm convinced that Motley will not hesitate to kill anyone who gets in his way."

"But Audrey—" Paden began to protest.

"No! Paden, I mean it. No heroics, do you hear?"

"I only want to—"

Audrey interrupted without ceremony. "Yes, to help. The way to do that is stay out of sight. Remain here unless you are called down. Sh! Here comes someone. Fulverton—Fumbo—my reliance is on you. Promise to inject some level-headed thinking into this imbroglio."

"Anything you say, Audrey. Count on me."

"Indeed I do," Audrey said, as Rose Flammock unlocked the door and entered, guarded by her son.

"Miss, oh, miss, they want you!" she cried. "You must come down alone and the boys stay here. Them's Motley's precise orders. I hope and pray no one gets hurt. Why, oh *why,* did I ever think the man could be trusted? He's holding the Marquis of Huxford at gunpoint. Yes, and Mr. Stubbs—Jeremy—slipped me this note; here it is: 'Am now working for Huxford' is what Jeremy wrote. What to do? Oh, *what* to do!"

Audrey's pounding heart threatened to choke her. Gideon was downstairs helpless under Motley's gun. As she'd suspected, this had turned into more than a simple kidnap and ransom case. Motley was out to kill the man she loved.

"We must stay calm, Rose. Now lead the way down, if you please. We may safely trust all to Huxford." Audrey wished she felt as certain as she sounded.

Audrey's first glimpse of her fiancé showed him standing squarely in the middle of the floor, his hands jammed in his coat pockets, lifting his head as she tread the stairs. A flash of his old grin, a reassuring nod of his head, and he demanded, "Are you all right, Audrey?"

Trembling like a bird in a trap, Audrey tried to read the intense look Huxford was giving her.

"I—I'm fine," she managed steadily enough. "Paden was shot last night and he and Lord Fulverton are being held, as I was, upstairs."

"Is Paden well?"

"Yes. Only a flesh wound."

"Silence!" Motley screamed, and waved his pistol.

Nothing about the interview had gone as Sir Malcolm had planned. For one thing, Huxford was here sooner than he expected.

After steeling himself to endure a week at Madsen Cottage, Motley had found himself confronting the marquis, who came strolling in behind Jeremy Stubbs, carrying a saddle bag full of money and demanding to see Miss Soames-Taylor.

Motley had jumped to his feet, grabbed his horse pistol off the table, and cocked and leveled it at Huxford.

But the marquis had seemed as calm as Motley had ever seen him gambling in the clubs or dancing at some great ball. "Motley," he'd muttered in greeting. "I must see Miss Taylor. Is she all right? And where is Paden Offutt and Fulverton?" Huxford had glanced casually about the sitting room of Rose Flammock's cottage, as if it were the most commonplace thing in the world to be down in Kent and bringing a fortune in ransom money.

"All in good time," Motley had snarled, cursing to himself and gritting his teeth. There was none of the fright he had anticipated—none of the desperation he felt Huxford should be suffering upon meeting the man who held the life of his fiancée in his hand.

He had turned to Jeremy Stubbs. "Have you searched him? Where's his gun?"

"Right here, your lordship." Jeremy had handed Gideon's gun to Sir Malcolm and from his inner pocket had produced another which he'd leveled at the marquis. "I took his gun before I brought him in, figuring as how that was best," Jeremy had told Motley, then fallen back to stand beside Rose at the end of Roscoe's bed.

Now, his eyes on Huxford, Motley felt his anger surge. His pistol was pointed at the marquis's heart, and Jeremy Stubbs stood armed and ready.

He slapped his hand flat on the table, making Audrey jump. "Cease this talk at once!" he snarled. "*I* will decide who talks here—you will speak when I give permission. Do you think this is some kind of damned tea party where the participants may converse at their ease? You are my prisoners—totally in my power; you will do well to remember that."

The implicit threat in his ragged voice warned them how close he was to losing control. Audrey jumped again when a nervous crack of laughter broke from Motley. Standing so close to him, she could see that he as shaking, laboring under strong emotions. What would happen if he were suddenly pushed over the edge? The wild glint in his rolling eyes made him look crazed.

"Here is the ransom money," Huxford said calmly, handing over his saddlebags.

"Of course!" Motley cried. "What does twenty thousand pounds mean to you, Huxford, compared with the girl?" He must have realized how shrill he sounded. He stopped and pressed his lips together, trying, Audrey supposed, to compose himself and regain some of his gambler's detachment.

Eyes narrowed on the marquis, Motley laughed wildly and broke into a shrill spate of words. "I've just thought of something very interesting, Huxford. You'd pay anything to see Audrey Taylor safe, wouldn't you? This has never been about money. We both know that. What will you give me for her life? Will you trade your life for hers?"

Huxford glanced once at Audrey, then looked straight at Motley. "I will, yes, if it's necessary." He stood squarely balanced on booted feet with his arms crossed over his chest.

"You're cool," Motley sneered. "Yes, quite cool when confronted with the loss of your money or your life. *Those* you'd willingly give to save her. You love her, I suppose?"

Gideon nodded curtly. "I do."

Motley gave a grunt of satisfaction and smiled thinly. He seemed calmer now. "Oh, you have just shown me your hold card, Huxford. Nothing matters to you except the girl's life. Very well! Since my object in all this has been to reduce you to the ranks of all the have-nots of the world such as myself ..." His voice rose. "I'll take her from you!" He suddenly crouched and swung his pistol toward Audrey.

She screamed and Gideon launched himself through the air.

But something in Sir Malcolm's stance, the way he tensed and twisted toward Audrey, had warned Jeremy.

Just as Kit Hartwell, gun in hand, burst through the door, Jeremy raised his pistol and fired point-blank into Motley's left side, exploding his heart. Gideon and Kit fired almost in the same instant, but Motley was already lying in a crumpled heap on the floor, his blood staining Rose Flammock's hearth rug.

Gideon whirled at a sound from Audrey and leaped forward to catch her, for she had fainted dead away.

She came to on Grannie Flammock's bed. They were all ringed about her. Rose shooed everyone out of the old lady's cubbyhole and closed the curtains behind her. Audrey discovered Huxford kneeling by her side and reached for him. Then at last she was wrapped in his arms, his mouth, his blessed mouth, on hers. "Gideon, Gideon," she cried. "I've been so afraid for you, my love."

"And I you." Gideon was holding her so tightly she couldn't breathe. "You're safe," he added, with a strange little break in his voice. "I want you, Audrey, need you."

Audrey broke into sobs, clinging to him, weeping as she'd wanted to ever since Motley had abducted her from the Baddingly home woods.

Gideon kissed her and let her cry. Then he kissed her again. Audrey struggled to control herself. His breath was warm in her ear as he whispered, "Sh ... sh ..." More lingering kisses, another short bout of tears. Audrey was wiping away the damage when Kit managed to make himself heard.

He knocked on the door frame before pushing the curtains aside. "I hate to interrupt, Gideon, but it's Toria. She's not at the Red Bull, not at Baddingly, and Lady Offutt hasn't seen her. I can't find her anywhere."

20

Motley's attempt to kill Audrey had revealed the extent of his derangement, and the very real specter of Victoria's death at his hands took hold of their minds.

While waiting for the justice of the peace to arrive in Madsen Lane, they made hurried arrangements to leave for Baddingly. "Yes," Gideon said. "We will establish a headquarters there to mount our search for Toria."

As they waited, Audrey repeated everything Sir Malcolm had said concerning Victoria. Jeremy Stubbs recounted what he knew of his former employer's meeting with her, but admitted he had no idea how much truth there was in Sir Malcolm's story of having left Miss St. Aubin safe at the Red Bull. "There's no telling, governor, what the like's of him would do."

This hardly added to their comfort, but at last, the local justice came, took statements, and—when he understood their rush—said they might be on their way.

The afternoon was far gone as they loaded up. The look on Chartley's face as he helped Lord Fulverton put Paden into Motley's curricle drew Audrey to his side. There were no words to express her concern without giving more alarm. She grasped his arm silently and Kit nodded his thanks and bent to kiss her cheek. Then she rode home to Baddingly in Sir Malcolm's curricle, crowded with Paden between her and Pinky Tadburn—who handled the reins. Huxford rode Erasmus alongside the vehicle.

Promising Rose Flammock he would return as soon as the young lady was found, Jeremy mounted Lord Fulverton's sorrel gelding, not bothering to hide his proprietary interest in his late, unlamented employer's rig, having fallen heir to it and the splendid gray team through the machinations of the grateful Marquis of Huxford.

Audrey glanced at Gideon, found his eyes on her, and flushed. He rode beside her like a centaur, masculine, sleekly beautiful. He'd offered his life for her today, had been prepared to kill for her, although Audrey couldn't be glad anyone—even Motley—was dead. She remembered Gideon's kisses—as if he wanted to devour her. Only when Kit had interrupted them had he left off kissing her. And his words: *He needed her.* Hope was like a golden wine, she thought. Had Gideon come to love her? She wanted him, wanted his love, wanted the strength and power of his body.

Beside Gideon rode Chartley, and beyond, Lord Fulverton—dear Fumbo. Audrey drew a deep breath, thinking of Gideon's sister. Kit's face was set, held in lines of worry. Would they find Toria? Was she all right?

When the cavalcade reached Rosedale, Lady Offutt was greatly shocked to learn Victoria was still missing. After assuring herself Paden was all right, she shooed them on their way, promising to send the little *ragamuffin* home if she should appear on her doorstep. "Toria's fine; I know she is. Ten to one she dropped by to visit someone, that old nurse of hers—Pimlot, wasn't it?—lives in the neighborhood of the Red Bull. Or perhaps Kit missed her on her way to London. Don't worry, we'll find her."

They arrived at Baddingly at dusk, and in the library, where he insisted Audrey take a small brandy, Huxford put Twickem in possession of the facts.

Kit stood by the fire, refusing to lay aside his riding coat, saying he was leaving immediately to look into the possibility that Victoria was indeed visiting her old nurse. Twickem had just assured his lordship that Lady Marpleby and Lord Higglesby were in happy ignorance of the unfortunate happenings when Kit stiffened.

There was the commotion of an arrival in the hall. The viscount leaped for the library door, followed closely by Gideon and Audrey. But it was only Lady Offutt, with Lord Fulverton attending Paden, who walked in leaning on a cane. Pinky Tadburn followed.

"These three would give me no peace until we came," her ladyship said, "and, to tell the truth, I couldn't bear waiting for news of Victoria either. Have you told your aunt what has gone forward here?' This last was directed at Audrey, whose attention was diverted by the fact that the porter was opening the front door again.

In the babble of speech about them—Lady Offutt debating with Huxford whether Lady M should be told immediately, and Paden arguing with Fulverton, who insisted on holding his elbow whilst tenderly guiding him toward the library—only two people witnessed Victoria's homecoming.

Audrey pressed her fingers to her lips to keep from crying out. Kit Hartwell stood still as a stone, not moving, even to breathe. His eyes were two coals pinning Toria in her tracks. White about the mouth, he had thrown up his head. His fear had turned to anger. Audrey suspected he was dangerous at that moment.

Everyone fell silent, their eyes glued to the prodigal who stood small in her long carriage cape. Slowly they drew back until a clear path lay between Toria and Kit. Huxford put his arm around Audrey's waist to prevent her from rushing to his sister.

"H—Hello, everyone," Toria said in a faltering voice. She tore her eyes from Kit's and handed the basket of duck eggs they'd given her at Giles Farm to one of the servants. She'd dreaded her return all day, hardly attending as dear old Pimmy dredged up stories from her childhood. She'd been unable to concentrate on anything except her arrival home. And now, it was even worse than she'd thought. She gave her bonnet to Bridget and looked at Kit again, her eyes widening as he advanced upon her.

"Toria," he growled through clenched teeth, "where the *devil* have you been?" He laid barely controlled hands on her shoulders and jerked her to him. His mouth on hers was cruel and hard, crushing hers in his need to punish, to love, to possess her once and for all. Finally, mercifully, his kiss softened and he lifted his head.

Toria, held quite off the floor and locked fast against his

body, raised glowing eyes. "Kit! You never kissed me like that before!"

Kit's appreciative grin was cut short; he'd become aware of their audience. He dragged her through the crowd of well-wishers while Victoria embarked upon a hurried, somewhat breathless explanation, while at the same time begging their pardons and denying she meant any harm. These utterances were somewhat garbled as Kit half shoved, half carried her in his relentless progression toward the library. Peering artlessly over his shoulder, Victoria endeavored to speak to everyone before he took her away.

"Tildy," she cried. "I'm sorry I had to use your name to throw smoke over my trail, but—" Her eyes grew large when they lighted on Paden's cane. "My goodness, are you hurt, Paden? Gideon! Thank, heaven you're back. I didn't mean to—Audrey?" Kit was behind her now, propelling her in a last determined push, but she clung to the door frame. "Audrey, I sent you a letter telling you where I was. Didn't Mrs. Simpkin's nephew bring it?"

Audrey started to answer, but Kit had succeeded in drawing Toria away at last. Not, however, before they heard her say, "Oh, Kit, kiss me again! I'd have run away long ago if only I had known—"

The bemused group standing in the hall stared at the heavy oak door Kit had slammed in their collective faces. There was a fascinating silence behind it until it was wrenched open and Kit thrust something, a folded document at Gideon. "Special license." He grinned at his friend. "Going to marry your sister," he added, shutting himself in with Toria again.

Once more, they were left staring at the closed library door.

Tildy Offutt broke the silence. "Well," she announced, "I won't have Victoria and Kit running off to get married. Come, Audrey. We'll go and put Letty into the picture. Yes, tell her everything. She'll be fine after she gushes at us for a few minutes. Then we'll decide on a wedding for Toria. I wonder where Madelaine's wedding dress is."

Halfway up the stairs, Tildy turned and leaned over the

railing. "Gideon," she yelled down. "How about a sunrise wedding in the chapel? That all right? Yes, I thought you'd agree. Audrey? Yes, Audrey thinks so, too. Send for the vicar, Gideon. Ask him to spend the night. We'll have a wedding supper. And Regis Shandy. The doctor should be invited, too. That'll make it an even dozen. See to it, Twickem," she commanded.

"First things first," Gideon heard her tell Audrey, as she swept his fiancée away, up to the third floor, to inform Lady Marpleby of the momentous events of the past twenty-four hours.

Gideon, dispatching orders left and right, gave Kit and Toria ten minutes. Then he knocked ruthlessly on the door and entered the library. "All right, you two. Tildy Offutt says you can't run away and get married. Says we'll have the wedding at dawn. If you have any protests, I suggest you make them now, because right at this moment, Tildy and Aunt Letty and Audrey are laying plans. None?" He laughed when Toria cried that she'd *love* a home wedding.

"Come here, little sister," he said, taking Toria in his arms and giving her a great hug. "All my best wishes. Be happy. I know you will."

Gideon shook Kit's outstretched hand. "Chartley, take care of her."

A look passed between them. "I will," promised Kit. "And you, old man. I hope everything comes about for you."

Gideon broke out a humidor of fine cigars. "It will," he said. "It must. Now—let's bring Paden and his friends from the hall. I've sent for Lord Higglesby, too. We'll blow a cloud and discuss what we've—or rather Tildy—has decided. Paden can show Lord H his wound and explain everything. Toria, would you like to go up to Aunt Letty and help plan . . . whatever brides plan?"

Gideon's face was soft with love, and Toria gave him another hug, shot a happy glance at Kit, and ran away.

The supper was scheduled for midnight in the lighted solarium. Tildy had ordered the menu while Audrey directed the excited servants. Audrey sent Toria up to dress, and, taking her lead from the willing Twickem, decided at once that they must have fresh-cut orange or peach blossoms from the forcing sheds—whichever were available. And candles. Dozens of candles.

"Very good, my lady," the butler said. When Audrey came down to check on the decorations sometime later, the arrangements were complete, the fragrance of peach blossoms hanging delicately on the air. A gentle breeze drifted through the windows; the room was cool and dusky. Only a few of the candles were lighted. The solarium was beautiful, the silver gleaming, the linen, crystal, and china complementing all. On the sideboard, the chafing dishes were ready. It was a small supper, only twelve covers, as Tildy had planned when she sent for the good doctor. He and the vicar, the Reverend Mr. Dutton, had arrived together not long ago, according to Twickem.

The butler now came into the solarium, received Audrey's thanks for the work he and his staff had done, and departed to supervise the basting of the capons.

Audrey stood alone for a moment, striving to keep the tears from gathering in her eyes. This was either her first or her last supper party at Baddingly. How well she fitted; how at home she felt.

"The room looks wonderful, Audrey."

The words startled her, coming as they did from over her head. Audrey looked up, straining to see Huxford on the curving balcony that wrapped the room. This was an elevated, second half-story to the solarium, quite unique, and—Audrey understood—a design of Madelaine St. Aubin's.

"Thank you," she called softly. The night, the silence, the lateness of the hour seemed to demand soft words.

"Come here," he said, in a barely audible growl. "I want to—to see you. I have some champagne." He sounded as if the wine were a bribe.

Audrey started up the stairs. As if Gideon would ever have to bribe her to get her close to him, or to share a secret glass of champagne. The party would be ready soon; in just moment, Twickem would return to light all the candles.

"Yes," she said. "I want some of that." *And you, Gideon St. Aubin. You can't look at me that way and not love me a little.*

Gideon watched Audrey come to him. She was wearing a white dress, close layers of silk banded in ice-blue satin, without ornament, low-cut, clinging, outlining her small high breasts, dropping straight and true to a demi-train that trailed as she walked slowly, deliberately, toward him. Her eyes, deep violet in the shadows, held his. Gideon's breath caught in his throat. He marveled at how she looked, how she was dressed, how her body, slender and sinuous, moved. And he smelled her. That mysterious musk-rose fragrance she always wore. He could recognize her perfume in his dreams.

Her hair was caught up in a twist on her head, secured with half a dozen diamonds, partly allowed to fall down her neck and back. The lustrous golden-red tresses swayed as she reached her gloved hand for the glass he held.

"Just a sip," he said. She glanced at him, then down, her eyelashes sweeping her cheeks. Elevating his glass, she turned it so she could put her mouth where his had been, repeating her own action at Lady Wrotham's musicale. "To Toria and Kit," she murmured, then drank, closing her eyes to savor the champagne. Did she realize how seductive her actions were? Gideon wondered, breathing deeply, feeling his nostrils flare. No other woman would ever satisfy him.

"To Toria and Kit," he responded. He'd have Audrey Taylor as his wife, he vowed, or take no wife at all. He crossed his arms over his chest to keep from reaching for her. He wanted his hands on her, and hers—he remembered how she'd run her beautiful hand up his belly on that fateful night in the tower. He wanted her low, sensuous laugh in his ear as he took her. But more than that, he wanted Audrey to grow old with him. It wasn't simply passion, although—God knows—he didn't discount that. Well he couldn't, not seeing her instant effect on him—even now, dressed in this formal evening suit. His body was raging for hers—when he should have been concentrating on his sister's wedding supper.

This had been a mistake, coming here, offering the wine. But he'd wanted a moment alone with her. He'd sworn he wouldn't touch her until he had a special license in his pocket. After all his insults, his boorishness, only a license would convince Audrey he'd changed, convince her that while she remained his sweet obsession, she was also the love of his life. It was true, he desired her in every way—holding him in the fury of passion, lying abandoned in his arms after their love-making was over. But most of all, he wanted her as his wife, his life's companion, for better or worse, forever and always. And he wanted the precious fruit of their love. Lately, he'd pictured her warm and round with his child cradled in his arms.

"I must go," he said abruptly. If he didn't get away, he'd kiss her and spoil all his plans to confront her with a marriage license, a formal declaration of love, and his proposal. If he held her now, it would prove nothing; merely that he wanted her physically, and Audrey knew that already.

No, Gideon thought, the next time he touched her, he must give her tangible proof of his love. Only then could he demand of her the words he longed to hear, a breathless, "I love you, Gideon." He took his glass from her. After drinking the dregs of champagne that remained, he set it on a side table. "I must go," he repeated and walked rapidly away.

Audrey stood silent, staring like a ghost on the dark balcony. He'd wanted to hold her—to kiss her; that was plain. Why had he not? She could feel his constraint. He'd been fighting himself. Was he still unwilling to love her? Had his kisses this afternoon at Madsen Cottage meant nothing? Audrey fought against an insidious thought. In all probability, he'd been carried away by the moment. That was the only conclusion she could draw. Her face burned. She'd obviously been ready to go into his arms; he must have seen that. She'd expected him to kiss her, had boldly offered herself, had let him see that she wanted him to hold her.

Audrey pressed trembling lips together. No more, she

thought. Never again would she lay herself open to such rejection.

She straightened as Twickem and two footmen came into the lower level of the room and began lighting all the candles. She lifted her chin; she couldn't cry now. Picking up her train, she descended the half-stairs. *First things first,* Tildy had said. They had guests; she must get through the wedding supper and tomorrow morning, the wedding. Only then could she concentrate on her broken heart.

21

In spite of Audrey's apprehensions, the wedding supper went well. Aunt Letty had made the seating arrangements. Audrey sat on Gideon's right, Tildy Offutt on his left. Toria, dressed beautifully in a formal blue gauze with a satin half-slip, sat with Kit in the place of honor at the foot of the table. Lady M, rigged out in mauve satin and feathers, was halfway down the table with Lord Higglesby, who kept reassuring her that she was in danger of outshining the bride. Her eyes were only slightly puffed from all her tears of happiness. However, Audrey thought her aunt's glance, from her to Gideon and back, held shadows. Although she'd never said a word, Audrey suspected she knew there was something wrong with her and Gideon's engagement.

Audrey let her eyes drift down the table. The men, including the vicar, Mr. Dutton, and Dr. Regis Shandy, were formally dressed. Tildy Offutt conversed with Lord Fulverton. Tildy's dresser had arrived with a round gown of sage-green serge, and although she wore a small diamond and jet tiara and was very elegant, she looked as if she'd just come in from the paddock. The air was one of restrained but joyous celebration.

Gideon seemed totally at ease, laughing and smiling. He kept Audrey's wine glass filled, watching her constantly. She was baffled by his close attention. She tried to concentrate on the excellent supper the staff had so hastily thrown together.

At the end of the second course, just as she thought all the toasts had been drunk, Gideon arose, pulled her up beside him, and proposed a toast to—of all things—her violet eyes.

Audrey blinked, staring at the man she loved. Yes, he'd asked her once if she knew what her eyes did to him. Glancing away, blushing, she tried to smile. She must look a perfect fool, she thought. But everyone was laughing—fondly, it seemed—standing, raising their glasses.

During the third course Audrey became aware of an exchange of glances between Tildy Offutt and Lord Farquar Fulverton. It was during a lull in the conversation; Tildy, fork suspended in midair, was regarding his lordship closely.

"You mean," Tildy demanded, alluding to some part of their conversation that Audrey hadn't heard, "you and Paden were shut in a room with Audrey for close onto twenty-four hours?"

His lordship closed one eye and squinted the other. "It was eighteen hours only," he pronounced judiciously.

Tildy gestured impatiently. "Whatever!" her ladyship said, waving her fork. "The fact remains—she spent the night alone with two young men and no chaperon."

"A night and a little over half a day—"

"Yes, yes." Tildy cut him short. "The thing is, if she were not an engaged woman, one of you would have to marry her!"

"Don't see the need," his lordship disclaimed. "Don't see it at all! *I* was there the whole time. The girl's m'sister, you know."

Serenely setting himself back in his chair, allowing the footman to serve him a collop of sirloin, Lord Fulverton missed the blank look on Tildy's face. For once in her life, Lady Offutt was speechless.

Audrey hid her amusement and looked at Gideon, wondering if he'd overheard this exchange. Seemingly oblivious, he was watching her again, his chair shoved back, a softened expression on his face. She smiled; he moved restlessly and smiled back, a gleam in his eyes. Audrey was now thoroughly confused. She wished the evening were over. Surely, she thought, it would end soon.

Her reprieve came. In a very few minutes, the supper

party broke up, Tildy directing everyone to get some rest, reminding them that the wedding would take place at sunrise.

The ladies were ready to retire. Gideon kissed Audrey's hand after they left the table, then he seemed busy directing the servants who were carrying Lady Marpleby's chair up the stairs.

Audrey trudged up two flights to her chamber, where Matty was waiting for her. As soon as she was in her gown, Audrey dismissed her. Last night she'd slept on Rose Flammock's attic floor. She was exhausted, but thought she'd never be able to close her eyes. However, the moment her head touched the pillow, Audrey sank into a dreamless sleep and awakened only when Matty called her.

In the cool light of dawn, she dressed in cerulean blue, a close-cut silk walking dress, severely tailored with a matching jacket. Her small velvet hat, gloves, and suede half-boots were pale gray. She and Gideon were the attendants—she the maid of honor, and Gideon giving his sister away and serving at Kit's best man.

Lady Tildy Offutt, bringing Paden, Lord Fulverton, and Pinky Tadburn from Rosedale, had already arrived when Audrey ventured down the stairs.

Twickem handed her a bouquet of vivid pink roses to carry. Audrey thanked him and looked about for Gideon. But, he, of course, must be with the groom.

Tildy stuck her turbaned head out of a side room and gestured to Audrey. "Here you are; don't you look stunning, my girl? Gideon will swoon, upon my word. But come look at Toria in her mama's wedding gown. The housekeeper has worked nearly all night, refurbishing it, you know. The size was perfect, but it needed new satin knots here and there."

Tildy hauled Audrey inside the room just off the chapel, shut the door, and flung her arm toward Toria. "Now, tell me if *that's* not a beautiful bride," she said, chuckling at Audrey's expression.

Toria stood in the middle of the room, clutching her mother's small white prayer book and a nosegay of pink

rosebuds. Her veil was thrown back, and her gown, a mellow, cream-colored satin *peau d'ange,* designed in the old
style, clung tightly about her tiny waist, belling to the
floor, shimmering in the morning light.

Aunt Letty, watching Audrey run across to hug Toria,
wailed again, seeking her handkerchief. "Oh, Toria," she
cried, "if only your mother could see you. You look exactly like she did when she stood up with your father in St.
George's. So happy—I'm so happy for you and darling
Kit."

"Yes, yes, Letty." Tildy's tone was brisk. "But you must
leave off that blubbering and brace up. You're ruining
your face."

She turned to Audrey. "Remember," she said. "You
march in first. The music will start, and a few measures in,
you may step out. Walk very slowly, don't rush," Tildy
warned. "Too bad there was no time for a rehearsal. Never
mind; everything will go perfectly. You'll come down the
center aisle, stand to the left of the vicar—who will be facing out. Kit will enter alone and stand to the right. Gideon
will bring Toria down the aisle, give her to Kit, and take
his place as first witness, to Kit's right."

Tildy stopped, tapping her teeth with one fingernail.
"What comes next?" she muttered, then shrugged. "I can't
remember. Mr. Dutton will direct all that. Now, then, I
must go and see if Gideon has the ring—it's Madelaine's
you know—and make all ready. Ten minutes; that's when
Twickem said the sun would beam straight through the
clerestory, bathing Toria and Kit in the sunlight on their
wedding day."

The rays of the rising sun were indeed shining for the
fortunate bride and groom. "Happy the bride . . ." Audrey
thought, waiting at the back of the chapel. She missed a
step when the pump organ boomed. A glance had shown
her Lord Fumbo Fulverton perched high on the bench,
calmly playing the rather wheezy old instrument, his long
legs pumping methodically. Audrey repressed a smile.
She remembered to walk slowly and managed to get to the
front of the chapel. Kit came from the right; they and the

cherubic Mr. Dutton stood in their places, and—as the music altered—it was time for Toria to march down the aisle.

Toria came, in a measured pace, clinging to her brother's arm.

Afraid to look at Gideon, Audrey tried to concentrate on Toria, and on Chartley's reaction to her. Audrey saw Kit swallow, couldn't resist a peek at Gideon, and found him looking straight at her. The organ majestically pealed the wedding march, and Audrey forced herself to watch as Toria looked in love and trust to her beloved Kit. Still Gideon stole glances at her.

When he gave his sister to Chartley, answering the vicar's benign inquiry as to who gave this woman, Gideon stepped back, so near to Audrey that she could actually feel him beside her. It was unprecedented, but Audrey saw a smile of understanding pass between Kit and Gideon. Had they planned that Gideon would stand by her? He was so close! A current—something!—seemed to encircle them, binding them as they listened to the age-old ceremony. Did Gideon feel it? Once, he looked down at her, a quick smile, then he concentrated on the ceremony. At one point, he stepped forward, gave Kit the ring, then returned to Audrey's side.

Kit and Toria knelt, rose, knelt again, and—suddenly, it seemed to Audrey—it was over. Mr. Dutton, smiling angelically, pronounced them man and wife, and invited Kit to kiss his bride.

Kit did, with all the enthusiasm of an expectant lover, and in that moment, Gideon's arm came suddenly around Audrey, his hand clasping her waist, squeezing her hard against his side. He released her so quickly that she gasped and looked wonderingly at him. But he was already laughing and clapping with the others, watching his sister and best friend break from their first married kiss.

They adjourned to the great hall, where the champagne punch awaited, where Toria cut her wedding cake and everyone milled about, carrying plates, eating from the breakfast buffet. In a while, Toria went up to change into her pink traveling costume.

Gideon found Audrey and grasped her arm. "Come," he said. "They're about ready to leave."

Her eyes teared up, and he nodded. "I expect you need some sleep. I want you to go to bed the minute Toria and Kit drive away. Time enough when you're rested to—to discuss this engagement of ours. Nothing stays the same, Audrey. We—we must move forward with our lives. This phase is over."

Audrey was to remember his words later, hear them again and again in her head, but at the moment, she was distracted. Everyone was rushing outside, shouting best wishes.

The carriage waited at the castle steps. As the wedding party prepared to depart, the morning sun climbed high above the horizon. Victoria, standing in the curve of Kit Hartwell's arms, bade Audrey and her brother goodbye. Lady Marpleby, Lord H, and all the guests had said their adieus. Now they stood back. Except for servants hurrying about, bringing baskets, carrying luggage, the couples were alone.

Tears escaped Toria's eyes and rolled down her cheeks. Audrey's vision misted as well; she was convinced she would never see the marquis's sister again. When Kit and Toria returned from their Italian honeymoon next spring, she would be long gone—home to America. She hugged the smaller girl and whispered, "Be happy."

The bride gulped back her tears and smiled brilliantly at Audrey while Kit gripped Gideon's hand. "You too," Toria replied. "I wish I could see you marry my brother. I'm so glad we're going to be sisters."

A side-glance at Gideon told Audrey nothing. He was wearing his most enigmatic look. She forced herself to smile and wave as Kit's carriage pulled away.

Gideon took her arm. "I hope you'll go to your chambers and get some rest, Audrey. I must run up to London. I plan to return tonight, if I can, but that might not be possible. At any rate, I shall be returning soon."

Yes, he thought. He would be rushed. It would mean moving half of heaven and all the lawyers in London. He'd spent hours at his desk last night, writing out the marriage settlements, making a new will in Audrey's favor. And he'd need to see a bishop for the license. With luck, it could all be done in one day. If everything went well, by this time tomorrow he and Audrey would be leaving in *his* carriage. He didn't think his godmama could stand the strain of another dawn wedding at Baddingly. Besides, he wanted Audrey to himself. He would find a country inn, call in the local vicar, and marry Audrey out of hand. Then he'd feed her a champagne breakfast and take her to bed, opening the door only for food until they were both satiated. He could imagine her swaddled in rumbled bedclothes, her hair a glorious tangle around her body, raising bruised lips to meet his.

Gideon kissed Audrey's fingers and wrenched himself away, never thinking to explain why he was leaving so soon, never guessing how she might feel, so intent was he on his goal: The special license. He must have it when he laid himself and his life before Audrey.

Inside the great hall, Audrey thanked Tildy Offutt, excused herself to her aunt, and said she was going to bed.

Gideon was right: she was tired, more so than she could ever remember. She had no place here at Baddingly; none of this could be hers. Nor happiness, she thought.

Audrey almost ran up to her bedchamber. After stripping off her dress, she fell into bed, shaking with sobs, abandoning herself to the grief that overwhelmed her. In time, she slept, and when she awakened, it was almost noon. Dr. Shandy was waiting to examine her briefly, and Gideon—Gideon was gone to London.

Wearily Audrey bathed, dressed in a light sprigged muslin, and went to see her aunt.

One look at her and Lady M said, "Don't worry, my dear. Gideon said he'd be back tonight. He told me so himself." She patted Audrey's hand, urged her to take some tea, and ordered them a light luncheon tray.

Audrey wasn't hungry. She chewed and swallowed, but the toast scraped her throat. Gideon had said he'd be back. He must want to talk to her, she thought, to resolve all this mess. Perhaps he could explain what his cryptic words of

the morning had meant. But she already knew. He wanted
this bogus betrothal over and done with, ended.

"Do you feel all right, Audrey dear?" Lady Marpleby
asked.

"I'm fine, Aunt Letty. There was no need to detain Dr.
Shandy." Restless, she pushed back her tray. She had to be
alone—to think.

"Oh, the doctor was Gideon's doing," Lady M said
brightly. "Although I'm sure I would have thought of it
sooner or later. Where are you going, my dear?"

Standing in the archway, Audrey gestured vaguely in
the direction of the ornamental pond. "I believe I'll take a
walk."

Lady Marpleby smiled her understanding and returned
to the letter she'd been writing to Ophelia Redfern.

Audrey never knew how she spent the rest of that day.
She remembered walking, walking, circumnavigating the
home woods and the ornamental pond. As she tread the
perimeter of the oak-lined lane, Huxford's answer to Motley's question kept pounding in her mind. "I do," he'd
said, when Motley asked if he loved her. Audrey leaned
her cheek against the rough bark of one of the oaks. No,
he hadn't meant that, she thought. He'd only said it to be
kind, a gallantry that only a gentleman would understand.

Audrey decided that it was possible Huxford was trying
to spare her the pain of his final rejection and was giving
her a chance to end it.

Sinking to the ground, she leaned against the ancient
oak. She looked down at the ring he'd given her, slowly
working it round and round on her finger. She would leave
the ring on his dresser, along with a note wishing him
well, and the business would be finished. If that was cow-
ardly, and she knew it was, she couldn't help it. Where
Huxford was concerned, logic fled and emotion ruled.

When she came in at dusk, her mind was made up. She
would pack and leave. At dinner, Audrey forced herself to
eat, calmly agreeing when Lord Higglesby remarked that it
had grown too late for them to expect the marquis that
night. After the tea tray came, she helped her aunt to her
bedchamber and arranged bed tables and pillows to ac-

commodate her and Egbertt's late-night card game. Then she kissed her aunt and startled Egbertt by kissing him.

In her bedroom, Audrey dismissed Mattie and packed her trunk and bandboxes. Finally, she sat down to compose a note for Huxford and another for Aunt Letty. It was almost midnight.

The shadows along the corridor to the south tower were deep, but Audrey hardly noticed, so intent was she on what she meant to do when she reached Huxford's rooms. Fortunately they were empty, with only a small light burning. The door stood open and she walked in, heading straight for his dresser. She propped the sealed envelope against his mirror and removed the ring. Audrey looked at it, then placed it in front of the note where she was sure he would find it.

She arrived back in her room without encountering anyone and dressed for bed. She was determined not to think about her situation until she was far from Baddingly Castle. If she did, she would start crying again. That wouldn't do, because she was through with tears. She was ready to go home; there was nothing to hold her in England now.

She dropped her robe across the foot of the bed and stood staring at her reflection in the mirror. Her breasts seemed to gather light from the candles, lifting and gleaming through the silken fabric of her nightgown, swelling above the plunging neckline, straining against the thin material which bound them. The silver and blue gown, clinging at the waist, flared full to hang in glimmering folds about her feet. Audrey grimaced. What good was a garment like this if no one saw her in it?

She whirled about when the door was thrust violently open. Audrey screamed as it splintered back on its hinges and crashed against her trunk, toppling her bandboxes and scattering them across the floor.

Huxford stood clutching her note, staring at her with a murderous glint in his eyes. His hair fell across his forehead where he'd run his fingers through it. He was coatless and his shirt hung open to the waist. Audrey could see his strong brown throat and the black hair that covered his chest.

She tried to turn away, but he took two steps and grasped her arm in a powerful hold. Breathing rapidly, he shoved the crumpled note under her nose.

"What's this?" he snarled. "Another example of your *American* manners? Or don't you think you owe me the courtesy of a personal rejection? What, you couldn't be bothered? Did you find it easier to write and run?"

Audrey forgot that she was almost naked before him. Her anger had risen with each of his questions, building until it exploded in a great rage. Eyes furious, hair flying, she raised her hand to slap him as she'd done once before.

Deflecting her aim with a casual block of his arm, Gideon wrenched her against him and pressed his mouth against hers as if he was trying to consume her. He paid no attention to her feeble attempts to push him away, but held and ravished her with kisses until she slid her arms around him and began kissing him back.

"Yes, hold me, Audrey. I've been wanting that for the longest time!" The words seemed to be torn from him, and only when he was in possession of her lips again did he loosen his grip so his hands could rove over her nearly naked body.

He lifted her and they lay across the bed, his weight bearing her down as he kissed her throat, eyes, then her lips again. When he pushed aside the silken straps that held her gown, the sudden exposure of her breasts made Audrey shiver until he warmed them, his mouth, moving from one to the other, kissing, teasing each erect nipple.

Audrey wasn't aware that she moaned his name, crying out: "Please, Gideon, please!" Instinctively, she raised her body toward him, almost insane with a sweet, wild craving for fulfillment. Lying under him while his mouth traced designs on her naked flesh wasn't enough. She ran her hands down his back, pulling him closer, until he groaned and drew away.

Quickly, almost brutally, he hauled Audrey to her feet. They stood beside the bed while he bundled her into a quilted robe and buttoned it to her chin. That was better, he thought. Get her covered up. Keep her safe until he could love her like he wanted. He'd very nearly lost control this time. Her reactions to his love-making had almost been his undoing.

She seemed dazed. Her eyes swept his face and settled on his mouth.

"Don't," he said. "Don't look at me like that, sweetheart, or I'll have to kiss you again."

Mutely she raised her mouth and he tasted it briefly, his tongue hard in her mouth. Then he put her from him and shook her in mock anger. "Stop it, Audrey, and listen! We must talk. You must know by now that I love you. I got a special license today and if you'll have me, I promise ours will be the kind of marriage you outlined so enchantingly the night Emmerhite caught us kissing."

It was what she'd dreamed of hearing him say. But now that it was actually happening, Audrey couldn't quite believe it. Was this a dream after all? Would she awaken alone and miserable, with her trunks packed and ready to go? She ran her hand up his flat belly, her touch making his muscles writhe, the thick curling hair on his chest springing back at her touch. No, she thought. This was real. She was one step closer to solving the mystery of that man-woman thing. Soon—oh, let it be soon, she prayed— she would take him inside her, and their bodies would blend until they were one. Gideon had shown her a glimpse of what passion could be. She knew what she wanted now, and that was to love him to completion. A great shudder passed over Audrey as he sat her on a chair and knelt to put her slippers on her feet.

"Wh—when did you realize you loved me, Gideon?" It all seemed too wondrous.

"I loved you from the first, but was too stubborn to admit it," he said. Standing, he pressed her close, her face against his chest. His hand idly, lovingly, smoothed her hair. "Do you remember the last time I held you like this? Your hair swirled around us then—a glimmering curtain."

Audrey shook her head to loosen that curtain now, making it cascade around them. "Gideon, at Lady Lancaster's ball, you said you didn't even like me."

"I was afraid you wouldn't forget that. Well, the truth is, I'd just discovered I was feeling more for you than desire.

Audrey, don't you see? I was falling in love with you all the time and making us both miserable by denying it. I've been the worst kind of fool, my darling."

"And yet—at one time, you were willing to let me break our engagement and go away. Back to America."

"Only because I was convinced it was what you wanted." He kissed her eyelids and murmured, "Your eyes have haunted me. That night in my room, with the storm around us—how I ever sent you away, I'll never know." His voice was a husky growl. "I wanted you, Audrey, as much as I want you now. That was the night I—"

"That's when you changed your mind about breaking our engagement. But why?" An enticing frown marred Audrey's brow.

When Huxford had kissed it smooth, he said, "It was the way you'd responded to my lovemaking all along. But more than that, it was the way you kissed me when I brought Christina Jeffers here. I knew then—in that moment—that I'd never let you go."

Audrey nodded slowly. "But when all that with Motley was over, and after Toria's wedding, why did you leave for London? Why didn't you tell me you loved me then?"

He kissed the tip of her nose. "I wanted to, but I was afraid. I thought you wouldn't believe I was ready to marry you until I laid a special license in your hand. Audrey, I've dreamed of saying 'I love you,' of hearing you say those words to me."

"I love you, Gideon." She tightened her arms around his neck. Her voice rang clear, as if she were reciting a sacred vow. "I love you now and ever more."

His kiss left them both trembling. "I won't—I can't wait much longer," he warned. She could feel the strong beat of his heart as he held her. His laugh was shaky. "In fact, it's a good thing you're packed, because we're leaving at first light."

"But I don't have the proper clothes for a honeymoon!" she wailed.

"No?" His teeth flashed as he grinned. "Who said anything about being proper? That nightgown you're wearing is all you're going to need!" He laughed as her cheeks flamed. Then he sobered. "Audrey," he said, "you don't want to wait, do you? You *will* let me take you away? You'll marry me tomorrow?"

Her eyelids drooped sensuously at the corners. "Yes. Oh, yes, my love."

Gideon caught his breath on her words. "Say that again."

"What?"

"Call me your love."

Audrey laughed. "My love," she said softly.

He gave her a quick kiss, then grabbed her about the waist and pulled her toward the door. "Let's tell your aunt," he said. "She asked me once if I was going to marry you. I said no. That was weeks ago, just after we'd come home from Vauxhall. I don't think she believed me. I have a suspicion that she wanted us to marry from the first. She was very happy when we got engaged, but I suspect she has had some doubts about our relationship lately. Now I want to let her know our betrothal is real, that I've come to my senses at last and my dearest wish—that you would love me—has come true."

Gideon's words came lightly, but his winter eyes—no longer cold—gleamed with a pure warm light.

"Yes." She smiled. "Let's tell Aunt Letty—I'd like to tell the world. I want everyone to know I love you."

But as he dragged her down the hall toward her aunt's room, Audrey recalled how she must appear in her robe and with her mouth swollen from his kisses. Her hair hung down her back and her cheeks burned hot. "Stop, Gideon," she begged, hanging back. "I must look a sight!"

"You look adorable," he whispered, holding her close to his side as they entered Lady M's suite.

Interrupted in her game of piquet with Lord Higglesby, Lady Marpleby shrieked at the sight of her niece's disheveled condition, dropping her cards and scattering them in every direction.

"Letty," Egbertt objected, "the cards! And just as I was about to—"

Overriding his lordship's complaint, Gideon addressed Lady Marpleby. "Dearest Godmama," he announced, "I have the honor to inform you that you niece has accepted my proposal of marriage."

Lady M clapped her hands, cooed lovingly, and extended her arms to Audrey, who flew into her embrace. Both ladies were happily overcome. They shared a few sentimental tears before Audrey went back to Huxford's arms. Finally, Lady Marpleby was able to compose herself and express suitable good wishes.

Throughout this performance, Egbertt had remained silent. Now he roused himself, and with a look of bafflement said, "Letty, did I understand St. Aubin to say he and your niece were to be married?"

"Yes, love."

"I'll tell you something you may not have noticed, Letty."

"What is it, dear?"

Lord H fastened an owlish gaze upon his bride-to-be. "I might be—not sure, but *might* be—getting a trifle absent-minded."

Gideon bit his lip and Audrey smothered a tiny sound deep in her throat.

Lady Marpleby's smile didn't falter. "How so, my love?"

"Well, it's a curious thing! Here I was thinking for weeks Huxford and Miss Soames-Taylor were *already* engaged." He swung around to fix the marquis with a suspicious glare.

Gideon felt Audrey shake with suppressed laughter and tightened his arm around her. "Oh no, sir," he said, with only the faintest quiver. "You mustn't fault your memory. Our betrothal was announced, all right. It—it was a hoax."

"Why?" asked Egbertt, who could cut to the heart of a matter when the need arose.

"Uh—spy stuff! Hush-hush affair! You understand, sir."

His lordship relaxed. "Ah! Government business, what?" He closed one eye and nodded sagely. "I detect Brumley's hand in this. Probably some scheme of his. Well," he said, laying one finger alongside his nose, "you have nothing to fear from me, m'boy! Wild horses and all that!"

Laughing, Gideon took Audrey to the castle roof to see

the stars. Leaning against a parapet, he pulled her into his arms. Her eyes shone mysteriously in the waning moonlight. "Never leave me," he said roughly.

"No, never," she promised. "I'll stay with you for all time."

"World without end," he vowed, and kissed her just as the dawn star rose.

Avon Romantic Treasures

*Unforgettable, enthralling love stories,
sparkling with passion and adventure
from Romance's bestselling authors*

FORTUNE'S FLAME *by Judith E. French*
76865-8/ $4.50 US/ $5.50 Can

FASCINATION *by Stella Cameron*
77074-1/ $4.50 US/ $5.50 Can

ANGEL EYES *by Suzannah Davis*
76822-4/ $4.50 US/ $5.50 Can

LORD OF FIRE *by Emma Merritt*
77288-4/$4.50 US/$5.50 Can

CAPTIVES OF THE NIGHT *by Loretta Chase*
76648-5/$4.99 US/$5.99 Can

CHEYENNE'S SHADOW *by Deborah Camp*
76739-2/$4.99 US/$5.99 Can

FORTUNE'S BRIDE *by Judith E. French*
76866-6/$4.99 US/$5.99 Can

GABRIEL'S BRIDE *by Samantha James*
77547-6/$4.99 US/$5.99 Can